Horned Jack: Never Say Never
Third Anthology

Book 1: Never Say Never
Book 2: The Truth Is Out There
Book 3: Into the Darkness
Book 4: The Impostor

M. R. Williamson

Horned Jack: Never Say Never
By M. R. Williamson

Story copyright owned by Marvin R. Williamson
Cover art and design by Laura Givens

First Printing, May 2021

Hiraeth Publishing
P.O. Box 1248
Tularosa, NM 88352

e-mail: sdpshowcase@yahoo.com
Facebook: Hiraeth Publish;
Twitter @HiraethPublish1

Visit www.hiraethsffh.com for science fiction, fantasy, horror, scifaiku, and more. While you are there, visit the Shop for books and more! **Support the small, independent press...**

Dedicated to my Wife, Connie Louise Gordin Williamson.
Through her encouragement, Horned Jack will live
on. . . . .and on.

Also by M. R. Williamson:

Horned Jack: The Early Years

Horned Jack: The Nephilim Chronicles

Bridges Into the Imagination

The Curse of the Monkey's Paw

Can You See Me?

The Green Lady

Book 1
Never Say Never

True love is rare and hard to find-
A blessing from God, a gift of fate.
But taken unjustly it plays with the mind,
Oft tempts one to tool with the perfection of hate.

Part 1
Never Say Never

There are none who could be more proud of their son than Rodney and Cinthia Goke. Even before Jason graduated from Memphis State University, he had found a wonderful girl in Drew Berry Rutland. The tall, green-eyed blonde was always a crutch to where he was weakest and supportive when he was sad or depressed, she was beside him since their first year of college. They were literally partners in everything they undertook. Coming from a middle-class family, Drew benefitted in the house Jason's parents rented near the campus and a good part of the money provided for their tuition. The fifty-year-old couple realized she was much more than a positive influence on their son, Rodney and Cinthia were always there for them. Four years at Memphis State and another two at UT at Nashville and the twenty-four year olds were back home in Memphis.

But not a single soul can be prepared for everything. JJ was about to find out that justice was sometimes the kissing cousin of vengeance, and if played correctly, they could sometimes be enjoyed at the same time. . .

Rodney Goke sat quietly in his livingroom, staring out of the big, picture window at the Memphis Zoo property on the east side of McLean Road. Noticing that his wife, Cinthia, was smiling at him, he slowly turned to her and returned the smile.

"Have you told them yet?" she asked, watching him nervously run his fingers through his sandy-colored hair.

Rodney shook his head in a silent 'No'.

"Have you changed your mind?" asked Cinthia, looking a bit worried.

"Not at all. JJ's track record all the way through MSU and UT would be hard for anyone to follow." He chuckled, looking at Cinthia. "I believe our Dew Berry has held his feet to the fire. She's the mortar that holds his building blocks together I believe."

7

"But what about--" Cinthia fidgeted with her long, red hair.

"Don't worry, Cinthia," interrupted Rodney. "Rowsey is supposed to deliver the furniture and stuff at noon. It's 11:30 right now and they haven't called yet. I gave them a diagram of where to put the stuff. If they want to change it around, that's their prerogative."

Cinthia nodded. "Did you opt for the apartments on South Bluff Drive?"

"I did," replied Rodney proudly. "They have 201. From there, they can see the river across Riverside Drive. Paid the rent for a year. By then they should have their feet on solid ground." He glanced at his watch. "JJ said he and Dew Berry would meet us there at 4:00PM. I believe he's figured all this out, but Drew is still in disbelief."

"I think you're right," replied Cinthia, laughing. "I heard her say nobody gets a house for Christmas, and that's only five days away."

*   *   *

Just over four hours later, Cinthia and Rodney pulled into the South Bluff apartments and immediately spotted their son's '63, yellow Mustang close to the front gate entrance. Quickly spotting Rodney's '60, white Lincoln, the manager trotted from the office, waving for them to go to the apartment. Being only two buildings to the west, Rodney proceeded with the yellow Mustang right behind them. Before either could get parked, the manager, a heavy-set blonde, was already briskly walking their way on the sidewalk.

"We got it all in, Mr. Goke," she said loudly.

"What all?" asked Drew as she and JJ got out of the Mustang.

"Haven't the foggiest," admitted JJ, his dark brown eyes giving her that 'I know something you don't' look.

"Well. . ." Cinthia smiled at Drew's confused expression. "Go and take a look. It's 201."

The manager quickly approached Rodney. "I'm the manager, Becky Jefferies," she said as she handed the keys to Rodney. "If I can be of further help, just call."

Rodney instantly tossed the keys to JJ, now at the door with Drew. "Take a look, he added."

"And feel free to move the stuff around if you want," said Cinthia.

JJ unlocked the door and slowly opened it as though he was almost afraid of what was inside.

"Myyy word," managed Drew weakly as she slid past him and on through the entranceway.

"It's a little early for Christmas," said Cinthia, "but Merry Christmas from Rodney and Me."

"No way!" Drew ran from the entranceway and straight into the living room. Stopping at a solid oak, antique coffee table, she looked back at Rodney and Cinthia in disbelief.

"There's a half board in the dining room," added Rodney.

JJ stood just inside the livingroom, watching Drew run from one room to another. "Have mercy," he finally managed. "She's so excited, she won't be able to sleep at all tonight. We'll be up 'till morning." He slowly turned and gave his mother a hug. "Thank you," he added, as he hugged his father as well. "I know I should say more, but words just fail me right now."

"Don't worry about that," chuckled Rodney. "The way Dew Berry is acting is thanks enough."

"This is one of our best homes," added Mrs. Jefferies. "We're not gated yet, but we have an armed patrol." She handed a window, ID decal to both Rodney and JJ. "Put those on your car and you won't get the guard all excited."

*   *   *

In three days, JJ and Drew had completely moved in their new apartment. With the Christmas tree almost finished, the two sat upon the couch and re-evaluated their situation. . .

Drew took a deep breath. "Can we finish this tomorrow? If I have to move, unpack, or hunt for another, single thing, I'll pass out."

JJ smiled, letting his head rest on the back of the couch. "No problem. It's close to 8:00PM. I think I'll get my shower right now if you don't want to go first."

9

"That's fine with me," replied Drew. "I'll slip out of these jeans and blouse, into a house coat, and then find us a movie on one of the Late Shows."

Then, just as Drew put on her housecoat, the doorbell rang. Tightening her robe, she walked straight to the door and looked through the peep hole. A young, black man dressed in a brown cap and matching shirt was standing there patiently holding a large box with UPS stamped on it.

"Ohhh my gosh," said Drew with a slight chuckle. "More stuff?" She quickly opened the front door.

The young man smiled. "I'm sorry I'm so late, Ma'am. This just happened to be my last stop of the day. It's a little heavy. Where would you like me to put it?"

"Well. . ." Drew glanced back toward the hallway. She could still hear the shower running. Unhooking the screen door she held it open for the man. "Just sat it by the coffee table."

The carrier nodded as he stepped into the livingroom and sat the box down. Turning, he held out a piece of paper. "Would you sign this for me and I'll be on my way." His smile was sincere enough, but he could hardly get his cap over his Afro hairdo.

"Sure." Drew took the paper and pen.

But just as soon as she put pen to paper, a pair of strong arms pinned her own to her body as a white cloth was pressed against her face. The odor on the cloth not only took her breath away, but her consciousness as well.

It seemed only seconds had passed as she started to awaken. She noticed the pain in her arms and wrists first, and then became aware that they stretched over her head and tied to something above her. She could hardly feel the floor with the balls of her feet.

"Oh-my-God. Oh-my-God," she groaned as she finally came to herself and opened her eyes.

But she could see nothing but a white cloth from perhaps a hood that had been snugly tied from her open mouth to the back of her neck.

"Well, well," spoke a man from somewhere in the room. "She's finally awake and with us."

10

The greeting was accompanied with a sharp poke to her lower abdomen causing her to grunt and struggle with her balance. Then, another man in the room laughed as the one nearest to her kept pushing her off balance.

"Grunt her again," suggested yet a third man. He sounded like a colored man. Possibly the one who delivered the package.

This garnered a sharp poke to her groin causing Drew to cry out in pain.

"Make her groan," suggested a man from across the room. He sounded young and punkish. "There's nobody home next door and the apartment below is vacant as well. Let her scream."

Now, Drew realized that she no longer had the robe on and could no longer feel her bra. But the elastic feel of her bikini panties was still there.

"One more time," chuckled the man closest to her.

Drew braced for whatever was coming her way, but it was hard to manage any kind of defense while being strung up so tight. With a quick swish through the air, a cane-like object was brought down hard on the top of her right breast. Drew
screamed out, causing all those in the room to laugh.

"Make her dance!" shouted the black man as the others applauded.

Again and again, from one breast to the other, the cane found its mark. It quickly became impossible to figure out which was more intense, the screams in her own ears or the intolerable pain the cane was delivering to her breasts. After more than a dozen blows, she lost count. Another dozen and she passed out completely. The darkness took away from the monsters in the room.

*   *   *

"Drew baby?"

The voice was that of her mother. That was certain. But it sounded distant and unusual somehow. Drew quickly went into the fetal position, almost afraid to open her eyes.

"Don't hit me. Please don't hit me again," she managed, keeping her eyes tightly shut.

"Mrs. Goke," spoke another person, a man perhaps. He was so close she could smell the garlic tomato sauce he had on his spaghetti.

"It's Bee and Jimmy, dear," spoke her mother with a warm hand on her right shoulder. "There's a policeman here with us as well. You're safe. They won't hurt you anymore."

"Excuse me," spoke even another man as she felt a cold, metal object on her chest.

Drew jumped at the man being so close.

"I'm the doctor on duty, Ma'am," said the man in a soft tone. "Just want to check your heart," added the blurry figure now hovering over her. "You're safe here. You're at the Methodist in Memphis."

"He's a doctor, baby," said another person quite close also.

Drew turned toward her mother's voice. Her parents, Bee and Jimmy Rutland, stepped to her right side as the doctor left.

"Mom?" Managed Drew as tears streamed down her face. "Where's JJ? Is he all right?"

"He's in surgery right now, baby," spoke another person from the left side of the bed.

"Mrs. Goke?" Drew wiped her eyes, her wet face, and then turned toward where she heard the voice.

Standing in the doorway, the portly Memphis Police Detective watched Drew closely. It didn't take him long to tell the smile she was working with was forced at best.

"You look worried," noted Drew as she studied Mrs. Goke's expression. "JJ's is hurt isn't he?"

Mrs. Goke lowered her eyes to the floor, searching for words.

"Ohhh my God," cried Drew as she threw the sheet from her legs and swung her feet to the side of the bed, stopped only by the IV she had in her left arm.

"No-no-no," objected the six feet plus doctor as he stepped past Mrs. Goke to gently grab Drew's shoulders. "You've got three fractured ribs. You really don't want to make them worse. Your husband is in good hands right now and the best thing you can do for him is lay right

12

there and get well. Just as soon as we hear the results on JJ, I'll be right back in her with the news."

Drew nodded as the doctor guided her back to her pillow. Only then did she feel the pain in her right side. Wincing, as she struggled to sit up, she noticed another person at the doorway. He was a young man in a doctor's, white jacket. He motioned for Mr. and Mrs. Goke to join him in the hallway.

"Mom?" Horrified, Drew turned to see her mother slowly sit down in the chair next to the bed. "Mom?" she managed again, pushing herself up against the headboard.

"Shhh, baby," replied her mother, slowly getting up from the chair. "I'm sure they'll tell us something in a minute."

But the closed door to Drew's room did little to comfort her. Hardly a minute had past when JJ's parents came back in the room. With the somber look on Rodney's face and tears streaming down Cinthia's, Drew's worst fear hit her like a freight train.

"Nooo!" she screamed, causing the nurse at the desk to come running down the hallway. Ripping the sheet back again, she exclaimed, "Take me to him! Take me to him!"

But the more she struggled, begged and pleaded, the tighter her father held to her until, once again, the dark came and took her away.

*   *   *

"Drew? Drew, baby, please don't cry."

Drew knew that voice. His lips were so close it moved the hair around her left ear. "JJ!" she shouted, grabbing her husband. She tightly closed her eyes, relishing the scent of his Aqua Velva shaving lotion. Quickly opening them again, she could see his smiling face directly in front of her. But the others in the room were, strangely enough, were gathered at the foot of her bed talking with the doctor who brought the bad news.

She looked back to JJ. "I thought you were--"

"Ohhh, let's don't go there," he interrupted with a kiss on her left cheek.

13

Drew hugged him tightly. "I thought I would never see you again."

"Never?" JJ gently pushed her to arm's length. "Never say never, my love."

That last comment was repeated over and over again like a skip in a broken record as darkness came once again.

*　　*　　*

"Drew? Baby?" Bee looked at her watch. It was already 1:45AM the next day.

The double question crashed on Drew like a Big Ben alarm clock after a sleepless night. Finding herself still well upon her pillow, she wiped her eyes and looked about the room. Her parents were still there as well as JJ's.

"Where is he? Where is he?" she asked. "JJ was right here just a minute ago. I touched him! He kissed me! Where is he?"

Running down the hallway, the night nurse quickly entered the room, glancing at Bee. "Is everything all right here?" she asked. "I heard her again all the way to the nurse's desk. Does she need another sedative?"

Bee quickly turned from where she was standing on the left side of Drew's bed. "She just had a bad dream, that's all."

"No!" exclaimed Drew, looking straight at Bee. "It wasn't a dream and I don't need any more pills. He was right here by my bed and so close I could smell his aftershave."

The nurse looked over her glasses at Bee.

"She'll be just fine," said Bee. "I'm staying with her through a good part of the morning."

*　　*　　*

Later that morning, a Monday on Christmas Eve and the Sheriff's office was just opening. Dianne had just started the first pot of coffee when the phone rang on her desk.

"Andy!" She looked at the tall, bear of a man behind the Sergeant's Desk. "Can you grab that?" she asked.

"Got it," answered Sergeant Jackson as he ran toward the dispatcher's desk across the lobby.

Dianne watched the squint on his face as he wrote down the information provided by the caller. "Outside trouble again?" she asked, tightening the rubber band on her long, blonde ponytail.

"Ohhh. . ." Andy glanced at her with a smile. "Maybe and maybe not," he quipped. "That was Memphis' West Precinct, the one on the river. They had a burglary in one o' those fancy apartments that overlooks the river. It cost one of the residents his life. They got a witness who said the perps were in a late model, Chrysler Newport with Tipton County plates--no numbers, just the county."

Dianne nodded. "Has Will heard from his new deputy yet?"

Andy shrugged. "Still waitin' on background checks. Memphis has already vouched for him. Seems he moved from there to Atoka. The trip out o' Memphis cost him his job. Fred's already helpin' Will with the paperwork though. The man left with sergeant's stripes, Dianne. We're gettin' a good one."

"Good," replied Dianne. "Is Fred back with us for a while, or has the got to go back to Memphis on that jury thing?"

"I think he's through," guessed Andy, "but you'll have to talk to him about that."

"Got a name for this newbie?" asked Dianne.

"Yep," replied Andy, still going through yesterday's papers. "Richard Watkins I think." He glanced at Dianne. "I believe he's called Bubba. He's about twenty years younger than me--about thirty or so."

Dianne instantly dropped a stack of coffee cups to the floor behind Andy, causing him to jump and look around at her.

"I know they call him Bubba," replied Dianne as a half-smile slowly changed her otherwise calm expression.

Andy laid his papers down and squinted at her. "All right. Spill it. Where's the grin comin' from?"

Dianne slowly shook her head, batting her big, blue eyes at him. "Do you remember, not that long ago, when Jack was on that Mississippi River submarine boat thing?"

15

"Of course we do," replied Fred. Dark hair, neatly combed, the forty plus Chief of Detectives stepped from his office and into the lobby. "It was called Low Rider I believe. That's the one Jack had to deal with those huge bull dogs."

"Exactly," agreed Dianne. "Well, the Coast Guard gave a 'heads up' to the Memphis West Precinct and they assigned two of their officers to patrol along the river all the way to the Tipton line."

Andy nodded. "I knew that," he answered as Fred nodded.

"Good. . ." Dianne's smile widened. "Anyone remember what happened when they crossed the county line while following the lights of a Coast Guard Cutter?"

Fred nodded. "It was way out in the river, close to the Arkansas side. All they could see were the lights."

"Who sent them back to Memphis?" asked Dianne.

Andy's chin dropped as a squint slowly marred his expression. "Will did," he finally got out. "But that was because the larger of the two policemen called him a. . ."

Andy's comment trailed off as his gaze slowly found the floor between Dianne and Jack's grandfather.

"The word is 'old goat," said Fred as he looked at Andy. "That was said by the one called Bubba."

"Ohhh-my-word," groaned Andy. "Do you think Will's made that connection?"

Fred smiled, not saying a word.

"He only talked to him on the phone," reminded Dianne, looking straight at Fred. "You filled out the paperwork to help Will speed up the process. I believe he's coming in to sign the documents today at 1:00PM."

"And start tomorrow?" asked Andy, drawing a nod from Fred.

Dianne looked to Andy. "You gonna tell him?"

"Uhhh. . ." Andy paused, hearing the lock snap on the front door.

"Good morning!" exclaimed Will as he walked in, adjusting the sling on his left arm. "Sorry I'm late. I had ta stop at Walgreen's and get a big bottle of Empirin."

"Still giving you trouble, Will," asked Dianne.

16

Will shrugged. "It's slowin' up some, but ever' so often, it comes screamin' back like a banshee," he added as he walked toward his office.

"Dianne looked at Andy. "Tell him," she whispered.

"Andy slowly shook his head in a silent but definite "No".

"Dianne. . ." Will paused, looking back from his office door.

"Yes-sir," answered the dispatcher.

"Any o' you heard from that new-hire, Watkins fella?"

Fred quickly turned and walked back toward his office.

"Coward," grumbled Dianne just under her breath. "Uhhh, no Sir," she replied with a quick glance at Andy.

*   *   *

About five hours later found Fred in the field and Andy sitting with Dianne at her desk eating their sack lunches. Will, opting for a cup of coffee and a McDonald's cheeseburger, was in his office listening to the police band on his Masterwork, short wave radio. Hearing the front door open, Dianne and Andy looked up just as Richard Watkins entered the lobby. Both froze with a mouth full of bologna and cheese sandwich and chips watching the six feet plus, dark-haired fellow pause in the middle of the lobby with his hat in his hand.

"Ohhh, I'm sorry," apologized Bubba as he fidgeted nervously with his beige Stetson. I didn't mean to disturb your lunch."

"No problem." Andy quickly retreated to his bottle of Dr. Pepper.

"Across the lobby and the door on the right," directed Dianne. "Will's expecting you I believe. Ohhh boy," she groaned softly as she looked to Andy with raised eyebrows.

"I hear ya, Mr. Watkins. Come on in," said the old Sheriff loudly.

Dianne and Andy laid their sandwiches down and watched the new-hire pause at the Sheriff's open door. His muscular frame, at least two hundred and fifty pounds, all but closed the doorway.

"What the Hell!" shouted Will as something banged against the office wall.

17

"Ohhh God, That's his chair," whispered Dianne. "It hit the wall as he jumped out of it."

The two quickly stood, gazing across the lobby.

"I had no idea it was gonna be you!" yelled Will.

Andy and Dianne, now standing, watched the big man almost wad up his Stetson.

"No Sir," said Richard, tightly gripping his hat. "That 'old goat' crack last month--I didn't really--"

"I took extreme exception to that crack, Mr. Watkins!" interrupted Will. "This place is not a place run by an 'old goat' or any other worn out cliché! My waddles may hang a little low and I might even walk with a hitch at times, but I can still out crow any other rooster in the yard! You got that!"

"Uhhh, yes Sir. I can see--"

"I have a good relationship with each and every one of my people here and the surrounding offices both in and out of Tipton County!"

"Yes Sir," replied Richard, still at the door, gripping his hat.

"IF you go to work for me, I expect the same respect as I'm gonna give you!"

"Yes-Sir," replied Richard. "Uhhh, if Sir?"

Will nodded, slowly sitting back down. "I know you lost your job when you moved to Atoka. I know you got a wife and two kids and one on the way. I also know that you have a brand new house note ta take care of."

"Yes Sir," managed the big man, still somewhat leery to step into the office. "I really need this--"

"Well. . ." For the first time, Will paused to look closely at the man. "You can put your hat on the rack before you completely kill it. Come in, close that door, and take a chair in front of my desk. We can discuss how you can worm your way back into my good graces."

Bubba glanced back at Dianne and Andy, stepped into the office, and then closed the door.

"Jesus on the cross," groaned Andy.

"Well. . ." chuckled Dianne. "At least he didn't shoot him."

*   *   *

18

Just west of Highway 14 on Highway 206 and about two miles north of the Tipton/Shelby County line sat an old farmhouse once owned by Mark and Mandy Isley. Being successful farmers all of their lives, left them with a paid off mortgage and a little time and money to enjoy what life they had gifted them. But, as Fate would have it, a tractor accident took Mark in the spring of 1961, leaving his son, Trey, to look after his seventy-year-old mother. Unfortunately, that obligation was far too short for Trey. She passed in April that following year. Now, with a failed marriage and even worse luck at farming, the thirty-year-old, collage drop-out sold three hundred acres of the family farm for a safety net until he could get his crushed ice business up and running. In the following two years, he formed a secret group called 'The Ice Men'. Using Trey's Crushed Ice as a workable front in the daytime, the dark-haired conman turned to their real profession-- preying on easy targets in Memphis at night. . . .

Trey Isley sat in the living room of his home on 828 Highway 206 West and looked out across the road in into the weedy fields of what was left of his father's farm. His close friends and tenants, Tony Burcher, Scott Henney, Steve Scott and Jimmy Sawyer were all sitting in the livingroom with him and waiting patiently for him to share what he was now planning.

You gonna make us guess?" asked Scott Henney. The thirty-year-old, sandy-haired ex Memphis policeman puzzled at Trey. "The take on the River Bluff place was an easy two thousand dollars and that's not counting the jewelry and electronics."

Jimmy Sawyer chuckled. "And we got a free show." The twenty-five-year-old red-head laughed at Tony. "Paddling her buttocks sure made her dance, Tony.

"Steve and me will take care of those other articles tomorrow," said Tony Burcher. The thirty-five year old college drop-out looked more like a Hell's Angel's biker with his coal, black hair combed back in a ponytail and a black, leather jacket.

Steve Scott, on the other hand, always acted like the leader, much to Tray's amusement. Well dressed, overconfident at times, and very arrogant. His Elvis-styled hair was never more than thirty minutes away from a comb.

"This next caper goes down tomorrow and right on Beale at the Gourmet Hamburger Restaurant." He looked straight at Tony. "It's a one-man job with a fast and invisible get-a-way for a motorcycle in the alleys behind the business."

"A restaurant?" Tony squinted at Trey.

"That's right," replied Trey, brushing his brown hair from his forehead with his right hand. "This is the day before Christmas Eve. They will be having a Christmas party all that day and will close at 7:30PM that night. It takes her about an hour to close out. The only other one during most of that time will be the head cook, and he will be gone by then. You go in and sit down at six or so, eat, get a feel for the place, and then leave. While there, and just before you leave, go to the restroom. The back door has an old fashioned, dead bolt lock with a thumb bolt. Trip it so you can get inside just after seven."

"You said 'her'," said Tony with a half-smile. What does she look like?"

"I'll go with you," offered Jimmy.

"Ohhh no," answered Tony. "One on a motorcycle is plenty, especially when you have to move fast." He looked back at Trey with raised eyebrows.

Trey slowly shook his head. "Tony, if you let your libido screw this up you're out of here."

Steve Scott squinted at Trey. In his early thirties, the blond-haired, trim fellow was quiet, moody at times, but had a twisted sense of humor. "There's no harm in thumping a good-looking girl every now and them. Most of them need tweaking anyway."

Laughing, Tony asked, "Just trying to ID the lady, Trey. I'd like to be sure of my target."

Trey rolled his eyes with his gaze ending up on Tony. "Her name is Cathy Sartain. She's in her mid-thirties, dishwater blond, green eyes, and about five feet, eight inches tall, and not a bad figure." He looked straight at Tony. "Concentrate on the money, Tony. Get in, get it, and then get out. There's an alley in the back of the place as well as on the south side. Like I said; get there a little early, have a bite and case out the place just before closing. That'll put you in the right time to unlock the back door."

Tony nodded, smiling as if well pleased.

*   *   *

The next day at 6:00PM sharp, Tony Burcher parked his Triumph Black Shadow in the alleyway just south of the restaurant. Taking extra time with his lunch, he watched Cathy work the tables. Her occasional smile at him only piqued his curiosity.

She-is-gorgeous, he thought.

He watched the way she moved, the way she cocked her hips when she stopped, and the constant tug on her short skirt drove him to distraction. Finally, at 6:45 and with the last two customers at the register, Tony got up, left a twenty on the table for a nine dollar and fifty cent bill, and then walked back to the restroom. Pausing right in front of the back door, he checked the front. The office door was closed as was the door behind the counter. There was not a soul in sight in the dining area. It took less than half a second to silently trip the lock. Straightening his shirt, he returned to his table and slowly finished his cup of coffee. One by one, the other employees leave except Cathy and one of the cooks. Nodding at Cathy, he pushed the bill and money across the table, got up, and then headed out of the front door. About thirty minutes had passed when the cook left by the front door, walking north and away from him.

"Showtime," he quipped as he briskly walked back toward the restaurant and then down the side alley.

Removing a three-foot cane, a coil of cotton rope, and a two foot by six inch oak paddle strapped on the back of his cycle, Tony trotted toward the back door and paused, looking at the lock.

"Now or never," he said as he slowly twisted the round, brass handle. Hearing the soft snap and feeling the door give brought a smile to his face. "Very good," he whispered as he opened the old door and peeped down the hallway toward the dining area. Both the office and the cooking area doors were still closed. Easing past the office door, he crept to the dining area, quickly let down the blinds, and then crept back to just past the still closed office door. The light showing beneath it was a quick reminder of the fun to come. Taking hold of the paddle with his right hand, he tossed it down the short hallway watching it crash against the nearest table in the dining area. As the shadow move in the light under the office doorway, Tony removed the either bottle wrapped in a white, cotton hood and quickly poured some of its contents on the hood. By that time, the office door gradually opened.

"Hello?" said Cathy, as she eased out of the office, looking toward the dining area. "Hello. We're closed," she added, stepping toward the dining area.

Tony silently stepped behind her, slipped his left arm over her head and under her chin. She barely had time to scream before the cotton sack was placed firmly against her face. Struggling, the little five foot, six inch blond could do nothing before the either robbed her of her consciousness.

Tony carried her to the dining area and eased her to the floor just under an exposed ceiling beam. Once her blouse and bra were removed, he cuffed her hands and then clipped the metal snap on the end of the rope to the chain on the cuffs. Now, with the hood in place, he took a short rope, placed in her mouth and then tied behind her head. Tossing the other end of the rope over the oak beam above them, he quickly hoisted her up until the balls of her feet barely touched the floor.

"Now to get paid," he said cheerfully as he trotted toward the still open office door.

And that was no problem. The money for the day was stacked neatly on the top of the desk with the paperwork and the safe was wide open. Using the bank deposit pouch, he hurriedly stuffed it full, zipped it closed, and then walked briskly back toward Cathy, still hanging in the dining area. Even before he got there, he could see her trying to struggle with both the cuffs and her balance.

"Wakie-wakie," he said as he walked up to her.

Letting his left hand ease around her bare waist, he paused over the button on her skirt. It was no problem, nor was the zipper just under it. He let it slowly fall from her thighs as he admired her pink bikini panties and the way she groaned as the either slowly relaxed its grip.

"Should I start with the cane or perhaps the paddle?" he asked as he retrieved the latter from under a nearby table. "You have a wonderful figure. Both your buttocks and breasts are most full."

Cathy instantly tried to object, but the thick, cotton hood was pulled well into her now gaping mouth by the rope.

"I think we'll start with the paddle," said Tony politely as he stepped behind her and pulled her panties well into the folds of her buttocks.

Squeezing her buttocks soundly, he lowered his chin to her right shoulder and listened to her groan.

"I like the way you groan, Cathy. Perhaps I can help you with that."

Then, with a half-step backward, he slapped the paddle hard against her bare buttocks. The loud, fleshy pop broadened the smile upon his face as Cathy's muted scream struggled to penetrate the cotton hood.

"Like that?" he asked as his left hand explored the front of her panties, tugging at the elastic near her groin.

Again, the paddle found its mark, sending Cathy groaning and struggling to keep her balance.

"Here, let me help you." Tony eased his left hand under her left breast, cupped it gently, and then squeezed very hard.

Gripping it tightly until she was making one, solid groan, he lifted it up until her left foot was almost off the floor. Again, the paddle found its mark, again and again until Cathy felt like her buttocks were on fire.

But then the spanking stopped. Cathy strained her ears. Had she heard another voice in the room? The sounds of her own, muffled screams had all but drowned it out. She turned her head to the right and away from Tony. But seeing through the cotton hood was impossible.

23

She felt Tony release his grip on her left breast. "Who the Hell are you?" he ask. "It can't be!" he added loudly as though afraid of the one she now knew was in the room.

Most desperate to see through the hood, it was all Cathy could do to keep her balance and, somehow, relieve the pressure the handcuffs were putting on her wrists. She could now hear Tony moving away from her, toward the hall perhaps.

"Get away from me!" shouted Tony as the sound of the wooden paddle swished through the air in front of her and crashed into one of the tables in the dining area.

But amid Tony's screams, the crashing of the furniture, and the dull thuds of fist against flesh, Cathy never heard a word from her savior. . .or was he? Hearing something heavy, perhaps a body, hit the floor fairly close to her, she braced for what could be coming next.

"Please! Please!" begged Cathy, hoping that Tony had not won the struggle.

Little by little, she began to feel someone working above her with the ropes. Suddenly, the pressure on her wrists was gone, sending Cathy dropping toward the floor. But she never felt the sudden contact with the hard, ceramic tile. Instead, she now felt a pair of strong arms cradling her gently and lowering her to it. At that exact time, she heard the burglar alarm go off, but the one helping her wasn't rattled at all. Gentle hands were now behind her and working with the handcuffs. They instantly fell off. As she fumbled with the rope that held the gag and hood in place, she felt something cool and soft being placed over her body. But she could hear not the first footstep.

"Memphis Police Department!" shouted someone now coming through the back of the Restaurant. At that same time, the front door was kicked in. "Memphis Police!" shouted yet another person.

"We got two down in here!" shouted a man as Cathy pulled the hood from her head and stared at the policeman kneeling at her side. "Are you all right, Ma'am?" he asked as she gathered the tablecloth closer to her body.

"Although she heard his question, all Cathy could manage was continue to tremble and cry.

"This one's dead," said another officer on the far side of the one kneeling at Cathy's side. "Looks like his neck's been broken and there's a cut all the way across the back of it."

Still gripping the tablecloth close under her neck, Cathy wiped her eyes, trying to see the face of the policeman so close to her.

"Clear outside," spoke another policeman as he entered the room. "Nobody in or out since we drove up."

"Looks like you got 'em Ma'am," said the policeman still kneeling by her side. "How did you manage that?"

"No," responded Cathy weakly. She nodded toward the handcuffs on the floor right in front of her. "I was in those and hanging by a rope from the rafter above you."

"What?" came the reply from the officer still at the door.

Cathy nodded. "I don't know who helped me." She pointed to the white hood. "That was over my face and I couldn't see him. But he fought with that man on the floor, and then untied me while you were coming in the back door. By the time I got the hood off, he was gone."

"Check outside again!" shouted the policeman now checking the restaurant. "He couldn't have gotten past us."

"Call an ambulance," said the officer at Cathy's side. "Looks like she's been beaten and is still badly shaken. Might better give the coroner a heads-up as well. Looks like her 'White Knight' gave us the slip somehow."

Part 2
Now You See Me

Siting in Uncle Bill's rocker in the living room, Jack watched Pico and Teresa pull the presents from under the Christmas tree. Shelley, watching him closely, smiled at his expression. It looked to be one of utmost happiness.

Jack smiled, looking at Shelley. "When do you want the turkey ready for the oven?"

Shelley shrugged. "Fred and Myrna will be here somewhere around eleven as will Andy, Will, and Becky. I told them we would have it on the table at noon or so." She glanced at her watch. It's a little after seven right now. We'll put it in at nine or so. I'll have the dressing ready by then. If you'll shuck the corn, I'll prepare the potatoes."

"What's for breakfast?" asked Pico, still fiddling with her last present."

"Got that covered also," bragged Shelley. "It's Jimmy Dean sausage and biscuits for this morning with a big glass of cold milk. They're in the oven right now. That'll hold us until dinner."

*   *   *

At approximately 11:00AM, Will's black Fairlane pulled into the Shoultz driveway. Seeing it first, Pico jumped from the couch and ran to the front door.

"Uncle Will! Uncle Will! she shouted excitedly, pulling on the brass knob of the door. Finally opening it, she peered through the screen as she bounced on the balls of her feet. "It's Christmas again! More presents!" she added, pushing the screen door open for Will, Becky, and Andy.

"Merry Christmas!" they exclaimed as they walked inside.

Pico's smile widened. "Mrs. Shelley's got a turkey in the oven and it's almost as big as me."

"Well. . ." Will handed her and Teresa their presents. "Why don't you put those under the tree and we'll take care o' that turkey in a little bit. Fred and Myrna are right behind us. Why don't you wait 'till they get here and you can open 'em all at one time?"

Will glanced at Jack as he sat down on the couch next to him. "I know this ain't exactly the time to talk shop, but I just got a call from Memphis' West Precinct on the river. Seems they sent another, young lady to the Methodist Hospital at Munford. Same MO, age and everything like the one they just beat at those river front apartments. But this time, they have a body ta go with it."

"The girl was killed?" asked Jack.

"No-no-no," replied Will. "They think it was the woman-beatin' burglar. Seems that someone came to the girl's aide while the burglar was beatin' the stuffin' out o' her but the police completely missed 'em." The young lady lives just over the Shelby County line in Tipton County. He smiled proudly at Jack. "I got our newbie on it startin' tomorrow. Bubba's no rookie. Gave 'em his stripes back I did. He's got over ten years in Memphis' West precinct. He'll be workin' with his friends on this thing, possibly with you from time to time."

"What?" Shelley stood at the living room doorway staring at the two on the couch. "I know you two aren't talking about work today are you?"

"Merry Christmas!" exclaimed Fred as he and Myrna opened the front door.

"Saved by the bell," whispered Will to Jack.

Pico was quick to help them with the presents as they walked inside.

*   *   *

The next morning around 9:00AM, and a beautiful, clear and crisp Thursday, Will and Jack pulled into the Munford Methodist Hospital parking lot.

"What do we have here, Will?" asked the young detective as he pulled up close to the entrance.

Will shrugged. "You got just about everything yesterday. We'll be tryin' ta add to that list today. We got a Mrs. Drew Goke and a Miss Cathy Sartain ta talk to today. The first one lost her husband at the apartments on the river during a burglary. The second lady was

27

robbed and beaten at her Gourmet Burger place just like the first. Both are young and pretty and the whoever that did it likes to beat the crap out o' tied up naked girls. Both were blindfolded by some kind o' hood and gagged by a rope pulled into their mouths on the outside of the hood and then tied behind their heads. The last one, a Miss, Sartain, got outside help from someone they haven't identified yet. Whoever it was, beat and killed the attacker. Mrs. Goke, however, said there were four, possibly five perps at her place when she was beaten and robbed. In the process, her husband was badly shot in the chest. She was out cold when that happened." He looked at Jack with a smile. "Let's go in and get our feet wet."

The walk to the main desk on the first floor of the hospital was short. Noting Will's quicker than average gate, Jack smiled at his enthusiasm.

Will flashed his badge at the young girl at the main desk. "Munford Sheriff's Department, ma'am," he added, smiling at a red-haired nurse of not much more than twenty.

"Can I help you?" she asked, almost smiling herself.

"We're lookin' for a Mrs. Goke and a Miss. Sartain," said the High Sheriff.

The young lady's smile widened as she batted her green eyes at Jack. Quickly thumbing through the admissions records, she stopped, staring at where she was pointing.

"They're both right here, Sir," she replied proudly, her gaze and smile making its way back to Jack.

"Well, at least we're getting' closer," quipped Will. "Want me ta guess which room?"

"Ohhhh, I'm sorry, Sir," apologized the young nurse as she looked back at her book. "Mrs. Goke's in room 203 and Miss. Sartain in 207. You can see Miss. Sartain right now, but to see Mrs. Goke, will be a little different."

Will raised his eyebrows. "Will we have ta make an appointment. . ." Will squinted at her nametag, "Miss Hensley."

"Of course not," she replied, motioning toward the elevators. "Just go up to the second floor nurse's desk and the head nurse, Mrs. Goodwell, will arrange your visits for you."

Will turned and headed toward the elevators.

"Thanks for your help," added Jack, quickly following him.

As the two stepped out of the elevator, Will slowly stopped, almost holding Jack back.

"See the heavy-set, dark-haired woman behind the desk?" whispered Will.

Jack nodded.

"That's our Mrs. Goodwell. For Pete's sake, don't get her riled. She's a bulldog when she's mad. Worse'n Banjo."

"Mrs. Goodwell," said Will cheerfully as the two approached the desk. "I need ta see two of your patients."

She slowly looked up from her paperwork and over her black, horn-rimmed glasses at Will. "I, Sheriff?" She glanced at Jack.

"That would be a 'we'," corrected Will, thumbing back toward Jack. "This young fella's Detective Shoultz. He'll be on the case as well."

She threw a quick glance up at Jack. "And just who will be blessed with your presence?" she asked.

"That would be a Mrs. Goke in room 203 and a Miss. Sartain in room 207," explained Will.

Nurse Goodwell squinted over her glasses. "You can start with Miss Sartain. Take your time with her. That'll give me some time to prepare our Mrs. Goke." She then pulled off her glasses and placed her left elbow on the desk. "Be easy with Mrs. Goke. She's on a sedative and has had quite a traumatic experience that included losing her husband. I believe her mother's still with her."

"Thank-you-Ma'am," replied Will politely as he turned away from the desk, tugging at Jack jacket sleeve. "Let's go see our lady in 207." "You wanna explain that smirk?" he asked without turning around.

"Did she just put you in the back seat again?" chuckled Jack.

Without looking back, the old Sheriff slowly shook his head as he slowed to a stop at Miss. Sartain's room. "Well. . ." he started with a deep breath, "Let's give it a try."

The Sheriff's knock was light, but it moved the partially open door of 207.

"Come in," spoke a young man as the door was slowly opened.

"I'm Bruce Sidewell, Cathy's friend. How can we help you?"

The trim, six-foot, sandy-haired young man stepped back, opening the door for the two.

Cathy Sartain, now sitting up against her pillows, was still picking at her breakfast on the over-the-bed roller table. She stared at Will's badge, but said not a word.

Will eased his Stetson off. "I'm sorry ta have ta bother you, Ma'am," he started with a half-smile. "I'm Sheriff Brumley and this young fella's Detective Shoultz. We're from Munford and working a case with Memphis' West Precinct. Do you feel like answering a few questions? I promise it won't take long."

Cathy nodded. "I didn't see much, Sheriff. He put a white bag over my head and drugged me with something that smelled horrible."

Will nodded. "That would be either, Miss. Sartain. "You said the bag was white?"

Cathy nodded.

Will glanced back at Jack. "The Goke lady said something about a white hood used on her." He looked back at Cathy. "You said someone came in as you were being beaten."

Cathy shrugged her shoulders. "I never heard him come in, God bless him. Just, all of a sudden, this awful man stopped beating me and said something to the one who helped me. It was, kind of like, he was surprised, if not horrified, to see him." She glanced at Jack. "I couldn't see a thing through the hood, but I heard the two struggle, and then someone hit the floor really hard. But the other man, the one the police couldn't find, was gentle. He untied the rope that held me up off the floor and gently

30

lowered me to it in his arms. He then took off the handcuffs. When I struggled with the rope that held the hood on, I felt him cover me with a tablecloth." She smiled, almost sheepishly. "I was mostly naked at the time. I could hear the police pounding on the back door when he put the tablecloth over me, but I never heard him leave."

"And the police didn't see this man who helped you?" asked Jack.

Cathy slowly shook her head. "They did not. By the time I got the hood off, the police were already in the room."

"I see," replied Will, smiling at her. "The one on the floor was the man who beat you. His fingerprints and your blood was on the paddle found near where you were lying." He patted her right shoulder. "You've been through a bad ordeal and we'll get to the bottom of it I promise. Thank you for talking to us." Will turned to Jack on the way out of the room. "Let's go back to the nurse's desk. Maybe our Mrs. Goodwell will let us see Mrs. Goke."

In less than five minutes, Nurse Goodwell had Will and Jack standing at the door of room 203 with her hand firmly on the door handle.

"You two be most careful here," she warned with a stern expression. "She's just lost her husband and took a severe beating as well. The doctor's given her a light sedative, but she should be able to talk to you if she feels up to it." She placed her hand on Will's right forearm. "She also insists her husband is still alive," she added softly. "She says she sees him every night." She looked over her black, horn-rimmed glasses at them both as she added, "Do not remind her that he is dead. That reality she will have to face soon enough." Turning, she eased the door open and peeped inside.

Will stepped to one side, looking in the room also. It appeared to be very dark. The TV was o, but no sound. The light from the curtained window on the far side of the room filtered through the reddish-brown hair of a lady standing on the far side of Mrs. Goke's bed.

31

"Can I help you?" asked the lady. In her mid-fifties, she stood, smiling at them both.

"Sorry to bother you both on such a strenuous day, Ma'am, but we're workin' this case with Memphis' West Precinct. I'm Sheriff Brumley with the Munford Sheriff's Department and this young man behind me is Detective Jack Shoultz."

Will's gaze made its way to Mrs. Goke. She was well up on her pillows, leaning against the headboard. Wiping her eyes, she looked to be trying to get a better look at her two visitors.

The lady stepped closer to the bed, looking at Will. "Since you're helping us, Sheriff, you can call me Bee." She nodded at the young lady in the bed. "You can refer to her as Drew if you like. I'm her mother." She patted Drew's left hand. "We have company, dear. Do you feel like talking to them? They're trying to find the ones who hurt you." She then eased to the foot of the bed, closer to Will and Jack. "She had another episode last night you know," she whispered. "She said her husband visited her again."

"Were you there?" asked Will.

Bee nodded. "I didn't notice a soul," she whispered. "I think the sedative is allowing her mind to dream a little."

"Uh huh," said Will just as a glint of sunlight reflected off of something dangling from the headboard's left bedpost.

Looking over his glasses, Will eased closer to the headboard. The charm on the silver chain depicted the head of a tiger, etched on a round piece of yellow ivory, and set in a round piece of silver about the size of a quarter.

Will removed the necklace from the bedpost. "Does this belong to you or your daughter, Mrs. Bee?" he asked.

Bee slowly shook her head. "No. . .I never really noticed it." She looked at her daughter.

"JJ brought it to me last night," explained Drew. Her voice weak.

Will stood there, fencepost still, staring at the necklace.

"Mr. Brumley?" Bee gently touched his forearm.

"Uhhh. . . I'm fine," he managed.

Now with raised eyebrows, he looked closer at the necklace. It appeared to have something caked into the links of the chain.

"Uh huh." Will slowly turned to Jack. "Gimme one o' your plastic bags. I'll bet my next check that this is the blood of the man the police found dead at that burger place." He turned to Bee. "We'll be takin' this thing if you don't mind, Ma'am."

Mrs. Bee nodded silently.

"You know. . ." Jack paused, looking at Will. "If that matches that dead man and it ended up where you just found it, perhaps JJ--"

"Don't even go there, Jack Shoultz," grumbled Will. "I barely escaped that 'Lady in Red' thing with what little hair I got left."

Bee squinted, moving even closer to the sheriff. "Do you really think that JJ did that?" She nodded to the plastic bag in Jack's hands.

"He does," answered Jack. "As for me, I'm just along for the ride."

*   *   *

The next day, a beautiful Friday the 27th day of December, Will dispatched Bubba to Memphis' West Precinct to collect whatever evidence they were willing to share on the Goke and Sartain cases. Still trying to rid himself of the 'old goat' remark, Bubba was most anxious to accommodate the Sheriff. But, all in all, things back in Tipton County at Trey Isley's place, Friday was not going nearly as smooth. . .

Trey sat across the breakfast table, barely making eye contact with Scott, Steve, or Jimmy.

"Maybe Tony had trouble with his cycle," suggested Scott, glancing at Steve and Jimmy.

"Perhaps he had money trouble," grumbled Steve. Flopping his napkin down on his plate, he leaned back in his chair and looked at Trey.

Trey slowly shook his head. "His Triumph is always in good shape, he has no family to count on besides us. I

33

don't think he would steal from the family he has in us. That leaves only one thing."

"They got him?" guessed Jimmy.

Trey agreed with a slight nod.

Jimmy squinted at Trey. "Can't we call somewhere and find out?"

Steve laughed out loud. "Sure we could, and that would lead them right back to us, knot head." He looked to Trey. "He hasn't even called us. He's got one call if they have him."

"That leaves us with two possibilities," added Scott. "Either he's afraid to use it and possibly expose us, or. . ." Scott's voice trailed off, as he looked up at Trey. "He's been shot while attempting this caper."

Trey slouched down in his seat, rested his head on the back of his chair, and then stared at the ceiling. "He's either in the hospital, in jail, on in the morgue. He lolled his head around and stared at Scott. "Get away from here, go to Munford perhaps, get on a pay phone, and then call every hospital in Memphis. He's gotta be in one of them if he's been hurt."

No sooner had Trey made that comment than Jimmy shoved his chair back from the table and begin to cough. "Something in the hash," he sputtered as his face turned red.

Scott jumped from his chair, pulled Jimmy to his feet, and then got behind his still choking friend. "Hold still!" ordered Scott as he grabbed him around the waist.

Now, with Scott's closed fist just under the front of Jimmy's ribs, he started a series of short and powerful thrusts into the young man's solar flexes. Somewhere between eight and twelve thrusts, Jimmy coughed up a wad of corned beef hash with something gold and shiny lying in its midst.

"Thanks for that," said Jimmy still trying to clear his throat.

"My God," said Trey weakly as he Steve stood from the table, looking at what they could see of the glittering object.

34

Scott immediately grabbed Jimmy's spoon, knelt on his right knee, and then moved the object from the pieces of biscuit and hash. "What tha. . ." Scott quickly stood up, tossed the spoon to Jimmy's plate, and then looked back down at a golden ring with a red stone.

Trey moved closer, staring at the ring. "That's Tony's ruby ring."

"Can't be," said Jimmy, backing away from those looking down at the floor at the dead man's ring.

But as Jimmy moved from the others, he seemed to trip and fall backwards against the countertop.

"Good God!" exclaimed Scott as he turned to where Jimmy was lying. Quickly kneeling by his side, he glanced up at the others. "He's out cold and bleeding all over the place! Hand me a towel quick!"

Trey snatched a drying towel from the dish rick and tossed it to Scott.

Scott glanced at Trey as he pressed the towel against the back of Jimmy's bleeding head. "He's got a six inch gash on the back of his head. Call an ambulance quick. He needs to go the Methodist at Munford ASAP."

"Got it!" said Steve as he pounced on the kitchen, wall phone.

Trey looked back at Scott. "Where the hell did Tony's ring come from?" I cooked that meal and I certainly didn't see any such a thing when I did."

Scott slowly shook his head as he continued to hold the towel against Jimmy's head. "Tony never took it off. It was the only thing his old man left him."

*   *   *

Batting his eyes wildly, Jimmy awoke and looked groggily about the perfectly, white room. Nothing looked so foreign to the young man as he lay there with his head pounding through the bandages. Finally finding a familiar face, he tried to push himself up on his pillow.

"None of that," said Trey. He quickly got up from his chair and stepped closer to the bed. "The Doc said to lay there while those stitches help the cut to heal."

"What does this cost?" asked Jimmy. "I don't--"

"Never mind the cost," replied Trey, smiling. "We got a company policy on everyone. Most of this is covered and I'll take care of the rest. The doctor said that your wound was made by something very sharp."

"Can't imagine that," managed Jimmy, gingerly touching the bandages on the back of his head. "Seemed like I got pushed, but all of you guys weren't anywhere close. I think I hit the edge of the counter."

Trey slowly shook his head. "You were about five feet from the counter, Jimmy. Plus, there was no blood on its edge at all. Scott found a butcher knife under you when he was trying to stop the bleeding. You damned near got stabbed as well."

"That doesn't make sense," grumbled Jimmy. "Those knives are on a magnetic holder right above the countertop." He added, as he lolled his head around in disbelief.

"Don't worry about it," said Trey. "The Doc said he might check you out tomorrow if there's no infection and the bleeding doesn't start again. Then he'll see you in five days or so to change the bandage and check the healing. Right now I've got to visit a place in Atoka and set up another caper. I got Steve running the Ice rout while Scott is in Munford checking on where the devil Tony is. By the time I get back, both of them should be at the house."

"What about Tony's ring?" Jimmy slowly raised his eyebrows.

"I have not a clue," replied Trey, almost apologetically. "I'll be back tomorrow and check on you."

*   *   *

Shortly after 1:00PM, with television becoming completely boring, Jimmy turned the set off to take a nap and hopefully enjoy the peace and quiet. In little time, he was sound asleep.

But sometimes, rest is an elusive creature. It seemed that no time at all had passed until he heard the room door open. Lolling his head toward the door, he could see Nurse Goodwell as she walked toward his bed.

"It's just me, Mr. Sawyer," she said softy as she held something close to his chin. "Just put this under your

36

tongue. Infection will cause you to run a temperature and we certainly don't want that do we?"

Jimmy shook his head as the nurse placed the thermometer under his tongue and looked at her watch.

Taking it out, she smiled. "Ninety-nine," she said as her smile held. "You just keep resting. It's a little after 2:00PM and I'll be in and out to keep tabs on your temperature."

With that, she left the room and Jimmy to return to his nap. About forty minutes later, the door opened again, but Jimmy was so groggy, he never bothered to take notice. Neither did he open his eyes when a pair of cold hands gently took his left hand and moved it to the guard rail of the bed. Seconds later, the same set of gentle hands were working with his right hand. He felt the cold, chrome rail against the back of his wrist.

"Nurse Goodwell?" he asked. But as he made an attempt to wipe the sleep from his eyes, he quickly became aware he couldn't move his hands from the bed's guard rail.

"What the--" Jimmy's comment was cut short as the blurry figure of a tall, sandy-haired man stuffed a knotted rag in his mouth and tied it behind his head.

Try as he did, Jimmy's complaints never got past the gag as he stared into the face of his tormentor. With clinched teeth bared and a smile that looked perfectly out of place, Jimmy looked into the face of the man now hovering directly over him. His eyes were so dilated they looked totally black. Jimmy tried to watch him as he moved to the wall where the headboard was, but he could only listen to something being removed from it. In only seconds, he was back with the armband of the blood pressure machine. Smiling again, the man gently tucked it under Jimmy's chin and fastened the Velcro snugly behind his neck. Now, nose to nose with the man, Jimmy could hear the pump-hissing sound of the inflation ball as the band became tighter and tighter. When it was all Jimmy could do to breathe, the pumping stopped.

"P-please," begged Jimmy, but the gag was doing its job much too well.

Jimmy could now feel his ankles being tied to the bottom rail of the bed. In one, smooth move, the elastic in his pajama bottoms was pulled down to join the top of the sheet still at his knees.

"No! No!" Jimmy's muffled screams were barely heard as his Fruit of the Looms were jerked down to join his pajama bottoms.

Now, completely wide-eyed and terrified, Jimmy recognized the man he shot at the river front apartments as he pulled Tony's three-foot cane from his belt. Gripping it firmly in his right hand, the man laid it gently against Jimmy's groin. Taking the time to check Jimmy's terrified expression and muted complaints, he began a series of blows that covered an area from Jimmy's lower abdomen to his mid-thighs. Again and again the cane struck until Jimmy had not the strength to scream. Then, when Jimmy would hardly flinch after each blow, the whipping stopped, and pumping sound began again. . . .

*   *   *

Outside the room and down the hall at the nurse's desk, Nurse Goodwell was finishing up a temperature tracking chart to display on the wall near Jimmy's bed. Succeeding in that, she turned toward the hallway and Jimmy's room. As she did, she noticed a young, sandy-haired man step from 205-the exact room where Jimmy was at. He was dressed in blue jeans with an orange, Rolling Stones tee shirt. With his gaze held to the floor, he passed the desk without a word.

"May I help you?" asked Nurse Goodwell, not recognizing the fellow at all.

Making not the slightest attempt to acknowledge her request, the young man stopped in front of the first elevator and pushed the down button.

"Lucy. . ." whispered Nurse Goodwell. "Did you see him check in?"

"No Ma'am," replied Lucy, now standing right behind the Head Nurse. "Two O Five is wide open. Shall I check it?"

"I'll get it," replied Mrs. Goodwell. "You keep an eye on our visitor. I didn't notice him come in either."

Not trying to show too much concern, Mrs. Goodwell walked briskly down the hallway toward Jimmy's room. In just seconds, she was inside and trying to release the armband under Jimmy's already blue face.

"Lucy! Lucy!" she shouted, tugging at the Velcro that held the armband tight. "Call security right now! Tell them to hold that young man at the elevator!"

Lucy looked toward the elevators as she picked up the phone. The young man was still there and acting as though he had heard nothing. On down the hallway, people were starting to look from their rooms—patients as well as visitors. Now, with the Code Blue alarm set in motion, the doctor on duty and a nurse's aide scrambled from the office. With the defibrillator's wheels clicking on the hallway's tile floor, Lucy watched the two race past the desk and on down the hallway toward 205. Still waiting for Security to pick up, Lucy turned toward the elevators again. The young man was still there. Now, hearing someone running, the young nurse turned to see Nurse Goodwell quickly approaching the desk just as Security answered the phone.

"This is Nurse Thompson on the second floor. We just had an assault on a patient and the assailant is about to step into the second elevator. He's about twenty, orange tee shirt, and has light-colored hair."

Then, just like a scene straight out of Nancy Drake's Mysteries, the Head Nurse raced passed the floor desk and headed toward the elevators. Her hands and the front of her white uniform were stained with blood.

"Gladys! Gladys!" shouted Lucy as she scrambled from her position in the desk area. "Don't go near that man!"

But the Head Nurse's temper was righteously kindled and she didn't even give Lucy a glance as the doors shut on the second elevator. Hesitating not a second, Mrs. Goodwell pounded on the down button and then stepped back to glare at the elevator doors as she tried to catch her breath.

"No-no-no!" shouted Lucy as she raced to her friend's side.

Now, with Lucy gripping the Head Nurse's right forearm, they both watched the doors as the elevator's bell rang again. But as the doors opened, it left them both staring at an empty compartment.

"The damn thing is as empty as my checkbook," grumbled Gladys. "Where the devil is he?"

"Stay here," ordered Gladys as she pulled away from Lucy. "I'm going to the first floor. He's gotta be here somewhere," she added as she stepped inside the cubicle and pressed the down button.

"Uhhh. . ." Lucy slowly backed away from the still open elevator and looked toward room 205. Jumping as the elevator doors shut again, she now found herself alone at the nurse's desk.

*   *   *

Inside the closed elevator however, Nurse Goodwell held to the cubicle hand rail, staring at the still glowing second floor button.

"Let's go! Let's go!" she exclaimed as she stepped forward and frantically pushed the first floor button over and over again.

"You shouldn't help him you know," spoke someone from behind and slightly to her right.

Slowly turning, she stared at the same, young man who had just came from room 205. His smile was as disingenuous as his eyes were black. . .

*   *   *

Downstairs and all around the submissions desk, was total chaos. Two security men were posted at the elevator doors, two had left and were racing up the stairs toward the second floor, and another two were trying to clear out the main lobby. With weapons drawn, the two in front of the elevator awaited the ring of number two's bell. When it rang, they stepped back, braced themselves, and watched the chrome doors slowly open.

"Where is he?" asked a puzzled guard as he stared at the nurse on the floor.

"We need a help over here," shouted the second guard. "We got one down."

40

That shout brought the floor doctor as well as the nurse at the main desk.

Kneeling at Nurse Goodwell's side, the young doctor helped her to sit up. "Are you all right?" he asked.

"Did he hurt you?" asked the security officer at the door.

Managing a weak "No", the second floor head nurse looked up at the officer. "He was right here with me," she managed. "I was looking right into his eyes. There was something about him--something, well, not normal. I guess I fainted."

"Take care of her, Doc," said the security guard. "We'll check the area again."

Part 3
Sometimes They Never Leave

Only seconds from the Munford Hospital's parking lot entranceway, the High Sheriff slowed to allow Jack's unmarked Ford all but slide in from the other direction. Lit up and with sirens wailing, they both raced toward the main entrance. Jack slowed to a stop hardly five paces from the people that were being ushered from the main lobby.

"In here!" shouted one of the security guards as he pointed through the doors, toward the main desk.

"What have we got?" asked Jack as Will trotted up to join him.

"Not a clue," admitted Will as they hurried through the main entranceway. Pausing, he looked at those in the crowd. "One o' the nurses here called it in to Dianne. Said one o' their patients had been assaulted and left in a bad way. The perp was a white male, young, and had light-colored hair. Nothin' like that here." Will turned and headed toward the submissions desk. "Dianne said the nurse watched 'em get on the second-floor elevator."

Slowing as the two approached the main desk, Will noticed Mrs. Goodwell sitting in a chair with two guards at her side.

"Right there," said the nurse at the desk, shaking a nervous finger at the elevators. "The man you're after was supposed to come out of the second elevator."

"Supposed ta come out?" grumbled Will as he headed toward Mrs. Goodwell. Will looked at the older security guard. "What's happened here?" He squinted at the nurse, but she just shrugged, glancing at the ceiling.

"I'm Richard Williams, Sir, senior guard here. I'm still trying to get a grip on that myself. I've got two guards stationed at room 205 right now." He nodded toward Mrs. Goodwell. "This lady is the second-floor head nurse. She came down from 205 with the assailant, but when the doors opened here, she was out cold and the perp was nowhere in sight."

Will slowly drug his hat from his head, ran his fingers through his thinning hair, and then looked at Mrs. Goodwell. With her hands still shaking, she wouldn't even make eye contact. "Wait just a minute," he said as he glanced back at Jack. "There's not a whole lot o' room between the first and second floor, guys." He looked back to the nurse. "Gladys, are you all right?"

She nodded, trying to force a smile.

"Did he harm you?" asked Will.

A silent "No" head shake came as she wiped her eyes and nose with a handkerchief.

"But. . ." Will paused, looking at the head nurse. "You said he was in the elevator with you?"

She shook her head. "Not at first. I mean, he went in and the doors closed. I wasn't close enough to catch the doors, so I hit the down button. When the doors opened, he was gone. So. . ." she glanced up at the old Sheriff, "I got in as Lucy called to warn the first floor. When the doors closed, the elevator wouldn't budge." She looked up at Will. "That's when he came back."

Will squinted, tightly closed his eyes, and then rubbed his forehead.

"Sheriff. . ." said the senior guard.

Will slowly opened his eyes, looking at him.

"These elevators have ceiling doors, and they all have security seals. The seal in number two was not broken."

Will looked back at the nurse.

"I know what you're going to ask," she managed in a low voice. "While I continually punched the first-floor button, he spoke from right behind me. Startled, I turned to look at him. I've never seen anyone with such an expression. His eyes looked like big, black marbles and his grin had to be borrowed from Satan himself."

"Where did he go?" asked Jack.

Nurse Goodwell shrugged, looking down at the wadded up handkerchief in her hands. "I'm not a weak person, Mr. Brumley, but I got so dizzy I could no longer stand. I felt him catch me as I passed out. He was very gentle.

That's all I remember until the guard woke me up on the first floor."

"Uh huh. . ." Fumbling with the Empirin bottle in his jacket pocket, Will looked back at Jack. "I'm goin' to the second floor in number one. Check this elevator out as quickly as possible so it can be used and then join me in room 205."

In scarcely a minute, the old Sheriff was stepping from the elevator and heading toward the nurse's desk.

"How is Gladys?" asked Lucy, quickly stepping from behind the desk.

"Shaken," replied Will. "But she'll fine. She got a good look at our attacker." Will glanced down the hallway toward the guards at room 205. They were both staring back at him.

"She got a good look at the attacker?" asked Lucy through a squint. "The man wasn't there, Sheriff. The elevator was empty when she got into it to go the first floor."

"Yep," replied Will. "Heard that as well." As Will looked toward the guards again, he felt a gentle hand on his back.

"Did you get him?" asked Lucy.

Will smiled, noting her desperate expression. Patting her hand, he replied, "No Ma'am, but we're workin' on it. Why don't you stay right here. I got a few things ta do down the hall a way a piece."

As Will continued toward the guards, a guard of forty or so, heavy-set, and with red hair took a half step toward him. "He's dead, Sir. We haven't touched a thing."

"Don't let anyone near that second elevator," ordered Will as he watched the older guard slowly shake his head. Trim, in his fifties, and mostly bald, he stared at Will. "Watch what you put your hands on in there, Sheriff. There's blood splattered on just about everything."

Will eased up to the doorway and looked inside.

"See that?" The bald-headed guard pointed toward the floor on the far side of the bed. A broken, wooden cane about three feet long lay there all but covered in blood.

"That fellow beat the crap out of that man. He's got whelps and cuts from his stomach to his knees."

Will nodded as he stooped under the yellow, crime scene tape that was attached across the doorway, stood up, and then stopped. The guard was right. The walls, ceiling above the bed, a good portion of the floor, as well as the windows on the far side of the room were all splattered with blood.

Will looked back at the guards. "Did you get the floor nurse's statement?"

"Yes, Sir," replied the bald-headed guard.

"Did she describe this fellow's assailant?" asked Will.

"In detail, Sir," answered the guard. "She was looking at him while she called it in."

"Uh huh. . ." replied Will weakly. "In that statement, did she mention that the perp had blood on him?"

"Uhhh. . ." The bald-headed guard looked down the hallway toward the nurse. "You know, I don't think she said that."

"Would you please go and ask her for me?" asked Will.

Without hesitation, the bald-headed guard left the doorway and headed toward the nurse's desk.

Putting on his blue, rubber gloves, Will picked his path through the blood splattering's in the floor and paused at the head of Jimmy's bed. The blood-stained, blood pressure band was still lying on the floor not two feet from the broken cane. Jimmy's face was still a dark shade of blue. Continuing to the head of the bed, the old sheriff pushed Jimmy's face toward the wall and pulled the back of his collar away from his neck.

"Ohhh Hell," groaned Will, now looking at what seemed to be fresh, reddened marks made by a necklace as it was jerked from the body.

"Coroner's here," said Jack, now standing at the doorway.

Will quickly looked up. "You finished with the elevator already?"

"Not at all," replied Jack, reluctant to step under the warning tape. "Kotts is helping Bubba dust for

45

fingerprints. They're on this floor right now. This place is a mess. Didn't anyone hear anything?"

Will slowly shook his head. "He was gagged. We got another room ta visit." Will pointed to Jimmy's neck.

"Find something?" asked Jack.

"Too much of somethin'," quipped Will.

"That would be a no, Sheriff," said the bald-headed guard now standing next to Jack.

Will looked at Jack. "Wouldn't you think that the one who pounded the puddin' out o' this fella would have blood on him as well?"

Jack nodded, looking about the room again, his gaze dropped to the near side of where will was standing. "There shouldn't be any blood there, Will. The killer should have been wearing what is now on the floor."

"Will rolled his eyes as he nodded. "There goes the rest o' my hair. The onliest thing that blood can't get on is somethin' that ain't there."

"I'm lost," said the bald-headed guard with a nod from his partner. "What are you saying?"

"I'm sayin' it's time for me to retire," groaned Will. "Have Kotts be sure to keep these ropes. They look like the one described in the last killing." Picking his way back to the doorway, Will ducked back under the warning tape. "Come with me." He glanced at Jack as he headed back up the hallway. "We're gonna take a look in on Mrs. Goke. If I'm right, we'll need ta get Charlie in on this."

"Charlie?" Jack squinted. "Was that man wearing a necklace?"

"Was is correct," answered Will as he paused at the closed door of room 203. With a gentle knock, Will eased the door open. "Mrs. Goke?" he said softly as he peeped inside.

But there were no visitors in the room, the drapes were partially open, and the patient appeared to be asleep. Then, just like the first time, the same, infamous glint seemed to yell at him from something hanging upon the near post on the headboard.

"Jesus on tha cross," said Will weakly as he stared at yet another tiger medallion.

Easing into the room, he crept to the headboard, took the necklace from the post, and then tiptoed back to the door and out of the room.

"Another one?" asked Jack, staring at the medallion.

Will glanced at Jack. "Didn't you say Bubba was here?"

Jack nodded. "He's helping Kotts right now in 205."

"Good," said Will with a slight grin. "You go right now and tell him he's assigned to this room until further notice. This character walked two, identical necklaces right into this room, killed a man hardly two doors down, and was seen as he passed right by the nurse's station to boot. Bubba is almost seven feet tall in his cowboy boots and weighs in at two hundred and sixty-five pounds and he does not believe in ghosts! I got a' feelin' if he can grab 'em, he's ours."

*   *   *

Shortly after 6:00PM, and back at the Insley home, Trey eased the phone down to its rest, staring at Scott. But he didn't say a word.

"Trey, I really don't think Tony ran out on us," said Scott. "Perhaps the hospitals are slow to update their records."

"Jimmy's dead," managed Trey, just above a whisper.

Scott slowly stood. As his chin dropped, a squint gradually formed in disbelief. "What?"

"How did this happen?" asked Steve, now standing also. "He was under the hospital's care for crying out loud."

"I know." Trey's stare slowly made it back to Scott. "Shortly after I left, the head nurse on the second floor said a young, sandy-haired man visited Jimmy's room. He was wearing jeans and an orange, Rolling Stones tee shirt. When he left, our boy, Jimmy was dead." Trey slowly sat down on the couch by the phone. "He killed him right there in his room."

"That don't make sense!" grumbled Scott. "What about security? What about the police? They're not five minutes from there."

47

"The nurse said security was there, but he escaped with the head nurse in the elevator on the second floor. Security was waiting for him on the first, but when the doors opened, the only one who was in it was the head nurse, and she had passed out for God's sake."

Squinting at Trey, Scott slowly sat down also. "You think Scott's dead, don't you?"

"I think someone's after us," replied Trey. "Someone either from the Goke or the Sartain family."

Steve stepped closer to the two. "Or anyone else of the others we have robbed in the last two years. Maybe we should just lay low for a little while. They might not know where we live."

*   *   *

But the incurable optimist, Steve Scott, didn't let the troubles of the day ruin his plans for a Friday night with his girlfriend. He had just spent five hundred dollars for her a good Christmas and he thought she was warming up to the idea of moving in with him in his Munford apartment. Besides, tonight was their scary movie with a pizza night and he wasn't going to miss that. Her parents, Doug and Pauline Glidewell, had left Janice the house for a weekend in Hot Springs, Arkansas. With them gone for the weekend, he knew he wouldn't have to leave until Sunday morning. . .

At 7:00PM sharp that afternoon, Steve pulled his '60, champagne colored ninety-eight olds into the Glidewell driveway at Atoka, Tennessee. Janice, a trim, brown-haired girl in her mid-twenties, opened the screen door, waving at him as he got out.

"How about a Sparky's BBQ tonight?" Steve asked, smiling at her.

Janice's smile widened. "Sounds good to me," she agreed as Steve stepped up the porch steps with a twelve pack of Bud Light.

Janice, now laughing, slowly shook her head. "You know how you are when you've had too many. If you break something around here, Dad will have your ears."

Steve laughed as the two entered the living room. "He's just a constable, Janice, not God Almighty."

48

Two hours, two BBQ sandwiches and fries later, Steve sat glassy-eyed next to Janice watching 'War of the Worlds'. About halfway through the movie, something heavy hit the back door, causing Janice to jump. Steve, barely affording it a glance, went right back to the movie.

"Steve. . ." Janice slowly sat up and looked toward the dining area.

"Ohhh Janice, for crying out loud," he grumbled. "Probably a coon or something. When you feed 'em, they come back forever." He threw her his 'don't interrupt the movie again' glance and then sat his half-finished beer on the coffee table to join the five other 'dead soldiers'.

Janice slowly stood from the couch, looking through the dining area and toward the kitchen where the back door was. "Watch your movie, Steve. I'm gonna take a look out of the back door window. If someone's in the garage, we're calling the police."

"All right," replied Steve, never taking his eyes from the movie.

Tiptoeing through the dining room and on into the kitchen, she eased the back door curtains apart and noticed the automatic garage door was opening.

"Steve," she said, trying to be as quiet as her excitement would allow.

"Great Scott, Janice," grumbled Steve again as he stood from the couch. "We're at the last part of the movie and--"

Steve's comment was cut short by a blood curdling scream from the kitchen. Steve, frozen in place, watched as Janice came running through the dining area to stop just a reach from him.

"Come on! Come on!" she exclaimed. "There's somebody looking through the back door window and he's 'not' one of our neighbors."

"What?" Steve took a groggy step forward and promptly fell over the coffee table.

"Get up! Get up!" encouraged Janice as she pulled him to his feet.

"I got this! I got this!" he said excitedly as he pointed toward the phone. "Call the Sheriff's Department while I take a look. Where's your bat?"

"At the right of the back door," replied Janice as she fumbled with the phone on the end table.

Wiping his eyes, Steve walked briskly through the dining area and on toward the kitchen and back door. Now wasting a minute, he pushed the curtains apart. The garage door was wide open.

He glanced back toward the living room. "Wasn't the garage door closed when I drove up?"

"Yes! Yes!" answered Janice. "I told you he was opening it just a minute ago."

"Ohhh. . ." Steve fumbled with the lock.

"Don't go out there, Steve," said Janice from the living room. "I've got the police on the phone."

Seeing no one at all outside, Steve opened the door, stepped out onto the back porch, and then eased toward the open garage, bouncing the Louisville Slugger in his right hand.

"Steve?"

Steve looked back at Janice, now holding the back screen door open. "Stay there, baby," he said softly. "I'm just gonna have a look."

With one foot on the small, back porch and the other still in the kitchen, Janice watched Steve tighten his grip on the bat and ease into the dark of the garage. Hardly a minute had passed before he appeared back at the opening again.

"Not a soul here, baby," he said, glancing about the back yard. "Maybe we scared--"

But Steve never finished his comment. Janice watched in horror as someone stepped from the dark behind him, looped something around his neck, and then pulled him screaming back inside. The Louisville Slugger lay there, rolling around on the concrete.

"Steve!" shouted Janice, but his screaming continued.

Wheeling where she was, she raced back inside and on to the hallway where her father's gun rack was. "Grabbing the first gun she could get to, she fumbled in the drawer of the gun rack for the twelve-gauge shells. Only then did she notice the flashing, red lights now being reflected off of things in the living room. Quickly putting the shotgun back in its place, she raced back up the hallway and on toward the front door in the living room. It barely slowed her down.

"Whoa-whoa!" said James as he caught her by the shoulders. "Is there someone in the house?"

"No-no," Janice finally got out through the tears. "He's got my boyfriend in the garage," she finally managed. "Hear him screaming?"

But try as he could, James could hear nothing. He looked back at Janice. "Stay right here Miss. Glidewell, I'll have a look in the garage."

So, with Sparky's BBQ lights flashing in competition with Mrs. Pauline's Restaurant, James could hear nothing but the traffic on Highway 51, hardly forty yards from the house. Moving from the porch and on toward his patrol car, James pulled out his flashlight as he eased around the corner of the house. Directing the powerful beam of the four cell Maglite toward the garage, he could now see and hear the garage door attempting to close. Easing closer, James watched the door come down to about a foot from the ground, hesitate, and then go up about a foot or so where it would, once again, try to shut. Opting for the regular door to the left of the roll-up, James pulled his . 357 Smith and Wesson and went in pistol first.

"Holy shi. . ."

James words faded as he held the beam of the flashlight on a man dangling from something around his neck that was attached to the top of the roll-up automatic door. He was slowly moving with the door's struggle. As his head hit the top of the door rack, it stopped the door from closing, causing it to repeat its effort over and over again. With a quick and careful look about the inside of the garage, James found the door button and pushed open. The door responded and lowered the man back down toward the floor to a pool of his own blood. There was no doubt that he was dead. The chain saw blade had cut well into his neck. There was little need to check for a

51

pulse. James got up, checked the area again, and then returned to Janice still waiting on the front porch.

"Stay here, Ma'am," he said firmly as he looked into her still wet eyes. "I've got to call this in."

Janice ran down the steps and grabbed his left arm as James tried to turn toward his car. "How is Steve? Did you find him?"

James dropped his gaze to the front porch steps. "Not so good, Ma'am. He didn't make it."

"Nooo!" Janice pushed James aside and tried to go around him.

"Please, Ma'am," said James as he gently grabbed her. "I wouldn't. We can't help him now and you don't need to see what's back there. Come with me."

James led her to his car where he seated her in the back. At approximately 10:15PM, and with James constantly at Janice's side, Virgil drove up with an ambulance right behind him.

"The Coroner is on his way," said the constable as he got out. The trim, six-foot fifty-year-old grinned at James. "He said something about Old Puff-N-Stuff couldn't be reached right now, but Lucy's still trying. "Want me to help you check this out?"

"He's back there right under the automatic door, but I'd wait for Kotts if I were you."

*   *   *

The next morning, the twelfth of December and a Saturday, the Sheriff officially assigned Deputy Bubba Watkins to a plain clothes, twelve hour shift from 8:00PM Saturday evening to 8:00AM Sunday morning. James would relieve him that Sunday morning and work until 8:00PM that night. Adding to what both the head nurse and ward nurse saw on the second floor of the hospital, was what Miss. Glidewell witnessed in the elevator. Holding to his belief that it was a slick serial killer, Will hoped to break the 'ghost curse' someone started at the coroner's office. . . .

Saturday morning, bright and early at 7:30AM, Bubba stepped from the second floor elevator at the Munford Methodist Hospital. Dressed in Levis and a red, plaid shirt, the light brown Stetson he was carrying in his hand screamed 'cowboy'.

The floor nurse glanced at the opening elevator doors and then quickly did a double-take at Bubba as he stepped out. Scrambling from her chair, she smiled at the big, Texas-looking guy.

"May I help you, Sir," she finally got out.

Bubba smiled, nodding to the young lady. "I'm Deputy Watkins of the Munford Sheriff's Department Ma'am. I'm here to keep an eye on room 203 without being overly conspicuous."

"Conspicuous?" The nurse's smile widened. "I'm Nurse Lucy Thompson," she said before she thought. In her mid-twenties, the trim brunette's chin slowly dropped. "No more conspicuous than a corn stalk in a bean patch I'd say."

"Ya think?" Bubba eased to the desk in front of her and rested his left elbow on it. "I don't wanna get in your way, Miss. Lucy, but I'll be here a good part of today."

Lucy slowly nodded. "What do your friends call you, Deputy Watkins?"

"Bubba," he replied as his smile widened also.

"I'll just bet," managed Lucy.

"Well. . ." Bubba nodded to her again. "I'll be in and out and I'll try not to get in your way."

"Ohhh you're not in my way, Bubba," assured the nurse. "I'll be here also. You can call me Lucy."

Bubba nodded to the young nurse again and then headed down the hallway.

Head Nurse Goodwell chuckled silently. "Lucy?"

Pulling her gaze from Bubba as he walked down the hall, Lucy's gaze finally found its way to Nurse Goodwell. "Ma'am?" she finally got out.

"Calm yourself," replied the head nurse. "He has a ring on and besides, you get off at midnight."

"So. . ." Lucy glanced back down the hallway. "I'll stay off the books," she added as she sat back down. "Why is it all the good ones I find are already spoken for?"

"I'm truly flattered, Ma'am," spoke Bubba from outside room 203.

"Uhhh. . ." groaned Lucy as she rested her forehead on the top of her desk.

Now standing in front of Mrs. Goke's room, he noted the door was slightly ajar. With a soft knock, he eased it open even farther.

"Come in," softly spoke a lady inside the room.

Bubba stepped inside, smiling at a middle-aged, red-headed lady sitting in a chair on the far side of Mrs. Goke's bed. Mrs. Goke, herself, appeared to be asleep.

"Deputy Watkins, Ma'am," whispered Bubba. "I'm here to watch over things for a little while if you don't mind." He looked at the headboard, but there wasn't a thing on either side.

The lady stood, offering her hand. "I'm Cinthia Goke, Drew's mother-in-law. I truly appreciate your efforts. These past few days have been much more than just a little rough on her," she whispered as she stepped away from the bed. "She still doesn't accept that her husband is gone and for the like of me, I don't know how to tell her. She's had visions of him visiting her almost every night. Our doctor still has her on a mild sedative and says he will keep her here until her nerves settle down a little." She paused, looking at him. "You know, the police found two necklaces that were left on her headboard at two different times. Strangest thing." She glanced at Drew and then looked back at Bubba. "Do you believe in spirits, Deputy Watkins?"

Bubba squinted. "You mean ghosts, Ma'am?"

Mrs. Goke nodded silently.

"I don't believe so, Ma'am," answered Bubba. "I have enough trouble with the living these days."

Mrs. Goke slowly looked back at Drew. "I can't tell her that JJ wasn't here, Deputy Watkins. I was here all last night. She gets so upset. I don't really know how to help her. I suppose God will have to do that somehow."

"I suppose so," agreed Bubba. "But I'll try ta keep and open mind on this 'ghost' thing. All I know is somebody with his feet in this world walked right in here and put those necklaces on that bedpost. Each one was taken from a murdered man less than a week ago. Now, there's a third killing in Crosstown. The description of the murderer matches your son perfectly. According to the dead man's girlfriend, he also had an ivory tiger's head necklace, but the coroner didn't find it on him."

Mrs. Goke eased back to her chair, sat down, and then dropped her gaze to the floor in front of her. "What do we do now, Deputy Watkins?" she whispered softly. "My son has never been a killer of any sort."

"I'm no expert on such things, Mrs. Goke, but considering what has happened to those two, I'd have ta say he has a mighty good reason to be angry."

*   *   *

The next morning, the 29th of December, James walked onto the second floor at promptly 7:30AM. Dressed in khaki pants and a white, polo shirt, he flashed his badge at the nurse on duty and proceeded toward Room 203. He immediately spotted Bubba two doors down. With his chair leaned back against the wall and his Stetson pulled low on his forehead, the big deputy raised his index finger to acknowledge his relief's presence.

"You're early," said Bubba as he slowly stood and stretched. "There hasn't been a soul on the floor except for an occasional patient after ice or somethin' or a nurse doin' her rounds."

"You check the room lately?" asked James, glancing at 203's closed door.

"Yep," replied Bubba. "No necklace yet."

"Well. . ." James scratched the back of his neck. "I just checked in with Dianne. "Stewart's working a homicide out on Highway 206 just west of Highway 14. The place is owned by one Trey Isley. The one killed was a Scott Henney. From what Will could tell, their crushed ice business was a front to hide their robbery endeavors. The Sheriff found a room full of stuff he thinks they had stolen."

"You mean. . ." Bubba pulled his hat off and wiped his forehead. "this thing is finally comin' to a head?"

James shrugged. "Your guess is as good as mine, Bubba. "There's one still left. We can't find Trey Isley.

When we do, perhaps he can fill us in on the missing pieces of this puzzle."

"How did this Scott fella die?" asked Bubba.

"He got sliced and diced," quipped James. "Seems he was tied and then run over by a John Dear tractor with a bush hog attached to it. Kotts is trying to put him back together right now I suppose."

"Mr. Watkins?"

Although the voice was very weak, Bubba caught it and looked past James toward room 203. Mrs. Goke was standing in the hallway, wiping her eyes. Dangling from her right hand were two, ivory, tiger etched necklaces.

"Good God, We've missed 'em again," groaned Bubba as he ran toward Mrs. Goke with James right behind him.

"I'm totally sorry, Ma'am," started Bubba. "I never saw a soul from out here."

Mrs. Goke dropped the necklaces in a plastic bag James was holding out to her. "You wouldn't have, Deputy Watkins," she explained. "The room door was never opened. I just yawned a minute ago and when I opened my eyes, JJ was standing right in front of me, holding out the necklaces as if I actually wanted them. Drew saw him also. Both of us begged him to stop the killing." She looked right into Bubba's eyes. "'You tell the Sheriff there is only one left,' he said. 'I won't kill him, but he will die, none-the-less.'" As she wiped her eyes again, she added. "When he finished saying that, he turned, and then walked right through this door. It was closed at the time."

Glancing at his watch, Bubba looked at James with a smile. "It's 8:15AM, James. "You wanna fill this thing out or. . ."

"I got it," grumbled James with an eye roll. "I'm used to this weird stuff anyway. Working with Jack has given me a new view of what life can be sometimes."

Part 4
True Believer

"Chopper ready?" asked a young man dressed in a black jumpsuit.

In his mid-thirties, the tall, black-haired fellow looked to be busying himself tending a camera under the nose of a completely black and unmarked helicopter.

An older man, dressed in maintenance overalls, looked down at him from atop a ladder at the rotor axle. "It'a a go, Sir. First day in 1965 and the rotor is in perfect shape." He eased down the ladder and walked toward the man at the nose. "It's Wednesday, Sir. Try to keep it in one piece through the rest of the week. Be mindful of the trees. This thing's not a Weed Eater you know."

"I'll do what I have to do, sergeant," replied the younger man in the black jump suit.

"Well, Sir, if that rotor takes another hit like the last one, I'll ground her. It's my call, not yours. It'll take at least three days to repair and even longer if it has to be replaced."

With an irritated glance, the younger man stood and looked about the hanger. "Where the Hell is Agent Logan?" he growled, glancing at the mechanic.

"Not my day to keep up with him, Sir. You know as much about him as I do," answered the mechanic. "Things that go bump in the night are not his cup of tea-- aliens either."

"I know where this alien runs, Sgt. Grube," argued the one in the black jump suit. "We're flying the south part of Insley Bottoms for starters tonight. If he's there again, I'll tag him for sure."

Sgt. Grube laughed as he looked over the older fellow's shoulder and watched Agent Paul Logan as he pulled into his parking spot outside the open hangar doors. "This 'Night Runner', as you call him, is not that regular anymore, Sir. How are you going to fly that one past him?" The Sergeant nodded toward Agent Logan as he approached. "He thinks you're checking Doc Hall's cattle mutilations again. How does that work with Insley Bottoms?"

"It doesn't," interrupted Agent Logan. Brushing his blond hair under his black cap, the tall and trim agent looked back at his cameraman. "Agent Butler is on his own vendetta, I think. That 'whatever' in the Bottoms is so elusive, he's became kind of a 'catch me if you can' kind of a thing with him." He glanced at Agent Butler. "We're after something you can see a lot plainer than that damned 'Night Runner'. It's the size of a Corvette, the shape of an almond, and glows so bright you can hardly take a picture of it without the whole damn frame washing out. They've been reported in Wyoming, Arizona, and Alabama. Not long ago, they were reported in El Paso and Eagle's Pass, Texas. Even a United States Air Force radar base in Eufaula, Alabama has tagged them. Now, we are getting reports of them here in south-west Tennessee. I'll be damned if someone playing hide and seek is going to take precedence over that." He looked to Agent Bugler. "Run your cameras along Insley Bottoms if you like, but we're not spending a lot of time and film in that area. Is that clear?"

"Crystal," grumbled Agent Butler.

*   *   *

Later that evening, at almost 4:00PM, Deputy Watkins busied himself by safety checking his patrol car at Munford Sheriff's Department. . .

"Bubba!" called someone from the office front door just as the deputy was about to get in the cruiser.

Bubba turned to see Chief of Detectives, Fred Shoultz, watching from the open, front door. "We've got two calls," said Fred excitedly. "Will's dispatched Jack to the Richardson Landing area. Millington N. A. S. has reported something went down in the woods. It had no flight plan. Dianne just got another dealing with a burglary right back at the Insley place again on Highway 206."

"Again?" complained Bubba. "But we were just there."

"Light it up and go check it out," ordered Fred. "Dianne said this complaint came from a neighbor."

"What a way ta spend New Year's," grumbled Bubba as he slowed on Highway 14 for the turn on 206. Easing closer to the Isley place, he looked for anything suspicious, but all seemed much more that calm--dead probably.

"A neighbor complaint?" grumbled Bubba. "The nearest neighbor's at least two hundred yards away for Pete's sake. James should be here. He knows about this place.'""

Slowly shaking his head, the Deputy pulled his cruiser into the small, circular drive of the Insley home and stopped right behind an old, 1950 Ford. With both of the barn's front, double doors open, it was fairly easy to see it was vacant. Looking toward the house, Bubba could see not a light on in the place.

"Well. . ." Bubba grabbed his flashlight, his hat, and then eased out of the cruiser. Heading down the concrete walkway toward the huge, screened in front porch, he kept an eye on the heavy, wooden front door. As he approached the huge twelve foot by forty foot porch, he noted the three chairs and a two-person swing on either side of the front door. There was no one their either.

"Hello the house!" he said as he tried the screen door. It was not latched.

Bubba stepped up the three steps and onto the porch.

"Munford Sheriff's Department! Anyone home?"

Not a sound.

"Burglars huh," he grumbled as he tried the front door. It was not locked.

A little reluctant to enter, he unsnapped the holster of his 357 Smith and Wesson, pulled it from its holster, and then eased the door open as far as it would go with the end of the barrel.

"Sheriff's Department! Comin' in!"

Still no answer.

"Don't go into the old, dark farmhouse, Bubba," he whispered to himself.

Bubba glanced back toward the cruiser and then looked through the living room and on toward the dining area as he eased inside. The two open rooms that entered the living room on the right appeared to be bedrooms. No one was there either. Easing through the living room, he paused at the entrance to the dining area and noticed a stairway on the right of a partially open door to a bathroom perhaps.

"It would have an upstairs," he whispered softly.

Checking the living room again, he looked back toward the kitchen entrance to the left of the bathroom. But, somehow, there was something different. Not only was the bathroom door now closed, but there was a light shining from beneath it.

"Munford Sheriff's Department I said! Don't play games with me. Come out o' that bathroom!"

Cocking his pistol, he held it down at his right side. A bit leery of his situation, the big sergeant took a quick look behind him at the living room again. But when he turned around, he noticed a shadowy figure of a man standing right in front of the now closed bathroom door. Not seeing his features that well, Bubba directed the beam of his four cell Mag Lite toward him.

"What tha Hell?" managed the deputy.

Now looking straight down the beam of the powerful flashlight directed at the man's chest, he could only see the closed, bathroom door. Slowly letting his gaze drop below the beam, he could see the man's waist and legs. Then, before his mind could deal with that bit of information, the man charged right at him. Bubba's chin dropped and his eyes grew big. The man's quick, heavy steps sounded like a base drum on the old, wooden floor.

Bubba quickly raised his pistol. "Stop right there or I'll shoot!" he shouted.

The repeated reports of the Smith and Wesson only stopped when the big man's head hit the door frame behind him, sending his Stetson tumbling into the living room and the big man, sliding back into it as well. Bubba rolled to his right side, trying to find a suitable target. Looking over the sights of his pistol, he spotted the fast-moving silhouette. It looked like steam from a hot bath as it passed right through the living room wall.

"Damn. . ." managed Bubba weakly as he pushed himself up to a sitting position.

Cocking the pistol again, he looked back toward the bathroom. The light was still showing under the doorway.

"Ohhh Hell," he said weakly as the beam of the Mag Lite was directed on the puddle of dark red blood now oozing from under the bathroom door.

Scrambling to his feet, he trotted to the door, opened it, and then stepped back with his pistol at the ready. Indeed, there was another person there. But this one was gagged and had his hands tied above his head to a heavy, brass hat rack near the top of the door, and he wasn't moving. Bubba looked on the opposite side of the door. There were four, chest-high holes in the door, but only one missed the man on the other side.

"Damn," said Bubba again as he quickly checked the man's neck for a pulse.

Although the body was still warm, there was no pulse to find.

Standing there with his eyes wide, Bubba felt his mouth going dry as he looked into the eyes of the dead man. The expression on his face was nothing less that raw horror. Looking down at the man's open jacket, he could see three bloody spots that certainly weren't there before he entered the old farmhouse.

Running his fingers through his hair, the big detective slowly backed away from the bathroom and on into the dining area until he bumped into one of the chairs at the table.

"Bubba?" spoke a man from the living room.

Wheeling, Bubba quickly raised his weapon for yet another target.

"It's me, Bubba! It's me!" shouted Virgil as he threw up both hands and quickly backed away, staring at the shaking barrel of the .357.

As Bubba's glassy gaze lowered to the floor between the two, so did the barrel of the pistol. "I killed 'em, Virgil. The damned thing baited me, and I just shot 'em."

Virgil squinted as he stepped forward and eased the deputy's pistol from his hands. "What do you mean 'the damned thing baited you'?" asked the constable.

Bubba backed to the door frame, slid down to the floor, and then looked back toward the man still hanging on the bathroom door. "Not that sure, Virgil. Don't really know just how ta explain it." He nodded toward the bathroom. "That door was closed when I entered this room. Thought I saw a man in front of it, but I don't guess I did. When he charged me, I shot at him four times, but I guess I missed."

Stepping just past where Bubba was sitting, Virgil spotted the man. "Holy crap," said the constable just above a whisper. "I heard the shots, but when I came in, I didn't see anybody but you."

Bubba looked up at Virgil. "I don't suppose you saw anyone leave the house when you drove up, did you?"

"Guess I missed him," answered the constable. "You come on outside and rest in one of the chairs on the front porch while I call this in. Kotts is gonna be pleased as peas when we hand him another DB." Watching the big deputy struggle to his feet, he added, "How are you gonna write this thing up?"

Bubba shook his head, slowly picked up his hat, and then looked at the Constable. "Not that sure, Virgil, and I don't think explainin' it will help much either."

*   *   *

At 8:00PM sharp, Deputy Watkins pulled his cruiser into the Munford Sheriff's Department parking lot. Even before he stopped the car, he spotted the High Sheriff's Ford as well as Virgil's maroon Oldsmobile 88. Spotting him from the window at her desk, Lucy eased from the chair, rushed toward and then out of the front door. Instantly spotting her, Bubba got out, shaking his head in disgust.

"Are you all right?" she asked as she slowed to a stop in front of him.

Bubba rolled his eyes, his gaze ending back up on her. "I'm toast, Lucy. Haven't been here but a week or so and I've already shot and killed a man."

"Well. . ." she tugged on his right arm. "Come on in. They're waiting in Will's office."

"No doubt," managed the big deputy with a worried tone.

Entering the lobby, Bubba noticed Virgil sitting in a chair beside Lucy's desk. He immediately got up and followed the two to the door of Will's office.

"Come on in," said Charlie Two Shirts, standing in front of Will's desk. Glancing back at Will at his desk, the old Indian looked at Bubba with a bit of a smile. "Is this the one who doesn't believe?" he asked.

Will nodded. Leaning back in his padded, swivel rocker, he stared at Bubba as a smile slowly grew on his face. "But, according to what Virgil had to say, we got another true believer amongst us."

"Take a seat," said Virgil. "We'll help you write your report."

Feeling Lucy's gentle push, Bubba hesitated, looking back at her.

"Right there," she said, pointing toward the nearest couch. You need something soft after what you've been through."

Charlie eased up and sat down beside him. "Did it say anything to you?"

Bubba squinted at the old Apache as he sat down. "It?" he finally got out.

Charlie's smile widened as he glanced at Will. "Nothing does a soul more good than putting an answer to something he can't explain."

"What?" Bubba's squint deepened.

"James told us what Goke's ghost said about the last man--that being the one you just shot," explained Charlie. "He baited you and you shot 'em. I would of shot 'em too, just like anybody else. The ghost as much said that would happen."

Will nodded in agreement. "You just killed the last of the Ivory Tiger Killers. At least that's what Kotts is calling them, and I think that name will stick, especially in the report."

Bubba shook his head as his gaze slowly drifted to the floor. "I thought I was toast."

Reaching into his jacket pocket, he pulled out his blue bandanna. As he did, something shiny fell to the floor beside his right boot.

"Well, I'll just be damned," said Virgil as he picked up the necklace and looked back at Bubba.

Bubba stared at the necklace as his mouth slowly opened. "Don't look at me. I didn't put it there. I swear I didn't."

"Let me have it," said Will. Taking the necklace from Virgil, he looked back at Bubba. "When you shot at that shadowy figure of a thing at the bathroom door, did you stop em?" he added.

"Nooo Sir," answered Bubba. "I was at the doorway to the dining room and he ran past me like I wasn't even there."

Will smiled, dangling the necklace in front of him. "That's when he gave you this I believe."

"Welcome to the club," said Charlie, smiling at Bubba's troubled expression. "This year's starting out with a bang," he added laughing. "Already one ghost down and Jack's wanderin' the fields of Richardson Landin' lookin' for some kind o' Black Chopper for Millington, who was lookin' for some kind of UFO thing for who knows what."

Will quickly sat up, looking at Virgil. "That's right. With all this levity, I forgot about Jack. You're still on the clock aren't you?"

"Yep. You know I am," replied the constable.

"Can you go and find our boy, Jack and send him home?" asked Will. "Lucy can't get 'em to answer his radio."

Virgil checked his watch. "It's only about 8:30PM or so. I'll find him for you." As the constable headed for the door, he added, "It's nice to be needed around here anyways."

Smiling, Will looked at Bubba. Tossing him the necklace, he added, "Keep this as a reminder, Bubba. Not everyone gets a present from a ghost."

*   *   *

64

Rolling out of Munford on the Drummonds Road, it didn't take Virgil lone to get to Richardson Landing Road. Constantly trying him on the radio proved fruitless. But when he pulled into Drummonds, he stopped at the Emporium--a favorite place for the young detective. Consisting of both a café and a crafts store, Shelley and the girls shopped there often. As luck would have it, the cashier said that Jack was there about two hours ago and told her he was heading to Coon Valley to check something along the Old River Road.

So Virgil proceeded west on the Landing Road. Seeing no sign of Jack's cruiser, at the Landing Park area, he continued south on the Old River Road toward Coon Valley. Slowing on the old gravel and red sand road, the constable turned his high beams on in hopes of catching Jack's taillight reflectors. Then, just when he was about to enter Coon Valley, he caught a glimpse of something red up ahead.

Why is it I feel like I'm one step from being back in the stew pot again? he thought as Jack's black Fairlane 500 came into view.

Virgil eased up behind the Ford and stopped. Keeping the Olds running and the headlights on, he reached to the floorboard of the back seat, retrieved his one-mile light, and then got out. Walking to the front of Jack's Ford, he put his hand on the hood.

"Almost cold." Slowly looking toward the woods on the east side of the road, he walked back to his Olds, sat down, and then picked up the mic. "Virgil to base. Lucy, are you there?"

"I'm here, Virgil," replied Lucy. "Have you found Jack?"

"Yes and no, Lucy," replied Virgil as he swept the woods with his light. "I'm sitting right behind his Ford just north of Coon Valley on the Old River Road. His engine is cold. I guess he's somewhere in the woods. I think I'll. . ."

Virgil's voice trailed off as he noticed a powerful light flashing from a hill, straight east of him, and a considerable distance away.

"Virgil?" called Lucy. "Are you still there?"

"I am, Lucy," answered Virgil. "I see a light signaling me from the east. I'm on a levy right now, so I'll have to ease down it and continue through the woods. Doesn't look to be a short walk."

"Virgil. . ."

"I know, Lucy. I know," said Virgil. "I'll be careful."

Turning off the Oldsmobile, he got out, locked it, and then looked down at his Cordovan slippers.

"Just great," he grumbled, "and my boots are still next to the bed."

Briskly walking to the back of the Olds, he opened the turtle shell, and then looked straight at a brand new box of .38 shells.

"Tell me this is not an omen," he grumbled. Quickly opening the box, he put a dozen or so in his jacket pocket, and then closed the lid.

The word, dark, seemed milk toast to what it looked like to Virgil in the woods beyond the levy.

"C'mon Jack," said Virgil as he directed the beam of the one-mile light toward the hill in question. An intermittent flash came right back at the same location.

"Well. . ." Virgil looked down the forty-five degree grade of the levy and then down at his new, Kaufman shoes. "Jack, you gonna owe me a brand new pair of sneakers after this."

Twenty minutes later put the constable almost out of the marshy scrub between the levy and the woods. Pausing at the edge of an opening in the trees, he flashed his light again toward the hill in question. The powerful beam in the distance responded again. But this time, it looked to be at the base of the hill and much closer.

"Hope you're moving this way," grumbled Virgil, glancing down at his wet shoes and soggy sox.

Another twenty minutes in an easterly direction, the constable paused at the top of a little rise. Resting at the base of an old white oak, and felt for the flashlight's switch in the darkness. As he did, the beam of another light shattered the darkness around him.

"And what brings you to these woods, Constable Forsythe?" spoke the deep and guttural voice from behind

66

the beam. Even though the beam was directed at where he was standing, he could plainly see the glowing, green eyes of the man he was still trying to understand.

"Letting the 'Beast' out again, Jack," asked Virgil, shielding his eyes from the flashlight.

"Yep," replied the man Jack as the beam went out. "It's easier to move in the woods when he's with me," he replied as he walked up to Virgil and dropped a black, canvas bag he was carrying to the grass. "I think I've got a tiger by the tail, Virgil," added Jack, plainly excited. "I'm going to need a little direction on this one. About three hundred yards from here, where you saw my first signal, is a downed chopper."

Virgil eyed the big Pitt as he trotted out of the darkness and promptly sat down beside the canvas bag at Jack's right leg.

"Banjo could have found the pilot and the others if there were any, but the thing was painted black and there weren't any markings on it at all. Besides, when it went down, Millington said it had no transponder, and no record of a flight plan could be found. Banjo could of found them I believe. But if he did, I would have been obliged to give them this."

Jack knelt, unzipped the bag, and then directed the beam of his flashlight into it.

"Looks like I've got three boxes of what seems to be Super 8 film, a thirty-five millimeter Cannon camera with a zoom lens, and a book of maps."

"Who do you think they were?" asked Virgil.

Jack shrugged. "I had Banjo track them for a little piece and then thought better of it. They were headed for Pryor Road not far from where the chopper was."

Virgil rolled his eyes. "You had better have a firm grip on that story, Jack. There's no telling who these folks are. It could be the FBI, CIA, Black Ops, or whatever. But it is the US Government for sure and they don't have a sense of humor when it comes to poking around in their business."

Jack nodded. "Let's get back to the cars and out of here. There's liable to be another chopper here any

67

minute. That one back in the woods was loaded with cameras. The next one, if it comes, could take our picture as well."

*   *   *

It was almost 12:30AM the next morning when Jack got back home. At 7:00AM that Thursday, Jack walked into the Munford Sheriff's Office with the black, canvas bag over his shoulder. Dianne immediately waved him over to her desk.

Seeing her check the partially closed door of the High Sheriff's office, Jack smiled. "Am I in trouble again?"

"Not sure," she answered with a smile of her own. "Check that with your grandfather. Millington NAS got a call early this morning from someone they wouldn't identify outside the base." She squinted at Jack. "What did you and Virgil find out there?"

"Not real sure, Dianne," answered Jack. "I think it was their Unidentified Flying Object. It was a black, unmarked chopper that went down on a hilltop just north of Coon Valley on the Old River Road. It was loaded with cameras and. . ." Jack shook the black bag as he added, "stuff."

"Well, old Puff-N-Stuff got a call just as he came in this morning from someone at the base. He wasn't connected with your UFO, but he said you were tagged by a motion-sensitive camera on that chopper you just burgled." She nodded at the satchel. "They know you have that, Jack, and 'they' are not amused. Better see Will. He and Virgil have two Super Eight projectors in his office. Better go right now. Will was told to expect visitors and they could be here any time."

Jack nodded and then walked straight to Will's office with the contraband. He paused just outside the door. Will was at his desk, but looking straight at him.

"Is it safe?" asked Jack.

Will squinted, glancing at the bag. "What tha Hell have you and Virgil got into now?" he asked. "You have tha films?"

Jack nodded, handing the bag to Fred.

"Can I help?" asked Dianne with Charlie and Andy right behind her.

68

"Sure," said Fred as he fished the three boxes of films out of the bag. "You know more about these projectors than I do."

"We only need one," poked Dianne as she put the nearest projector on a small table and turned it toward the white-painted wall of the office.

"This film's got UFO's on it?" asked Charlie. "Those black choppers follow those things around you know."

Will quickly picked up a Super 8 camera from the top of his desk and handed it to Dianne. I want a copy of whatever looks interesting on these tapes, Dianne, and don't mention it to anyone."

Everyone scurried for a seat except Will as Dianne threaded the film through the projector. The old sheriff busied himself by going through what was left inside the bag.

"Here we go," said Dianne as she flipped the switch on the projector and then turned the room lights off.

With a soft, clicking hum, the show began. Woods and plenty of them was first. But as the film progressed, it became plain to see what those in the chopper were after. Looking closely down through the trees, a tall, shadowy figure of a man could be glimpsed here and there running remarkably fast. Each time he slowed to look up at the chopper, those glowing, green eyes forced the Beast out of the bag.

"Good God," softly spoke Will with a glance toward Jack. "They've tagged you, son."

"Not really," corrected Charlie. "They still don't know who he is. Fast forward that thing. Let's see if they've spotted the Pitt."

Following Charlie's directions, Dianne ran through the film. In little time, the glowing eyed silhouette disappeared into the thick of the woods and Banjo was never spotted.

Will picked up the film tin and looked at the hand-written label. "Insley Bottoms Shadow Man – Mid 1964," it says. He looked at the second one. "Coon Valley area," this one says. He paused as he squinted at the third, all but reluctant to pick it up."

69

"What's that one?" prompted Charlie.

"Not that sure," admitted the old sheriff. "It says Silver Streak – Stl un id crft - Mississippi Delta – Cattle Samples." Will handed the tape to Jack. "Decipher please. It's got some kind 'o code on it."

Smiling, the young detective took the tin and immediately handed it to Dianne. "I'd like to see this one. I believe that's our UFO. I think it says 'still unidentified craft'."

"I would as well," added Charlie. "If I am correct, these are the Sky People who occasionally make trouble for the Nations."

"Put it on," said Will with a nod to Dianne. "We'll lose everything if these government folks catch us with this stuff."

In less than a minute, Dianne had the film threaded and running. Again, there was nothing but woods at first. Then, Charlie leaned forward and pointed out something glittering in the moonlight behind a huge white oak, a good ways ahead.

"There's your black chopper," said Charlie. "One o' those who ride in the thing is making the movie. They've landed where there is cattle."

Will sat up and leaned closer to where the projector was focused on the wall. "I see 'em, Charlie. There's about a hundred yards away."

Suddenly, and so quick the human eye could hardly follow, another glowing craft approached from the south and hovered well above the field over the cattle. Shaped exactly like and almond and about fifteen feet long, six feet wide, and about four feet tall, it lowered itself very close to the ground. As it did, static charges shot from the craft in a loud, sizzling light display that caused most of the cattle to quickly move away. Noting the same scene was running long, Dianne sped up the projector.

"What's it doin?" asked Will, squinting at the glowing object.

"Can't tell," said Andy. "That darned thing is too bright to see anything close to it."

70

Upon seeing the strange craft rise from the ground, Dianne took her finger off the fast-forward button.

"As I thought," said Charlie, leaning forward a bit. "It goes away. Now, look what it leaves."

As the craft sped off in a southerly direction, everyone leaned forward for a better look at a reddish-brown lump in the knee-high winter grass. Amazingly, the cameraman from the black chopper moved toward the suspicious lump in the grass.

"It's a cow," said Virgil.

"My word," groaned Dianne. "It's been disemboweled. Its udders are gone."

"Look closer," advised Charlie. "Where's tha blood?"

"There is none," replied Andy. His tone weak.

"Blood should be everywhere," said Will. "Where is it?"

"Good question," said Charlie. "Already seen this movie. It happens at least once a year in the Nations all along South Texas. They come, they take, and then they leave."

"The helicopter and that glowing thing?" asked Dianne as she rewound the tape.

"The Greys," explained Charlie. "They fly the thing the government calls the Silver Streak. But the government doesn't work with the thing with no soul."

"No soul?" Will sat up on the edge of the couch and looked at the old Apache. "What tha Hell does that mean?"

Charlie smiled at Will's confused expression. "The Greys are human-like creatures about four feet tall with light, greyish bodies, smooth, cold skin like plastic, bulging heads, and large, black eyes. When they look at you, you can't see a pupil at all, only black, like the dark sunglasses the agents who watch them wear." He looked at Will. "There are two kinds of Government in the States--the ones you vote for and the ones you don't, but get anyways. The white man now lives in the big city and is blinded by the lights in their work-a-day world, I think. They have forgotten what it is like on the outside. The ones you don't know, the Black Ops people, work with these creatures and tolerate their presence. For that, the government is given knowledge in return, I think."

"Wait a minute!" interrupted Andy with a squint. "You mean they work with those alien things?"

With a bit of a grin, Charlie slowly shook his head. "No," he finally said. "The Greys live, but are not real. I have said, 'They have no soul.'. The Black Ops people work with the others who use the Greys who fly the Silver Streak. We call them Clones because they all look very similar—light hair, tall and trim, and their eyes have a yellowish tint to them like a mountain lion." He smiled, glancing at Jack. "But they do not glow. These Clones are sent by others, I think, to effect some kind of change in this world of ours. They bleed like we do, but the Greys do not."

"Wait a minute," Will looked to Dianne. She was frozen with her mouth wide open. "Run through that second tape. If there's nothing on it, put them all back in the bag for whoever is coming for them." He looked to Andy. "When he or they or whoever get here, send 'em to me. And for Pete's sake, don't let 'em know what we just did." Looking back to Dianne, he added, "Hide those projectors in the storage room in the back. If they ask you anything, just reply that you have no idea what they are talkin' about." Will slowly shook his head as he smoothed his thinning, grey hair back with his right hand. "Never thought we'd make the jump from ghosts to somewhere between reality and the Twilight Zone."

Book 2
The Truth is Out There

Be proud of those who seek the truth--
To persist, to endure, and never quit.
But when the answer is finally revealed,
Beware of the few who find it.

Part 1
Seeing is Believing

Eleven AM, Thursday, the second of January, Will sat quietly in his office listening to Andy joke with Pico over 'his' donuts again.   Shelley's little shopping spree had ended up at the office to 'check on her friends' as she said. Unable to concentrate on his work, the old sheriff pondered his situation. . .

What would be worse than an FBI investigation?" he mused as he stared mindlessly out of the window, watching the puffy, white clouds drift by.

"Will?"   Shelley stood at the door and stared at the back of his chair. The very top of his almost bald head was all she could see.

But when Pico rattled the peppermint jar, he immediately swung the swivel chain in her direction.

"You just missed Fred," said Will, smiling at Shelley. "Covington's car thieves are at it again. But what a great surprise. It'll be noon in a little bit. Is Teresa with you? Have you eaten?" He glared at Pico. "Get out o' my candy!" he snapped.

Shelley returned his smile as did the undaunted Pico. "That would be, I'm sorry I missed him, yes, and a no. Teresa's fell into the donut box on Dianne's desk I believe."

"Dianne!" said Will loudly as he stood and walked toward Shelley at the door.

"Here Will," answered the day dispatcher as she walked toward the two at the office doorway.

"How 'bout ordering two large garbage pizza pies from Tony's? I'll pay for 'em if you go and get 'em."

"Garbage?" Teresa mouth slowly opened, looking at an equally puzzled expression on Pico's face.

"That's a Supreme, sweeties," explained Dianne. "It's got just about everything on it but anchovies."

"Pies?" asked Pico, looking at Shelley.

Will chuckled.   "I'm sure that's the only thing you heard, baby doll, but we're talkin' pizzas right now."

"Call it in," said Dianne to Andy. She looked back at Teresa and Pico. "Come on and we can spend Will's money on a pecan pie and some cold Mountain Dew to go with it."

*   *   *

Thirty minutes later, almost noon, Shelley was setting up the pizzas on a small, folding table behind the Sergeant's desk. Dianne immediately carried a two pieces on a paper plate with a cold Mountain Dew to Will in his office. He was already smiling when she walked through the office door.

"I could already smell the sausage, cheese, and onions before you came in," he said as he quickly reached for the plate.

Hearing the front door open, Dianne stepped back from Will's desk to take a look. "Ohhh wow," she said weakly.

Will froze, mid-bite, looking straight at her. "It's them, ain't it?" he managed through the pizza.

"I think," whispered Dianne. "I don't know them. I'll stall them a little."

"Them?" Will ripped the bite from the slice. Quickly chewing, he placed the piece back on the plate.

Taking another bite, Will listened to Dianne's "Can I help you?" and "He's in his office." but couldn't understand what else was said. Giving up on the quiet, but not the meal itself, he leaned back in his chair and continued to work on his piece of pizza.

"Mr. Brumley?" spoke the first of two men now pausing just outside the doorway. "I'm Agent Clay Colter of the Department of Defense." He glanced at the black man right behind him. "This is Agent Joe Eldred."

Agent Colter took his ID wallet out of his suit pocket, opened it, and then held it up to the old sheriff. The American eagle on a light blue background seemed to scream 'Let 'em have the stuff!'."

"Interesting." Will took another bite and then chased it with a good swallow of Mountain Dew. "Well, boys. . ." Will took another bite. "Good pizza. The pies are right behind the sergeant's desk. Go get you a slice and then we'll talk about why you came."

76

"No thanks, Sir," replied Agent Colter. Medium build, black hair, and about thirty or so, the agent stared at Will with a kind of 'I got you' half smile.

"Well, if you won't have any, you'll excuse me while I do," said Will. "Why don't you have a seat and tell me why I'm blessed with your presence? Did you retrieve your chopper yet? You know, you really should fix that IFF thing on it. Next time you might draw a fighter from Millington instead of an officer from Munford." He managed a smile with a half-full mouth. "One might just take you for a UFO or somethin'."

Agent Colter quickly glanced at him as he took a seat in one of the two, wooden chairs in front of the desk. Agent Eldred remained standing at the side of the second chair.

"The chopper was handled by someone else," answered Agent Eldred. Now looking a bit irritated, he reached into his suit pocked, pulled out a photo, and then placed it on the Sheriff's desk. "Do you know him?"

Will placed his piece of pizza back on the paper plate, wiped his hands, and then picked up the picture. It was dark and blurred. Slowly pulling his reading glasses from his shirt pocket, he put them on and looked again.

"Yes," replied the old sheriff as he took the last bite of his pizza. "Where'd you take it?"

"A motion sensitive camera caught this sometime last night," answered Agent Colter. "He took something of ours and we would like it back."

"Do you know him?" asked Agent Eldred again.

"Yesterday, we responded to a request by Millington NAS to check out a downed aircraft in our area. They said it had no flight plan and no IFF response." He reached under his desk, pulled out the black satchel, and then plopped it down on the left side of his desk. "You boys just saved me the trouble of findin' out who belongs to this stuff."

Agent Eldred instantly took the satchel and started examining its contents.

"I hope none of its contents are disturbed," said Agent Colter. "We never intended to upset anyone here."

Will smiled, finishing off his Mountain Dew. "In this profession, I've learned never to say never about anything. It always leaves you with pie on your face. Speaking of pie, we also have two, nice pecan pies on that table behind the sergeant's desk. You sure you won't have a slice?"

Agent Eldred immediately took the satchel and left the room without another word.

"We appreciate your co-operation in this matter," said Agent Colter as he stood. "We would also appreciate it if you would refrain from discussing any of this or what you might have seen with anyone outside this department."

"Sounds reasonable," replied Will as he followed the two agents from his office. Watching them drive off in a black, Ford station wagon, he looked over his reading glasses at Dianne and Andy standing at the dispatcher's desk. "Department of Defense? Really?" he said, slowly shaking his head.

Dianne shrugged. "Millington said they were coming and they did."

"Well-well," replied Will with a bit of a smile.

"I know that smile, Will Brumley," she said. "Why is it that I'm starting to feel uncomfortable again?"

"I kept their book of maps," answered the old sheriff. "There's writin' all over them. From Insley and Black Bottoms to Richardson Landing and on south into northwest Mississippi those UFO things are startin' to get active." He looked at Dianne. "They're on my desk in a large manila folder. I'd appreciate it if you would get them and take them to Hewlett Packard down the street and make two copies of all of 'em. I think there's six." He nodded to Andy. "Give the originals to Andy when you get back. When, and if, those folds come back, he can say I forgot 'em and hand em' right over without a fuss. . . hopefully."

The old sheriff spent the rest of the day in his office, making notes and talking on the phone. Nobody ever questioned him about why he looked troubled to the point of obsession. That evening, he left the office without a word to anyone.

*   *   *

78

Bright and early the next morning, a beautifully clear and crisp Friday the third of January, Will marched into the lobby, barely glanced at Andy or Dianne, and went straight to his office. Seeing him, Fred stepped to the doorway of his office but never even got a nod as the old sheriff passed.

"Something's afoot," said Andy. Quickly stepping from behind his desk, the Sergeant joined Dianne at hers.

No sooner had he done that, than Will appeared at his office doorway with an open, eight-by-ten-inch spiral ringed notebook in his hand. "Is Jack here yet?" he asked, hardly looking up from the notebook.

"On his way," answered Dianne. "He's stopping by the Hewlett-Packard place to pick up those copies."

Will nodded. "Tell 'em to come to my office when he gets in." Without another word, he returned to his office and closed the door.

"That does it," grumbled Dianne. She shoved her chair back and struck a trail straight toward the High Sheriff's office.

At that exact time, Jack walked into the lobby with the maps, causing Dianne to stop.

Fred held his hand up for the dispatcher to stop. "Let's let Jack handle this, Dianne. He'll clue us in later."

Sensing he had just stepped into a situation, Jack stopped just a reach from Dianne. "What have I just walked into here?" he asked just above a whisper.

"Will kept those Black Chopper maps," said Dianne. Her tone soft.

"That's a gimme," replied Jack, shaking the maps in his right hand.

"No-no-no," grumbled Dianne. "Will said there were notes all over them. Something about those notes has him in a tither and he won't say a word about it."

"Jack!" called Will loudly. "Are you out there?"

"Present," replied the young detective.

Will marched out of his office, hardly looking at anyone. Barely slowing as he passed Jack, he said, "Pull out that number one map, have Dianne hide the rest of

79

the copies, and then give the originals to Andy. You're with me in your car."

Jack looked Dianne with raised eyebrows as he placed all but the copy mentioned in her hands. "What's up with him?" he asked.

"Not a clue," answered Dianne as Jack all but trotted to catch the old sheriff now leaving the lobby. As he headed toward his car, Jack noted that Will was reading something in the notebook.

"What's happening?" asked Jack as the old sheriff got into the unmarked Fairlane 500.

Closing the notebook, Will flashed a smile. "Gonna take a little ride, Jack. You good at puzzles?"

"Better than most, I guess," answered Jack as he backed out of his parking place.

"Head out toward Drummonds. We're goin' ta Guilt Edge." He glanced at Jack. "Where's Banjo"

"Left him with Donnie. I think Shadow's pregnant."

"Well, I'll say," chuckled Will. "I'm not really a dog person, but I'd like one o' those pups if you have an extra."

"I think we'll have several," replied Jack, laughing himself. "What's at Guilt Edge?"

"That would be a 'who'," replied Will, looking at the young detective. "We're gonna visit the Call place, Jack. I'm not real popular with those folks right now. I put their youngest son in jail back in November of 1962. He's in Fort Pillow Prison right now." Shaking the number one map in his right hand, he added. "This may just prove I made a bad mistake."

Jack squinted. "You mind explaining that?"

"Not at all." Will looked back toward the road. "Didn't much believe in UFO's back then. Still ridin' a fence right now. You saw that film where the fellow in that glowing thing sliced and diced that bull didn't you?"

"I did," replied Jack.

"Well. . . That bull was a Black Angus and if I'm right, one of Doc Hall's prize possessions. The more I think on it, the more I believe it was the one Larry Call happened on already killed. He just helped himself. Don't think that's much of a crime." He glanced at Jack. "Larry's

80

brother, Big Jim, said something about gettin' a visit from two men dressed in black because Larry tried to explain his version of what happened to the bull. Does that sound familiar to you?"

"Sounds like the DOD men you talked to earlier," replied Jack.

"The same," said Will. "All this puzzle thing is startin' to come together piece by piece. I went over the court transcript yesterday. Larry said the bull had just been killed, but he all but refused to say how. That bein' so, I believe he saw our glowin' thing as well, but was afraid to speak of it."

"And that's what prompted the visit from the men in black," guessed Jack.

"Exactly," replied Will. They threatened him, or possibly his whole family, if he talked about it. Now step on it. We gotta straighten this mess out with the Call family."

Now on Highway 178 and pulling into Guilt Edge, Jack slowed to a stop where it ended on Highway 59.

"That's it." Will pointed across the road to a gravel drive leading up to the top of a six foot bank. Once there, it turned right and stopped at the side of the porch to a little, farm house. A short, stocky fellow slowly stood from his chair on the porch and looked toward the unmarked Ford. There was hardly room for a part in his curly, brown hair. Jack immediately read the confused expression on his face. It screamed, 'Back again?'.

Noting the man's expression, Jack slowly looked to Will. "They didn't know we were coming, did they?"

"Not at all," answered the old sheriff as he got out. "Marshall, I'd like a word with you if I could," he asked.

Marshall Call stepped from under the tin roof of the old, wooden porch. Stopping in front of the unmarked Ford, he eyed Jack and then looked at Will. "You're not after Jim, are you?" he asked, still holding the troubled brow.

Will slowly shook his head. "No, Sir. I'm here for Larry."

"He's in Fort Pillow for Pete's sake," grumbled Marshall. "You of all people should know that."

"That's right, that's right, Marshall," said Will. "But I'm here to help 'em right now. But to do that, I need help from you and your family."

Hearing the front porch screen door slam, Marshall turned to see his wife, Dorothy Call, step onto the porch. "Marshal. . ." She stepped from the porch and eased up behind her husband. "What's going on?" Heavy-set, about five feet and six inches tall, she pushed her dark brown hair up under the thin scarf that held it.

"Dot. . ." Will smiled with a tip of his hat. "Somethin' good I hope. Yesterday, I ran across some papers and other things that proves I was wrong about Larry. This just might get him out of jail. Now that I've got you two here, I need to get statements from you both." He glanced at Jack as the young detective got out his pen and pad.

"Jack here is gonna be takin' some notes on what we will talk about. If you agree with them, I'll ask you to sign them. Is that all right with you two?"

"Yes," said Dot as Marshal nodded in silence and what looked to be, disbelief.

"Very well," continued Will. "Do you remember that night when Larry came in with the meat he had taken from the dead bull on Doc Hall's place?"

Dot's eyes grew big as Marshall's confused look deepened.

"You believe the bull was already dead?" asked Marshall.

"I do now," answered Will. "I read the trial transcript about what Larry said happened. I believe he was intimidated to the point that he left out some very important parts that would have probably cleared him. I think he was intimidated by strangers dressed in black."

Dot nodded. "They saw him in a place where he shouldn't have been," she admitted with a nod from Marshall. "They warned us not to say anything about what Larry said or what he had seen. If any one of us did, Larry would go to jail for a very long time."

82

Will's smile widened. "Was one of them men white and the other black?"

Marshall's confused look was right back again. "How did you know that?"

"Had a request from the Millington Naval Air Station to investigate a craft that went down near the Coon Valley area the other day. We now know that it was workin' some kind o' way or another with a UFO--a very bright craft about the size of a sports car. I think Larry got a good look at that same ship but was scared out o' talkin' about it by the same folks that gave you a visit."

"You saw it too?" asked Dot, holding her fingertips to her mouth.

Will nodded, holding out his hand toward Jack. "This young man is my detective, Jack Shoultz. He found an abandoned black chopper in the Coon Valley area the other night and brought back a few things from it to ID the owner of the craft. You see, it was solid black without any markings at all."

Dot immediately backed up and sat down on the edge of the porch. Her eyes welled up with tears as she asked, "Do you think that will get my Larry out of jail?"

"We'll certainly see," replied the old sheriff as he unfolded the number one map and held it up in front of Marshall. "Jack here is workin' a case on Doc Hall's cattle mutilations." Will pointed out an area on the map to Marshall. "That's south of Richardson Landing and marked 11/62. I believe that's November of 1962."

Marshall nodded. "That's where Larry said he got the beef."

"Excellent," replied Will. "I got a strange visit yesterday from two men from the Department of Defense." He glanced at Dot. "That's our men in black who scared Larry off. They were a might kinder to me than they were to you, but I got the same message none-the-less. I'm taking all this evidence, with your statements to the District Attorney's office and re-opening Larry's case. I'll try to commute whatever charges that still linger, if any, to time served."

"You can do that?" asked Marshall.

83

"No," replied Will, "but the DA can."

"We need your help as well as your son Jim," added Jack. "I am told that Jim's work takes him all over these parts."

"It does," replied Marshall. "He works for Hearts Bread. He's delivering right now."

"Good," replied Will. "Perhaps if he or his friends spot either the chopper or the UFO, please call us immediately." Handing Marshall a dozen business cards, he added, "Ask Jim to pass these out and tell him why if you would."

"We'll do it," said Marshall, finally with a bit of a smile. "Jim works early in the morning and sometimes it takes him well up into the day before he finishes his route."

"Good then," replied Will as he turned to leave. Pausing at the open door of Jack's cruiser, he looked back and added, "If that DOD team pays you a visit again, tell them nothing. Hand them one o' those cards and say I'm handlin' the whole damn thing for Tipton County with MUFON. Give me a call just as soon as they leave." He glanced at Jack. "I'd give a week's pay to know where their office is."

*   *   *

A little after 4:00PM, Jack and Will were well on their way back to Munford. Seeing the old sheriff's head rested on the back of the seat with his eyes closed brought a smile to Jack's face.

"Satisfied?" asked Jack softly.

"I'm on my way there," replied Will. He rolled his head around to face Jack. "Wanna let the 'Beast' out and run the woods a little come Monday evening?"

"That works for me," replied Jack with a smile. "I'm sure my 'help' would like it as well."

On the way back, Will never asked what 'help' meant. He eventually drifted off to sleep for the rest of the trip.

*   *   *

After a long weekend with his family, Jack checked in with his grandfather and started off his evening, watching one of Doc Halls grazing fields on Richardson Landing Road just south-west of Guilt Edge. Turning up the collar of his jacket to the cool night air, he leaned back against the front of the Ford and listened to Ji Woo's version of a whippoorwill as she glided somewhere high above the fields. Little did the sheriff know of the ramifications of asking the young detective to "let the Beast out" especially at night. . .

The night. . .. Jack looked up and watched the steam from his breath swirl about as he pulled his cap off and laid it upon the hood. *Not a cloud in the sky and the stars are countless.*

"Can you not move?" asked a voice so close to him it made him jump.

Slowly running his fingers over his hair and over his horns, he looked searched for the voice's owner but he could see not a soul. But Banjo's attention was on her, somewhere high above them both, and there was little doubt who it was. The little girl voice in his head was a dead giveaway.

"Woo. . ." Jack smiled, searching the sky directly above him, but he couldn't find her.

"I'm off!" exclaimed Jack so loudly that it made the pit bull jump and look back at his master.

Bounding away from the cruiser, Jack headed across the field and toward the stretch of woods between the pasture and the river. Old, soft Levis, plaid shirt, and faded jean jacket never felt so good.

"Come, Banjo!" he said. "Now's the time to let the animal out in you!"

Ignoring the one he knew was above him, the Pitt broke out in a dead run toward the running Nephilim. The breeze grew stronger and stronger as he ran. Now seeing the night as a human would see late afternoon, he turned south and continued to run parallel to the woods. Then, quickly approaching a field where about three dozen Black Angus were settled down, he slowed and hugged closer to the woods and away from them.

The solace of the night—only a few could enjoy correctly, he thought.

That night, or for the next three, there was not a thing special save for the joy of running the 'Beast'. But on the

85

tenth of January, a Friday, and about 10:00 p.m., at exactly the same place, he noticed something that definitely wasn't there before. Drifting in from the south on the breeze was the pleasant aroma and sound of grilling beef searing on the grill. Now, completely curious, Jack knelt at the edge of the woods by Banjo. From where he was, he couldn't see the cattle. A thin strip of woods stretched out across the field about fifty yards away and between him and where they were bedded down. But the steady breeze was in his face, bringing with it the scent of the cooking beef. Jack slowly stood, but before he could start toward the cattle, the limbs of the old oak above him rattled and down came Woo with a thud--leaves, limbs and all. It surprised Banjo so much that he ran about ten yards away from Jack, stopped, and then looked back at Woo.

"Ji Woo?" said Jack. He watched her rub her arms as she sat on the ground, looking disgruntled.

Frowning, she slowly looked up at him. "What do you say when you get really mad?"

Jack laughed. "Dammit, I suppose."

"Well. . ." Woo slowly stood and brushed the grass and leaves from her hair. "Dammit, I suppose."

"What happened?" Jack grinned. "It looked like someone threw you through the tree."

"It's there, Jack! It's there!" She pointed a shaky finger straight toward the jetty of woods between them and the cattle. "And that thing is there as well."

"It? Thing?" Jack laughed silently. "What are you talking about?

"I don't know," shrugged Woo, looking somewhat irritated. "The 'It' was standing by this solid black 'Thing' about the size of your green car. The 'It' was working on the 'Thing' I think, and there was a cow there as well. I don't think the animal was alive."

"What does this 'It' look like?" asked Jack.

"Scary," whispered Woo. "It was a little taller than me, grayish-green skin, funny looking head with huge, black eyes. It had skinny arms and legs as well."

"Is it still there?" asked Jack as he and Banjo started trotting in that direction.

Woo quickly flew past him. "We'll see," she answered as she flew toward the strip of woods.

Although Jack was well into the 'Beast', there was no way he could keep up with the little flying girl. As he approached the jetty of trees, Woo flew out of the darkness and landed so hard she all but tumbled in front of him.

"Get in the woods! Get in the woods!" she exclaimed, as she grabbed and tugged on his right hand.

"What now?" asked Jack, now at a trot in the direction she was pulling.

"That black, propeller thing has just landed close to the 'It'."

"Helicopter?" asked Jack.

"That's it! That's it!" replied Woo excitedly as they drew close to the woods. "There are also two men with it and they are helping Mr. Gray Skin work on his ship."

*   *   *

Now, easing through the woods and toward the open pasture, Jack walked behind a righteously disturbed Woo. With every, fifth step, she would pause as if searching for a movement in the open pasture ahead of them. Then, with only ten yards to the edge of the woods, she stopped and held up her hand.

Looking in that direction, Jack could not only see the chopper, but hear the engine as it revved up. Extremely quiet, the DOD chopper lifted from the grass and headed west. He watched it as much as he could until it disappeared into the night, still heading toward the Mississippi River.

Jack knelt by the little bat girl. "C'mon, Woo, let's get a closer look. I don't see the UFO ship glowing yet. Perhaps they just brought a part or something."

Woo slowly looked back at Jack. "I'll follow you this time," she whispered.

Stopping at the edge of the clearing, Jack could plainly see that the Gray Man's attention was completely taken up by working in a small, compartment on the side of his ship. So far, their presence went unnoticed. As they

87

watched, the alien opened a brown, cardboard box and took something made of a chrome-like metal from it. Removing a like object from the open compartment, the strange being replaced it with the one from the box and closed the door. As he put the old one in the box and dropped it to the grass, he paused and looked toward the woods, almost in their direction. Jack froze, holding tight to Banjo's muzzle. Then, as if touched by something one couldn't see, Woo sneezed so hard she sat down in the grass in front of him.

"Eeeeeahhh!" exclaimed the Gray as he instantly turned toward them.

Seemingly without being prompted, a glowing seam appeared horizontally around the entire, black ship. When the glowing line connected to itself, the top half of the ship opened and the entire craft raised to about foot above the grass. With one more look toward Jack, the Grey dove into the ship and closed the top. With static sparks flying between it and the ground, the glow of the line slowly spread until the entire ship became so bright one could hardly look at it. Rising until the static charges stopped, the ship turned and then shot off toward the river without a sound at all.

"Dammit, I suppose," said Woo weakly, looking toward where the 'Silver Streak' and went.

"Exactly," added the man, Jack. His gaze drifted from toward the river to where the strange craft had been sitting, about thirty yards from them.

Ji Woo squinted as Jack stood. "You're a man now. You're not going out. . ." Her voice trailed off as she watched the young detective walk toward the edge of the woods. "Yes, you are, aren't you," she added weakly.

Keeping an eye on where the two ships went, Jack looked back to where the Gray's ship was once sitting. "They left it," he said, just above a whisper.

"It?" Woo eased toward him, tightly clutching Banjo's collar. "What 'It'?" she asked, looking straight at Jack.

"Don't know," admitted Jack as he knelt beside the still open, cardboard box.

"Awww, nuts!" complained Woo.

Jack instantly looked back to see that Woo had shut her eyes tightly. The sneeze that exploded from the little winged girl left her sitting in the grass once again.

"Are you all right?" asked Jack as he peeped inside the box.

Woo slowly shook her head, still keeping her distance from Jack. "It's Mr. Gray Skin," she complained. "I can't stand the way he smells. It's like burnt motor oil and black pepper. He moves. Even when he stands still, he still moves. I can't tell what he's thinking--too many thoughts, much too many. Can't hear his heartbeat, yet he lives."

Checking the skies over the river once again, Jack pulled the strange, chrome object from the box.

Woo moved closer, but still over a reach from Jack. "What is it?"

Jack shrugged, holding up the object. "Centre Blocken is on the outside of the box. It looks like some kind of a weapon. I guess it's fired from inside the ship. But, it's got a handle, what looks to be a trigger, what looks like cooling louvers before the barrel starts. And there's a red button over the trigger."

Jack looked at the dead Black Angus heifer lying in the grass. Its udders had been cut away and with them, parts of the exposed entrails. There was no blood at all on the ground.

"Let's get out of here," suggested Woo, looking toward the river again. "When that thing realizes he left it, he might come back."

Jack nodded. "Guess you're right. Let's go back to the car and take this thing to Will. If those DOD fellas come for it, they're gonna get more than they bargained for. Will's gonna be plenty pissed about what just happened to Larry Call and they stood by, without a word, and let it happen."

*   *   *

That night, while Jack lay next to Shelley, he couldn't keep his mind away from what had just happened. He knew if the FBI could find whatever they wanted, then the CIA, or DOD, or whoever could do as well if they had a

89

reason.   Perhaps in taking the thing in the box, he had just given them one--one that would bring them right to Will's office. Woo's attitude was also just a puzzling. For the first time, she had showed him that she could fear something. . .

"Jack?" Shelley sat up, lightly touching his right arm. "It's 1:00AM. You know you've got to go to work in six hours from now. You can't sleep?"

Jack briskly rubbed his face.   "I need to clear my mind." He turned toward Shelley. "Would it trouble you if I ran for about an hour or so?"

"The woods, Jack?" asked Shelley.

Jack nodded, got up, and then grabbed his faded jeans.. "I'll be back at 2:30AM or so.

Shelley turned on the table lamp and sat up. "Are you all right?"

Jack shrugged, smiling.   "That's what I'm looking for right now--my version of normality."

Part 2
Strange Visitor

The next morning, a cloudy and cold January 8th, Jack pulled Uncle Bill's Ford into the Munford Sheriff's Department parking lot shortly after 7:00AM and parked. Yawning, he looked about the lot. Dianne's car was already there as well as Andy's. His grandfather's black Ford cruiser had been moved to the front door. Smiling, he noted Charlie's Airstream.

"Well. . ." Jack picked up the Gray man's forgotten box as he got out of his vehicle.

The promise of a heavy rain had started with its heavy drops here and there as Jack walked toward the front door. Noting the huge, dark gray clouds right above him, he picked up his pace with Banjo keeping time as always. Once inside, Banjo trotted straight to Dianne's desk where she was working the daily crossword puzzle. Will's door was closed, but Fred's was partially open. Andy was making coffee behind the Sergeant's Desk.

"Where's Will?" asked Jack, looking at Andy.

"He's stopped by the DA's office to talk with Charles Davidson. Will's re-opening an old case back in '62." He noted at the box in Jack's hand. "What's that?"

Jack smiled. "Not sure myself. I would normally give this to you since you're next in the chain of command, but this comes with baggage you might not want to deal with."

"You found something last night, didn't you?" asked Fred as he walked toward his grandson. "Will had me put you on something to do with his 'Men in Black' but. . ." Fred's words trailed off as he looked into the box. "What the devil is that?"

"This came off Will's Silver Streak UFO thing that's been giving Doc Hall a fit."

"Silver Streak?" Andy walked up and handed Jack a cup of hot coffee. "Two sugars and two creams," he added. "That thing looks like a weapon."

"Woo led me to in on Doc Hall's land. The UFO and a Gray was there, as well as another dead Black Angus. That black chopper brought in a replacement for this thing and left. But the Grey spotted us. He left so fast he forgot to take the old one he replaced."

Dianne quickly got up and walked to Jack's side. "Ohhh boy," she groaned. "Will's bound to get a visit over this."

"Centre Blockhen, the box says," noted Andy as he reached in and picked up the heavy, chrome instrument. "Looks like a real ray gun, Jack. It's got three barrels, cooling louvers behind the barrels monitored with a red light. He gripped the handle, holding it out toward his desk like a pirate's pistol. There's a red button above the handle where the hammer should be and trigger right in front of my index finger."

"That's an alien thing, Andy," warned Fred. "Be careful. Don't touch anything. You might blow a hole in something."

"Or worse," added Dianne as she eased behind Jack.

Andy lightly shook in. "It's heavy enough to be a weapon," he surmised.

"Andy," warned Fred. "Put that damned thing back in the box."

"Awww Fred," chuckled Andy. "Should be safe enough as long as you don't touch the tri--"

But the big sergeant's heavy thumb was already on the red button and the blinking, red light on the cooling louvers stopped Andy's comment immediately.

"Point it toward the window!" shouted Fred as Dianne backed even more behind Jack.

"It's humming and vibrating," said Andy, now directing the weapon toward the window closest to the front door.

"Damn it, Andy!" exclaimed Jack. "The light is solid now. Whatever you do, don't touch the trigger." He quickly looked at Fred. "Go and open the back door of the cell block."

Without a word, Fred ran toward the cell block door, opened it, and then ran inside and out of sight.

"Follow him, Andy," directed Jack, "and don't touch that trigger."

Andy immediately walked briskly through the cell block and then outside the back door where Fred was waiting in the alley.

"Point that thing in the air and press the red button again," said Fred.

Doing that, everyone watched the red light atop the cooling louvers start to blink again and then it went out.

Taking a slow and deep breath, Jack looked to his grandfather. "Who do we know that could tell us what this thing is?"

Fred slowly shook his head. "Professor Miles at Memphis State University. I overheard Will speaking to him yesterday. He's some kind of big wig in at a UFO center based there. He's gonna meet Will here around noon or so."

"Come with me, Andy," said Dianne. "You can put that thing in Will's safe. Professor Miles can look at it when he gets here. And for God's sake, don't touch that button again."

*   *   *

That afternoon, Jack made sure he was in the office at 12:00PM. Teresa and Pico were at school, so Shelley opted to come with him. Since he had been working at the office most of the day, and his case was going better than expected, Fred opted to put him back on days. . .

Following Jack inside, Shelley took a seat near Dianne's desk.

Jack paused near the desk as well. "Are Will and our UFO expert here yet?" he asked.

Dianne nodded toward the sheriff's office. "They're in there right now and waiting for you."

"I'll stay right here with Dianne," said Shelley.

Jack nodded and then turned and walked toward Will's office. Stopping at the partially open door, he peeped inside. Will, and his grandfather were there, as well as a red-headed man with his back to the door. The UFO expert looked to be in his early forties, just under six feet, and heavy set. Will's smile instantly gave his quiet arrival away.

"Well. . ." Fred turned toward the door as did the red-headed man.

"I heard you had more than just a little luck last night," said Will. "I got us a man who might just know a little something about what we're dealin' with here."

"I had a little help," admitted Jack, glancing at the stranger.

The red-headed fellow quickly stood and offered Jack his hand. "I'm Professor Eddie Miles. My friends just call me Eddie. I'm over the Tennessee branch of MUFON—that's Mutual UFO Network." He glanced back at Will's desk where Jack's alien weapon was lying in its box. "I'll be personally responsible for that thing if you loan it to me for a week or so."

Before Jack could answer, Eddie picked up a small, black box with a chrome wand attached to it by a spiral cord. "Know what this is?" He looked up at Jack.

"Geiger counter?" guessed Jack.

Eddie nodded as he held the wand close to the thing in the box. It immediately began to click, but didn't seem to alarm its operator.

Eddie directed the wand toward Jack. "Your hands please."

Although the clicking sound was weak, it was there none-the-less.

"Andy's already scrubbed," said Will. "You can use my bathroom."

Jack paused, staring at Eddie. "I took this thing home with me last night."

"Did anyone else handle it?" asked Eddie.

"No, Sir. I left it in the trunk of my car. I took a bath before I touched anyone."

Eddie smiled. "I wouldn't be alarmed, Jack. Your exposure was minimal at best."

"Then. . ." Jack cast a jaded eye at the box. "Do you know anything about the cattle mutilations in Montana, Oregon, Texas, and now here in Tennessee?"

94

"Yes. . ." Eddie glanced at Will. "I was told about them. Wish I could have been there with you." He looked to Will. "You say you were visited by two from DOD?"

Will shrugged. "That's who they said they were," replied the old sheriff. "Their ID's looked official to me."

Eddie looked back to Jack. "Those cattle were killed by an intense blast of RF energy. The three round burn marks were mostly on their foreheads. I believe the radioactivity is what kept most of the predators and scavenger animals at bay."

"Then we're through with this UFO stuff?" asked Jack.

"Not by a long shot," replied Will. "I got pictures of that weapon thing with me and Eddie and DOD maps showin' where Doc Hall's prize bull was killed by that Silver Streak thing. I have reopened the Larry Call case with this new evidence and I ain't stoppin' 'till I get that boy out of Fort Pillow Prison." He looked straight at Jack. "But you're off it for a little bit. Your grandfather's got a tiger by the tail right now and needs a little help."

Fred smiled. "This is right down your alley, Jack. You like to work in the woods and this vehicle theft problem in Covington's driving me to distraction. They mostly target four-wheel drive trucks and ATV's."

Jack squinted. "Chop shop or outright thefts and sales?"

Fred shrugged. "Don't know yet. Every time I think I'm getting close, I hit a dead end. Last Friday afternoon, this character hit in broad daylight at a shopping center and made off with a four-wheel drive sports utility vehicle. As I pulled into Covington, it drove right past me. But when I finally got turned around, he had two, three blocks on me and made a hard left. In less than a minute, I made the same turn but couldn't spot him anywhere."

Jack smiled, almost laughing. "And this is a woods thing?"

"It is, Jack," answered Fred. "I found two places where three or more have met up with some kind of heavy truck, loaded what appeared to be vehicles, and then drove away weighted down." He smiled again at Jack and then added, "Wanna hear something strange?"

95

Jack nodded.

"The one driving the GMC SUV was a young, red-headed girl in her twenties, I'd say, and she drove that thing like she owned it. What's worse, when we passed, she smiled right at me as if to say catch me if you can."

Jack smiled at his grandfather. "She knew who you were?"

Fred nodded. "Red hair, light complexion, and green eyes."

Jack burst out laughing. "You noticed her eyes?"

"Yes. I'm not dead yet, Jack," grumbled Fred.

"Boys, boys, play nicely," quipped Will, laughing himself. He looked to Fred. "There's not a thing more pressing that the case you're on right now. Keep Jack with you until we run these people down."

*　　　*　　　*

With Covington only thirty minutes down Highway 51, Jack wasted little time. Remembering what his grandfather said in the briefing about the truck tracks, he headed to the west end of the Hatchie Wildlife Refuge where Highway 14 hits 54 from Covington. According to Park Rangers, deer hunting in that area was most popular.

Perhaps I should concentrate on something enclosed that could carry two or more cars, he thought as he turned east on Highway 54 and headed toward the Refuge. *But what if it's not a big, enclosed truck?* he pondered as he watched a rather large cattle truck as it passed.

Slowing as he approached the Highway 14 intersection, he pulled into a Texaco service station and parked close to the road and picked up the mic.

"James, Jack here. Come in."

"James here," responded the radio loud and clear. "I'm cruising Covington. Where are you?"

"Texaco station where Highway 14 hits 54," answered Jack.

"Heads up, Jack," added James. "Got a possible headed your way. Just turned east on Highway 54 and trailing a new, four-horse trailer pulled by a red, F 250

Ford. It's new also. No hay in the trailer and the wheels look a bit muddied."

Fifteen minutes later, the rig in question turned into the Texaco station and pulled up to the pumps. Seeing a brown-haired girl of twenty-five or so get out of the driver's side and go into the store, Jack did the same. Passing close to the rig, he noted the Tennessee, Tipton county plates. To make things more interesting, the trailer was equipped with a retractable ramp and the two, side doors were secured with heavy padlocks. Snugging his Munford Sheriff's Department hat down over his forehead, he entered the store and smiled at the young blonde behind the register.

"Can I help you?" she quickly asked, looking up at him with a smile. Her hazel eyes stared as he paused at the register.

"Do you have Juicy Fruit gum?" asked Jack, returning her smile.

"I am. Uhhh, I mean I have." Her face turned red as she produced a large, yellow package of Wrigley's. "You must play basketball."

Jack's smile widened as he checked the brunette now at the soft drink dispenser. "Not that coordinated," quipped Jack. "Can't walk and chew gum at the same time." He nodded at the big rig at the pumps. "Does that rig come in here very often?"

The clerk shrugged. "Once a week I guess." She looked down at the ring on Jack's finger. "Just my luck," she grumbled. "Here lately, it seems like every young man I meet is married."

Jack smiled, noting that the brunette he had followed in was now right behind him. "Raise horses?" he asked.

"In a way," said the woman as she paid for her gas.

Knowing that she didn't have time to pump it, he looked outside to see yet another girl. Blond, in her late twenties, and with an impressive figure, she waited beside the truck for the brunette.

Jack turned toward the brunette as she walked toward the door. "Do you ride them or show them?"

"We just move them," she answered, holding the smile.

97

Later that evening, around 8:30PM at Jack's home, he listened to Shelley negotiate with the girls about the bathroom. Settling on Pico first, Shelley prepared her bubble bath. Hearing the window slam shut in Pico's room, Jack got up to see Shelley walking briskly down the hallway toward it. Pausing at the hallway entrance, he noted she had turned toward him.

"Better come and see what's upset Woo," she said, nodding back toward the bedroom. "She's under Pico's bed and won't come out."

Even before Jack entered the bedroom, he could hear the little batgirl sneezing. Kneeling beside the bed, he peeked under the edge of the bedspread. She was there all right and completely covered by her black, leathery wings.

"Woo?" Jack's tone soft.

"He's back! He's back!" exclaimed Woo, still tightly hidden under her wings.

Jack squinted. "Who's back?"

"That shiny thing is in the woods just past the back gate and the Grey Man is in the garage."

"Now?" Jack quickly stood.

"Don't know about now," she replied.

Woo slid from under the bed and stopped directly under the window. Easing to its lower, right corner, she peeped out toward the back yard and then glanced back at Jack. "He thinks."

"Thinks?" Jack's looked puzzled at Woo.

"Yes-yes-yes!" answered Woo. "What's a Cinder Blocker?"

"That's Centre Blocken, Woo," explained Jack as he trotted from the room with Woo fluttering in the air right behind him. "That's the thing the Grey Man left the other night. It's a weapon of some kind."

Straight to the nightstand ran Jack, unlocked it, and then removed his Smith and Wesson .357.

As the two left the bedroom, Jack paused to look at Shelley and Teresa at the hall entranceway. Pico was wedged in the middle, wrapped in a towel.

98

"What's going on?" asked Shelley, notably worried. "Something peeped in the bathroom window at Pico. She's scared stiff."

"Somebody's in the back yard, Jack," said Teresa. "He's making a lot of noise in the garage."

"Stay here," said Jack as he ran past them and on to the back door with Woo right behind him, glancing off the wall as she sneezed.

"Wait a minute," said Shelley. She quickly held out a three-cell flashlight. "You'll need this."

Just as soon as Jack opened the back door, Woo brushed past him, stopping a short way in the yard. "He's at the gate! He's at the gate!" she exclaimed, tumbling to the grass behind him.

"Let's go," said Jack as he started running toward the back gate.

"What?" Woo looked back at the girls, now holding the screen door open.

"We're not going," said Shelley as Pico and Teresa shook their heads in a definitely silent 'no'.

Woo sat tight in the grass.

Slowing as he quickly approached the gate, Jack could see the little, grey man looking back at them as the top half of his ship was starting to open up and glow.

"He's getting away!" shouted Woo, now hovering closely behind him.

The two eased closer to the gate, now only twenty yards or so from the ship. As the top started to close, the glowing, horizontal line was already starting to spread causing the ship to hum softly.

"Stop right there!" shouted Jack as he kept the pistol behind him. "Who are you and what do you want?"

Paying him no mind, the little, grey man busied himself with the controls of the ship as the door closed. Now, completely illuminated, the craft started to slowly rise in an array of static sparks to the ground. Woo dropped to the grass and eased up close to Jack's right leg, gripping it tightly. When the craft was about ten feet from the ground, Jack noticed the compartment on its left side had come open and the strange weapon was sliding

99

out and into place. Jack quickly raised his .357 as the craft started to turn toward them.

"Power down! Retract your weapon!" shouted Jack.

Then, as if in a bad dream, the red light on top of the weapon started to blink.

Jack instantly fired his Smith and Wesson three times, striking the strange craft in the nose.

Visibly shaken with each shot, the craft's nose rose slightly, directing the weapon away from the two. Now, spewing blue sparks from the area it was struck, the craft seemed to lose part of its glow. Patches in the nose, each side, and in the top of the ship quickly became dark. Struggling to rise above the trees, it looked as if it was losing power. Jack and Woo watched as it pulled away from them and started to weave around the tops of the trees. As it did, the strange craft exploded loudly in a bright array of white smoke and sparks.

"What did it do?" shouted Shelley from the back porch.

"Not sure," replied Jack as he gently tried to free his leg from Woo's arms. "I think it just blew up." He looked down at Woo. "Let's go and see what's left."

The little batgirl's grip tightened. "Go?" Woo looked up at him and then at the little fires scattered here and there under where the ship exploded. "You first," she said weakly, releasing her grip on his leg.

Quickly concentrating on stamping out the burning leaves here and there, the two also looked for parts of the ship.

"You'd think there would be some big parts," complained Jack. "But all I see is little pieces of shiny metal here and there."

"Jack. . ." came Woo's weak summons, almost as a warning.

The young detective looked to his left where the little batgirl was standing. Her gaze was transfixed on a black, smoldering lump in the grass about thirty feet from her. Ten feet past it was a glowing, red light nestled in the leaves and grass.

"Don't touch it!" warned Jack as he trotted toward her.

100

"Don't worry about me," replied Woo, weakly. "You shouldn't touch it either. It's probably really hot."

Jack looked back toward the house. "Shelley! Call the dispatcher and tell her to send an ambulance with back up. Tell her to call Will also and tell him the Silver Streak is down and one dead. . .I think!"

"Look at his head," whispered Woo as she eased closer to what looked to be a charred eight-year-old boy lying in the grass. "It looks normal right now."

"You're right."

Jack directed the flashlight's beam to something very close to the head of the lifeless body. Although badly damaged, it appeared to be some kind of helmet. Shaped like a stem-down pear, its dark lenses were lying on the grass in front of it.

"Good Lord," groaned Jack as he slowly knelt by the helmet and picked up the two, dark, oval lenses. "I've really stepped into it now, James."

Jack quickly stood and looked back at Teresa, still on the back porch. "Tell Shelley to have my back-up step on it. I need the coroner here ASAP. We're gonna have company."

"Company?" Woo looked up at Jack.

The young detective nodded. "Do you Remember the black chopper?"

Without a word, the little batgirl took to the air, flew past the gate, and then continued straight to Pico's partially open window.

*   *   *

Now sitting in the warm living room, Jack swiveled the big, padded rocker to face the couch. "All right," started Jack, noting the blank expressions on the faces of all, three girls. "Let's hear your questions."

"What is he?" Pico finally asked, as Teresa and Shelley sat there in silence.

Jack smiled. "Not that sure, Sweetie," he replied. "But he won't be troubling you anymore."

Pico quickly sat up to the edge of the couch. "He had big, black eyes and his skin didn't look right."

"We heard you shoot," said Teresa. "Did you kill him?"

101

"In a way I guess," answered Jack. "I shot his ship when he pointed his weapon at me. He died when his ship crashed in the woods."

Then, quick as a flash, Pico jumped from the couch and ran to the big, picture window. "Someone is here, Uncle Jack!" she exclaimed.

Even before Jack could get up, he could see a cruiser's red light being reflected off of the window.

"Hello the house!" hailed someone outside as Jack walked toward the door.

"It's Bubba," said Jack as he opened the big, wooden door.

"Well. . ." Bubba looked through the screen door and waved at Pico. She looked as if she was glued to Jack's right leg. "What's this Lucy's sayin' about little, green men and a glowing UFO?" His blank stare ended up on Jack. "She was so excited I hardly understood her. Said you shot the thing down?"

"He was here!" exclaimed Pico as she pushed the screen door open. "He wasn't green. He was grey and Uncle Jack shot him."

"Uhhh. . ." Jack hesitated, glancing down at Pico. "I shot the UFO. The Grey Man died in the crash."

"Crash?" asked Bubba as he stepped back to let Jack onto the front porch.

"Jack?"

The young detective looked back to see Shelley offering him a three-cell flashlight again. "You'll need this if you go back there."

"Thanks." Jack took the light and then eased down the porch steps. "C'mon, Bubba. The little man, or what's left of him is back here past the gate. He almost landed the thing in my back yard."

"Why would he do such a thing?" asked Bubba.

Jack shrugged. "I think he was looking for that weapon MUFON has right now."

Bubba ran his hand under the bill of his cap and scratched his head. "Well. . .the Chief's on his way. Lucy said he was gonna show me Horned Jack." He stopped the detective as they slowed for the gate. "What in

102

tarnation did he mean by that? Every time that name is spoken at the office, somebody always looks at me like I've got the measles."

"Will told you that?" asked Jack as he noted another set of red, flashing lights had just pulled into the driveway.

"Yep," answered Bubba. "And he added something that didn't make no sense at all. "If you see 'em in the 'Beast' you just might shoot 'em. What tha blazes does that mean?"

"I'm comin'. I'm comin'," said Will as he trotted toward the two from the garage. "Are you all right?" he asked, looking at Jack.

"Never better," answered the young detective.

Will nodded as he trotted up. "Lucy almost passed out tryin' ta tell me you shot down somethin' in your back yard," he added as he looked about the yard. "I don't see a thing and she's got Kotts on his way with the ambulance. What tha Hell's goin' on?"

Jack shrugged as he opened the gate and walked into the woods. "Come with us and I'll try to explain. We had a burglar. He looked into Pico's bedroom window. I caught up with him about thirty yards from here." He glanced back at Will. "I caught up with him as he got into his ship. It was a Grey Man, Will. When I shouted for him to stop, I saw the weapon compartment open as he turned the ship toward me. I shot first and the ship crashed back there a ways in the woods.

The old sheriff grabbed Jack's right arm, stopping him. "You mean we got a DB back here?"

Jack nodded. "Kotts needs to get here before that black chopper does."

Will immediately looked to what he could see of the sky through the limbs of the trees. Looking back at Jack, he asked, "You showed 'em yet?"

"Uhhh. . ." Jack glanced at Bubba. "That would be a no."

Bubba rolled his eyes, ending up on Jack. "Why do I feel like a third thumb here? Show me what?"

103

"Well, here goes," said Jack as he looked at Bubba. "Have you ever heard of what folks in these parts call Horned Jack?"

Bubba eyebrows slowly raised. "No, but my wife has. She was raised in Drummonds. Says he's some kind o' Batman or somethin'."

"Batman?" Will laughed, glancing at Jack. "That would be a Woo I think."

"Woo?" Bubba rolled his eyes. "Here we go again."

"All right-all right, Bubba," replied Will. "You just stand right there. Jack's got somethin' ta show you."

"Very well," said Jack as he turned off his flashlight.

Closing his eyes, he concentrated on bringing the fever.

The big deputy squinted through the darkness at Jack just as something tapped his chest.

"Take it," came a voice he had never heard before. Deep it was and unrealistic.

As Bubba took the flashlight that was being pressed against his chest, he looked up at two, glowing, green eyes, the color of which he had never seen on any animal.

"What the Hell?" said Bubba weakly as Will took hold of his right arm.

"Don't touch that gun, Bubba," instructed Will. "Turn tha light on."

Bubba turned on the Eveready and slowly directed its beam toward Jack's face. "Jack, is that you?" he asked at a whisper.

"I'm still Jack," answered the young detective in the same, low tone as he held his, now taloned, hands close to the beam.

"Holy shi--" Trying to back up, the big sergeant only found Will's strong arms.

"That's enough," interrupted Will, almost laughing out loud.

Jack snatched the flashlight from Bubba and turned it off.

"Jack?" Bubba's right hand found Will's left forearm.

"Are you back, Jack?" asked Will.

"I think," replied the man Jack.

104

Still laughing, Will took the flashlight, turned it on, and then directed the beam close to Bubba's face. He was still very much wide-eyed.

"Awww c'mon," grumbled Bubba, hearing them both laugh. "Nothin' much shakes me up these days. But this. . .this got to me I'll have ta admit. Jack, what tha Hell are you?"

"Nephilim," answered the young detective. "We don't have time now, but tomorrow when you have time, drop by old Doc Rhea's office and have him explain me. I'm sure you'll understand him a lot better than me."

Part 3
Catch Me If You Can

Back at Jack's back yard, the levity of the moment was broken by four, little words from the County Coroner as he walked up. . .

"What's Jack into now?" asked Kotts as he stood there grinning, with his leather bag slung over his left shoulder.

"No time to explain, Doc," replied Will. "This is one of those 'You'll have ta see things'." Will turned to Jack. "We're wasting precious time. Show us what we need to get and we'll get it and get the Hell out o' here."

Jack turned and started toward the woods with the rest in tow.

"What's the hurry?" asked Kotts, now at almost a trot.

Will glanced back at him. "You read the report, Don. That damned black chopper shadows these things. If it catches us here, we'll most likely lose everything. And I don't want another visit from those DOJ guys."

Everyone then slowed, watching Jack look about the grass for something.

"It's still glowing," said Jack, glancing back at the others.

"Ohhh Hell," grumbled Will, glancing back at Bubba. "Memphis said you were some kind o' weapons expert. Go and take a look at what Jack's found."

"Yes sir," replied the big deputy as he stepped around the others and up close to Jack. "What'cha got?"

"Not sure," replied Jack, holding the beam on the red, flashing light in the grass. "Hear that hum?"

Bubba nodded as he eased forward. "Just guessing here, but whatever it is, it seems to be charging up I think."

Bubba knelt down and lightly touched the chrome instrument. "Still warm, but not damaged maybe."

No sooner had he said that, then the red light went to steady on.

"Ohhh Hell," grumbled Will. "Watch what you're doing, Bubba. "That damned thing's liable to blow up."

Gently picking it up, the deputy directed it at a nearby pine tree and pulled the trigger. The weapon went off like a cherry bomb, shooting out three beams which quickly joined to form one solid, bright orange streak of light. Striking the tree like a close-fired shotgun, it sent pine bark flying, leaving the four staring at a smooth and smoldering bare spot.

"Well. . ." Bubba walked toward the tree.

"Leave it be," ordered Will.

Bubba stopped but a reach from the bare spot and looked back. "Didn't even make a hole."

"Not one you can see," replied Kotts. "I think it was shooting more than just energy."

"This way." Jack turned and with no less than a dozen steps, stopped and directed his light toward the small cadaver.

"Mother of Pearl," said Bubba, his tone weak. "You killed a kid."

"Don't think so," said Jack as he watched Kotts kneel by the corpse.

"He's a Grey Man," added Jack. "What we thought was his head was a helmet I think."

The coroner nodded as he looked closer. "His eyes are kind of slanted, like he was some kind of oriental. But. . ."

Kotts' comment faded as he reached down in the grass about a foot from the alien's face and picked up two, oval-shaped pieces of what looked to be lenses from sunglasses. "Good Lord," he said weakly as he held one of them up. "They magnify the light--some kind of night vision I think." He quickly handed them to Bubba and nodded toward the big satchel. "Wrap them up. I got paper and plastic bags in there. Pull out that big, black plastic bag first if you will. We need to get this little fellow in there and leave right now. I haven't been this nervous since they killed the last president."

No sooner had they got the cadaver back to the ambulance, than Jack stopped and looked back toward the woods. "Shhh!" he hissed as he turned out his flashlight. "Something just flew in low and over the woods. It's hovering just past where we found the body.

Jack ran to the back porch where Shelley, Teresa, and Pico were still standing. "Go in the house and turn all the lights off."

"Are we in danger?" asked Teresa as Shelley and Pico ran into the kitchen.

"No," replied Jack. "But I don't want anything we found out there to be connected with any one in here. Where's Woo?"

"She's under the bed in Pico's room," answered Teresa. "Something scared her again."

"Shhh. . ." hissed Bubba as he trotted up to the back porch. He pointed back at the woods, toward a powerful beam of light directed at the ground about a hundred yards from them. "They're not landin', but they're sure lookin' for somethin'."

Will walked up, nodding at Teresa. "We're out o' here, Jack, and nobody lights up. If you and yours don't feel comfortable here right now, I'll sign off on a room at the hotel for you."

"We're fine, Will," replied Jack. "I'd like a second look when our visitors leave."

Bubba looked to Will. "I'm stayin' here for a little while if it's all the same to you. "That thing's lookin' for somethin' and I don't think he's gonna find it. I took a quick look and there's not a piece left of that ship bigger than an apple out there."

"Well. . ." Will looked to Jack. "If you find somethin', bring it in with you tomorrow. And if those girls get nervous about all o' this, you put em' up in the Munford Hotel. You hear?"

"Thanks, Will. We'll do that," replied Jack.

*   *   *

Standing on the front porch, Jack and Bubba watched Kotts and the Sheriff leave. Obviously uncomfortable, Bubba kept looking back toward what he could see of the woods between the house and garage. The powerful spotlight of the black chopper was not hard to pick out.

"What do you think?" asked Jack, amused at the big deputy's nervousness.

"I'm goin'. I'm goin' just as soon as that thing leaves," grumbled Bubba. "He can't land it in the woods and he dare not land it in someone's yard." He glanced at Jack. "But I'd feel heaps better if the guy who actually shot down a UFO would back me up."

"Well. . ." Jack nodded at the chopper now pulling away and heading south-east.

"Let's go then," said Bubba as he started walking toward the back gate. Arriving there, he stopped and looked back at Jack.

"What?" asked Jack. "You're not getting cold feet at this point are you?"

"When we get back there, you're not gonna do that Horned Jack thing on me are you?"

Visibly tickled, Jack held to the gatepost, looking at the big man. Although Jack was almost a head taller, Bubba was well over six feet and two hundred and fifty pounds of solid muscle.

Jack squinted. "You're still shaken by some over-blown urban legend?"

Bubba slowly shook his head, grumbling, "Urban legend my foot. What I saw just a few minutes ago wasn't no Jack Frost prowlin' the forest or some Confederate soldier called Old Green Eyes. What I saw was somethin' I ain't never seen before and absolutely do-not-understand."

Jack smiled silently at Bubba's troubled expression. "I am a Nephilim, Bubba," he explained. "I'm just one of many who are allowed to watch over this world of ours. Please, do not be afraid of me."

Now the confused look was back on the deputy. "Nephilim huh?" Bubba looked down at the grass and shook his head again. "One of many? Guess I'll have ta look that one up."

"Start with your bible," suggested Jack. "Go to Genesis in the days of Noah. That will give you an idea of what one is. I was just blessed with the gene and it sprang to life when I turned sixteen."

Jack pulled of his cap and directed the light on the top of his head.

"God bless me," said Bubba. His tone weak. "And if I read about this, I'll understand what you are?"

Laughing again, Jack shook his head. "Probably not. I've had twenty-four years to do that and I still don't."

"Well, all right then." Bubba looked toward the woods. "Let's go and see what that chopper was lookin' for."

*　　　*　　　*

So, on a cold, January 8th, Wednesday morning at 12:20AM, Bubba followed Jack through the gate and on into the woods with their flashlights on.

Passing where they found the charred body of the Grey Man, Jack stopped and glanced back at Bubba. "That chopper seemed to hover over one spot. Did you notice that?"

"Yep." The big deputy stepped around Jack and continued south. "Not far from here at all. Seems that somethin' had its attention under there." Bubba pointed the beam of his flashlight at a huge, old bodark tree about forty yards away.

Quickly checking of what he could see of the sky through the limps of the trees, Jack then looked at Bubba. "I don't think it's coming back. Let's see what we can find and get this over with."

After searching for fifteen minutes or so, the two had found several, lemon-sized pieces of what looked to be polished aluminum. It was then that Jack noticed that Bubba was staring down at something in the tall grass on the far side of the bodark tree.

"Jack," called Bubba quietly. "You might want to come and have a look at this. Looks like some kind o' radio."

Jack eased up beside the big deputy and looked to where the beam of his flashlight was directed into the grass. Slightly charred and dented here and there, lay a black, 3" by 6" by 12" piece of electronic equipment. Carefully picking it up, Jack noted what looked to be ten inches of insulated, two conductor power cord still attached.

Jack glanced at Bubba. "I'll bet MUFON can get this thing to work. We'll get Will to call Eddie just as soon as we get back." He smiled at the big deputy. "Good work. The sheriff will like this. This will probably get you out of the doghouse."

"Ya think?" quipped Bubba.

*   *   *

That afternoon, around 4:00PM or so, Jack pulled his cruiser into the Munford Sheriff's Office parking lot. Bubba's patrol car was parked right beside what looked to be Will's cruiser. But the cruiser looked to be freshly painted white over black with Chief lettered on the front doors.

Interesting, thought Jack as he headed for the front door.

Once inside, he paused and looked toward Dianne at the dispatcher's desk. She was already smiling at him.

"Will had that Mr. Miles from the UFO center in Memphis here today. When Will told him what you two had found, he dropped what he was doing and came right away.

"Bubba found the thing," replied Jack. "We also found several pieces of metal."

Dianne nodded. "He's got those as well. I'm to tell you there will be a MUFON team at your house the first thing tomorrow morning." As she laughed, she added, "There will also be a reporter from the Memphis Press Scimitar with them. Eddie Miles is exposing this UFO thing as much as possible." Her smile widened. "You're all gonna be in the papers, Jack."

"Ohhh boy," groaned Jack, rolling his eyes toward the front door. "What did Will say?"

Dianne shrugged. "Something about get it all out in the open I think. Fred says Old Stuff 'n Such wants to see you right now." She looked at him with, "Did you see the new paint job on his car?"

Jack nodded.

"Well, whatever you do, don't say a thing about that. He still preferred the unmarked version."

Hearing Jack's discussion with Dianne, Bubba turned from the sergeant's desk and walked quickly toward them. "That UFO fella's got our box, Jack," he added. "He said it was a transponder--somethin' you gotta have when you fly a plane."

Jack squinted as the big deputy stopped just a reach from him and Dianne.

"That glowing, UFO thing was one of ours?" asked Jack.

"Nope," replied Will as he walked toward them from his office. "Our Mr. Miles has already fired the thing up at his lab. He said a regular transponder broadcasts on one of three frequencies to identify planes--private, commercial, or a military aircraft." He looked straight at Bubba as he walked up. "What you found, Bubba, has added a mysterious forth frequency to his records and one that he has no knowledge of. What's more interesting, is the fact that it is a military box complete with a serial number. That's what the black chopper was lookin' for. Eddie said the box was equipped with a backup power supply, but it was probably depleted before the chopper could locate it. Nice work," he said, smiling broadly at Bubba. Glancing at them all, he added, "I'll handle anything that comes our way from the DOD. When asked, just say you can't comment on an on-going investigation and direct them to me. And for Pete's sake, don't mention Eddie Miles or MUFON. He'll handle his own advertisements."

Bubba scratched the back of his neck as he looked at the old sheriff. "Then, all o' this UFO stuff is on the up and up?"

Will slowly shook his head. "I could o' swore you were with us last night when Kotts scooped up that charred fella, took him and his funny pistol, and then drove away from Jack's back yard." He stepped right in front of Bubba. "That was you, wasn't it?"

"Uhhh. . ." Bubba glanced at Jack. "Yes, Sir. I was there. I just didn't see the ship."

"Really?" grumbled the old sheriff. "Well, Bubba, he didn't just come up with the dew or fall from the sky with the rain."

112

"Yes, Sir," replied Bubba. He reached into his pocket and pulled out a half-dollar sized piece of silver metal.

"Freeze right there!" exclaimed Will, looking somewhat astounded. "Please, don't tell me that's a piece of the Grey Man's ship."

"Not real sure," said Bubba. "Jack and me found several pieces like this under a big, old tree right where the black chopper thing was lookin'. It was real close to where that transponder thing was found. Guess I forgot ta--"

"Gimme that," growled the sheriff as he snatched the piece of metal from the deputy's hand. Shaking it at the big deputy, he added, "If one o' those DOD Agents caught you with this, it would put us all right in the stew pot, and we're gonna be there soon enough, I'm sure. You don't, by any chance, have any more souvenirs do you?"

"Nooo Sir," answered Bubba. "That one just skipped my mind I guess."

"Uh huh," replied Will. "Then go on out there and get started. I want you two ta be fresh as daisy's if they catch up ta you in the field."

"Where are you going?" asked Dianne, noting that Will had his hat in his hand.

"I'm goin' ta see Kotts. Maybe by now, he can tell us somethin' about that charred DB. Eddie Miles from MUFON is gonna be there at five sharp and that's only thirty minutes from now."

*   *   *

At just a minute or two after five, Will pulled his now black and white cruiser into the Coroner's lot. Sure enough, Eddie's Chevy Bellaire was already there. Entering the office, he paused just inside the doorway, looking at Kott's sectary. . .

"Well, come on in, Will," said Carmelita Hipshire. The little, forty-year-old Hawaiian smiled at the sheriff's reluctance to enter the room. "You know you've made Kott's day. He's back there now with what he calls Jack's dead alien. There's a man from a UFO place in Memphis with him right now."

"Anybody else?" asked Will.

"Not a soul," answered Carmelita. "Kind of dull really until Kotts brought that alien thing in here." Her eyes narrowed as she looked at the old sheriff. "Now, it's just plain spooky."

"Spooky?" Will quickly looked about the room. "How so?"

"Well, the phone rings and nobody's on the dang thing. And when it does, the lights flicker and the printer starts up but doesn't print a darned thing. Just rolls out blank sheets. Now, that's just plain spooky. You better go back there and check on those two. They know you're coming."

"Will! Is that you?" yelled Kotts from the examination room down the hallway.

"I'm comin'," answered the old sheriff as he headed toward the hallway. "Gimme some good news, Doc. I'll need all I can get ta get that boy out o' Fort Pillow."

Eddie stepped from the examination room and into the hallway with Kotts.

"We sure got a puzzle here, Will," admitted Kotts.

"Talk plain English," said Will. "I haven't got my pocket dictionary with me."

"Never seen anything like it," started Kotts. "He's half a living being and half a machine--loaded with implants. One of them kicked in about an hour ago and had all of us jumping. Eddie had to bribe Carmelita to get her back inside. The thing in his abdomen was about as big as my Zippo cigarette lighter. Eddie took it out and wrapped it in aluminum foil. He said it looked like some king of radio transmitter, red light and all."

"That's great," grumbled Will. "How long did it take you ta find it?"

Kotts shrugged. "About twenty minutes," he answered with a nod from Eddie."

"Think someone picked up on it?" asked Will.

"Never sure about that," replied Eddie. "Better be on the watch for vehicles with a strange, circular antennae mounted on the top."

"And they would be?" asked Will with raised eyebrows.

"Uncle Sam probably," chuckled Eddie. "Since that transponder had a government serial number on it, they

114

probably know of this little fella also." Eddie started to chuckle. "I love it, Will. It's about time we get to slap back at the dark side of Washington."

"What can I expect?" asked Will, slowly glancing back down the hallway.

Eddie shrugged. "DOD I guess, or worse. After all, they already know that Jack's onto them and are aware he shot one of the ships down in his own-back-yard."

"All right then," grumbled Will. "What's the 'worse' part?"

"That's the wild card," answered Eddie, still laughing. "You might get a close encounter with Black Ops and you won't even know it until it's over." He glanced at Kotts. "This is better than that Sci-fi show 'Outer Limits'."

"I'm still listenin'," grumbled Will, staring at Eddie.

"There are two kinds of aliens we're dealing with here, Will," started Eddie. "This one Jack came up with is called the Grey Man and pilots the UFO they call the Silver Streak. We picked up their transmissions, but couldn't get a bead on them. The darned thing they fly is just too damn fast."

"They were talking English to this thing we have in there?" asked Will.

"Yes," replied Eddie, "and he was speaking back to them. Those who give our little Grey Man his orders are clones we believe, and look just like us. The Indian nations have had several run-ins with them and are now in a running battle every time they locate one."

Will squinted at Eddie. "You mean ta tell me that they all look alike?"

Eddie shook his head. "They're not identical, Will, but they are all about six foot tall, trim, and with light-colored hair. The few that we have took pictures of all have icy-blue eyes."

"Goood Lord," sighed the old sheriff. "That is right out o' 'Outer Limits'."

"Yep," chuckled Eddie. "And your detective just shot down one and as far as they know, their little, Grey Man is still alive. That's going to drive them to distraction. I'd say that the next few days is going to be more than just a little interesting."

*　　　*　　　*

Sometime after 6:00PM that evening, Jack left Bubba in Covington and headed toward Brownsville to meet with a young man who had just lost a new, light blue, four by four Ford pickup. About halfway there, he spotted what looked to be a custom 1957 red Chevrolets Apache. Heading toward Covington, it flew by him well over the speed limit. . .

Seeing the bright red Apache fly by him, Jack slowed dramatically, looking for a place to turn around. The snapshot he got of the driver was a perfect match of the redhead his grandfather couldn't catch. Sliding into an Exxon station, Jack gunned the 390 cubic inch interceptor and spun the Fairlane around.

As he jumped back out on Highway 54, he jerked the mic from the hook. "Bubba, are you out there? Come in, Bubba!"

"Bubba here, Jack," answered the big deputy. "What's up? Over."

"I got a 1957, red Apache pickup headed toward Covington like a bat out o' Hell. Be careful and cut her off if you can. She's one of our car thieves, I believe."

"Just left Covington, Jack," explained Bubba. "Comin' your way. If you can see her, make sure to see if she turns on Highway 384.

Thinking his 500 could catch the older vehicle, Jack pushed the big engine to almost a hundred miles an hour. But the best he could do was to see a flash of red ever so often almost a mile away. Knowing Bubba was on his way toward him, Jack held the Fairlane on the century mark, but still couldn't manage to close on the Apache. Topping a little rise, he slowed to a stop where Highway 14 crossed from the south-west. What added to the confusion, was a large, gravel road leading into the woods to the south-east made it a four way. The young detective pondered his ever-changing situation. Then, with the roar of Bubba's cruiser quickly approaching, he got out of his Fairlane and

116

looked toward the gravel road. There was not a sign of dust.

"Lose 'er?" hollered Bubba as he stopped in front of Jack's Ford.

Jack shook his head as he laughed. "I didn't know an old Apache could run so fast, Bubba. I never did get that close."

"Who was it?" asked Bubba.

Jack shrugged. "I think she was the pretty redhead that gave the slip to Fred. But this time, she was in a hot rod." Jack looked back at the intersection. "Honestly, I don't know which way she went."

"Red, '57 Apache huh?" asked the deputy.

Jack nodded.

"Yep." Bubba slowly shook his head. "I got the call just before you radioed me. She nabbed it at a car show in Brownsville. The owner was tryin' ta empress her by lettin' her sit in the cab and start the thing. The next thing he knew, she gunned it and took off."

The big deputy slowly turned toward a slowing vehicle approaching from Covington. "What's this, Jack?"

The late model, dark green, Ford station wagon pulled right up behind Bubba's cruiser.

"Not a clue?" answered Jack, just under his breath.

"Can I help you?" asked Bubba as he walked toward the vehicle.

"Quite possible," spoke the young man with an unmistakable, English accent. About six feet tall, with light colored hair, and dressed in a hound's-tooth sport coat, he got out of his vehicle, continued right past the deputy, and then walked up to Jack.

"You lost, mister?" asked Bubba as he walked up behind the man.

"Long way from home," answered the man, still looking at Jack. "It seems those I work for lost something yesterday and we've been given permission to search for and retrieve what we can."

"Permission?" grumbled Bubba. "Why don't you drop by the Munford Sheriff's Office tomorrow and--"

117

Jack held up his hand toward Bubba, watching the man closely. "Could you describe what you lost?"

He slowly shook his head. "I don't think I have to, Jack Shoultz. Keeping any part of what you might have found, would endanger a very important agreement the Department of Defense has made and might also prove costly to those who propose to keep the material."

Bubba slowly backed away from the two and checked the plates on the station wagon.

"And your name is. . ." asked Bubba as he walked back to join the two.

Casting an irritated look back at the big deputy, the mysterious man handed Jack what looked to be a business card and then added, "Waiting to make contact with this man would be a mistake. I would do it now if I were you."

The man turned, walked past Bubba without a word, and then drove away toward Brownsville.

"Who the devil was that?" asked Bubba as he watched the station wagon pull away. "Jack. . ." The deputy patted Jack's left shoulder.

Jack rolled his eyes to the sky and then looked at Bubba. "I don't think that was the DOD, Bubba."

"Yea, well, he had a Government tag—Washington 103. What's on the card?"

"It's got Army Colonel Harold G. Withers, Special Ops. Department of Defense on it." He looked troubled at Bubba. "He knew my name, probably knows where I live, and is after everything we took from the woods back at my place." He scratched the back of his neck as he stared at the deputy. "Call Lucy right now and tell her to be watchful and call Kotts as well. Then light up and go straight to the Coroner's Office. He has the Grey Man's body in the first cooler."

Bubba hesitated, staring at Jack. "You think this guy knows where it is?"

"He knew where we were, didn't he? Now get going. I'm going to call Lucy and get her to call Shelley. This sounds too much like a threat to me."

"Yes Sir," replied Bubba.

Bubba jumped into his patrol car as Jack got into his unmarked. In just seconds, the two were heading northwest on Highway 54 toward Covington and Highway 51.

*   *   *

About halfway back to his home, and still on Highway 51, Jack's radio sounded off.

"Jack! Jack! Are you out there? Come in." Lucy's unmistakable voice sounded obviously excited.

"Great Caesar's ghost," grumbled Jack as he grabbed the mic from the hook. "I'm here, Lucy, and on the way to my house."

"Good," replied the dispatcher. "Bubba's already clued me in and is headed toward Kott's well. Shelley's at your neighbor, Mr. Wiggley's house with the girls. "When they got home from shopping, someone had gotten into the house. The front door was left wide open."

"On my way," replied Jack as he lit up and hit the siren. "Bubba! Did you hear that?" Come back."

Already ahead of Jack and lit up as well, Bubba replied, "Loud and clear," he replied. "I'm goin' straight to the Coroner's Office. James is at our office already."

*   *   *

At about 7:25PM, Jack made the turn off Getwell and onto Willow View. He quickly turned his lights off, duffed the siren, and tried to lighten up on the pedal as much as his anger would allow. Still, after all of that, he barely made the turn into his driveway. Jumping from the Ford, he noticed Shelley and the girls were already standing with Wally on his front porch. He also noted that his front door was still open.

Holding his hand up toward the girls, he mouthed "Stay there," and then continued toward the back of the house.

Stopping at the back corner, he quickly checked the open garage and the back yard. The back porch light was still on.

No one out here, thought Jack as he crept around the corner just far enough to see the back door.

The screen door was shut, but the heavy, wooden door was left wide open. Ever so slowly, Jack pulled his pistol,

119

eased the screen door open, and then peeped into the dark kitchen. There was not a light on in the house. What little light there was from the neighbor's front porch, filtered through the kitchen and dining room windows giving the whole place an uncomfortable look he had never noticed before.

"Come in, Jack."

The voice sounded like the person was in the living room. The English accent was a dead giveaway.

"Who are you?" asked Jack as he eased into the kitchen, eying what he could see of the dining area.

At that same time, Jack noticed the lights of another car as it pulled into the driveway. He eased on into the dining area.

"Let's just say that I'm a concerned citizen and leave it at that," replied the Englishman.

Jack quickly stepped into the entranceway with his pistol at the ready, but there was not a soul there. Now turning toward the still open front door, he could see the man from the second car and he was standing at the foot of the porch steps.

"You won't need your weapon, Jack," he said. "I'm here as a friend."

"Really. . ." Jack eased the screen door open and held the .357 Smith and Wesson on the Englishman. "Friends don't break into friends' homes and scare their families. Again, who are you?"

The man smiled. "There is nothing broken here, Jack, and your family wasn't there at the time I came to visit. We have what we want and no one was harmed in the process."

Jack lowered his pistol. "Again and one more time, who tha Hell are you and more to the point, who are you working for?"

Holding his smile, he replied, "You are a Watcher, Jack Shoultz. And for that, you have my admiration. Although I am not like you, I am a kind of Watcher as well. We are here to keep the balance of power on what you call Earth tilted in the acceptable direction. You have your job and we have ours. Let's keep it that way, shall we?"

Having never seen an alien, Jack watched the young man back away from the steps and head toward his automobile. Doing nothing wasn't usually in the young deputy, but for some reason, he felt as if he had best leave well enough alone.

"Jack!"

Jack jumped and spun around toward the end of the porch. There stood Shelley and the girls with Wally Wiggley holding them back.

"Is everything all right, Jack?" he asked.

Jack smiled, noting the baseball bat in Wally's right hand. "Not sure, Wally," he answered, glancing at the girls. "Remember last night when you saw that shower of sparks just after the gunfire?"

Wally nodded. "You told me it was some kind of ship."

"Well, it was, but it wasn't one of ours." Jack gestured with his raised thumb toward the sky. "It made what looked to be a threatening move and I shot it."

Wally raised his eyebrows. "Looked like you hit it good."

Jack nodded. "I did, but I'm afraid that all of the fallout from that has yet to be seen."

"Jack! Jack!" came the call from the radio in the Ford.

Scrambling from the porch, Jack opened the door and snatched the mic from the hook. "Jack here, Bubba. Where are you?"

"The Coroner's Office. But--"

"The Grey Man's gone isn't he?" interrupted Jack.

"Well. . .yes," managed Bubba. "But how'd you know?"

"I think I just spoke to the man who took him. He was the same one we just saw out on the highway. I'm gonna give Will his card and let him handle it."

"What the Devil's goin' on Jack?" asked Bubba.

"Not sure, but I think I just poked a hornet's nest and I feel like the stings are just starting to come."

Part 4
Pretty Poison

The next day, a cloudy and cold Thursday afternoon, Jack pulled into the Munford Sheriff's lot with Banjo riding shotgun. Quickly getting out, they both headed for the front door. Banjo, a little quicker than Jack, waited patiently at the door for his master. . .

"Well," started Jack as he opened the door and looked down at Banjo, "aren't you the eager. . ."

The young detective's comment was curtailed as he watched the big Pitt run in and head straight for Dianne's desk. Not acting surprised at all, the dispatcher laughed at Jack's confused expression as she opened the donut box.

"Right here, sweetie," coaxed Dianne as she laid a paper plate with one sausage and biscuit and a donut on the floor in front of Banjo.

"How long has this been going on?" asked Jack.

Dianne shrugged, watching Banjo gobble up the treats. "If Shelley and the girls are not visiting with him then Donnie is with his mom. I think he likes donuts."

Jack slowly shook his head.

"Ready to go?" asked Bubba as he walked briskly through the front door. "You know, I could o' swore I saw your Apache on Highway 51 a little while ago, but it was mint green. The one that out-ran you was red wasn't it?"

"Cherry red," replied the young detective. "Where was this one headed?"

"North toward Covington and just about an hour ago," answered the deputy.

"You sure it was a '57?" asked Jack.

"Yep." Bubba looked away, a little disappointed. "I always want one o' them."

Jack looked at his watch. "It's about a quarter to four right now, Bubba. Let's head that way. Maybe we can spot it again."

Noting Will, standing at his office door, Jack reached into his jacket pocket, pulled out the Colonel's card, and then walked toward the old sheriff.

"Did you read the report I wrote up last night?" asked the young detective.

Will nodded. "I think we just got warned off by your Colonel. You got that card?"

"Yes, Sir," answered Jack as he handed the card to the sheriff. "I hoped you would notice it in the report."

Will nodded with a bit of a smile. "Guess I had best call him and see what we've stepped into."

*   *   *

Thirty minutes later, Jack watched Bubba slow his cruiser as he eased into Covington. Slowing even more, as he approached The Donut Man's bakery, Jack followed him to the back of the store and parked by his cruiser.

"See it?" said Bubba as he trotted to Jack's unmarked Ford.

"See what?"

Bubba rolled his eyes. "That mint green Chevy is in front of Harriet's Diner just two doors down."

Jack quickly got out, looking toward the rear of the restaurant. "I'd sure like to get a closer look at it."

"Then let's go," agreed Bubba as he quickly pulled his shirt off.

"All right," replied Jack, a bit tickled. "Looks like you've got a plan. What is it?"

"When I saw it earlier, there was a young girl behind the wheel. But I'm not that sure she was your redhead. If I can pick her out in Harriet's, maybe it'll give you enough time ta look at the Apache."

"Good," replied Jack. "I'll give you five minutes and then take a look at the pickup."

"Deal," agreed the big detective as he straightened his black T-shirt and doffed his deputy's hat.

In just seconds, Bubba was entering the back door of the restaurant.

"Stay," said Jack to Banjo. Lowering the window a bit, he eased the door closed on the big Pitt.

123

As he turned to ease down the side of the diner, he immediately spotted the green Apache parked in the alleyway on the side of the restaurant. It was in plain sight of their cars. Trotting over to it, he quickly checked the driver side door. It wasn't locked. Opening it, he checked the rubber molding on the door.

"Got-cha," said Jack as he noted the cherry red was still there under the molding.

He was about to check the front of the restaurant when he noticed a black folder lying on the front seat. Thumbing through it, he could see pictures with names of not only everyone in Munford and Drummond's Sheriff's department, but the local police as well. Jack's heart jumped as he turned to Munford. Bubba, the new hire, wasn't in it. But just as he closed the folder, he could hear Banjo barking excitedly. Standing from stooping inside the truck, he looked toward his own cruiser.

But the sharp blow on the back of his head prevented him from seeing it. Reality seemed to be just out of his reach as the ground tilted and his world turned black. He never felt himself hit the pavement. . .

*   *   *

"Jack! Jack! Are you all right? Can you hear me?"

Even before the young detective opened his eyes, he could still hear the Pitt barking.

"Bubba?" Jack struggled to a sitting position, rubbing the back of his head. "Please let Banjo out while I still got a seat left," he managed through a grimace.

But as Bubba opened the door, Banjo muscled past him, and ran straight to Jack. Offering the young detective only a quick sniff and a lick, the Pitt turned to where the truck was parked and started sniffing around on the pavement. Bubba snatched his shirt and hat from his cruiser.

"It's gone," grumbled Jack. "The damned thing is gone," he repeated as he struggled to his feet.

"Not completely," said Bubba, closely watching Banjo.

The Pitt's nose seemed to be glued to the ground as he moved back and forth from where Jack was standing and where the Apache was parked. Then, just as quick as a cat's sneeze, he bolted from between them and headed toward the back door of the restaurant.

"Well, I'll just be damned," said Bubba as he trotted toward the Pitt. "Maybe we haven't lost out girl yet. There were three of 'em in there, but the redhead said she had to go the powder room." He glanced back at Jack. "Are you all right?"

Jack nodded. "To take a powder is more like it," he quipped. As he quickly followed, he fumbled in his pocket for a BC powder he had been keeping for just the occasion.

"Let him in, Bubba," instructed Jack as he downed the white headache powder with a grimace. "But keep close behind him. I don't want him eating whoever he is following."

"You bet," said Bubba. As he opened the back door, he glanced at Jack. "I don't see how you can take that bitter stuff."

Jack shrugged as he stepped inside and leaned against the wall close to the men's restroom door. Trying to shake the cobwebs from his head, he could hear the customers complaining about the Pitt, but he never heard a growl or bark.

"Keep your seats!" he finally heard Bubba address someone in the dining area. But who was he talking to?

"Jack, are you back there?" asked the deputy loudly from the dining area.

Jack quickly rubbed the feeling back in his face. "Coming, Bubba," he replied, stepping away from the back door. "I'm still a bit woozy."

"Well, come on if you can," replied Bubba. "We've got two treed in here, but Banjo won't move so I can cuff 'em."

Entering from the short hallway, Jack paused to look at the two young girls at a table on the far side of the room. They looked horrified. With their eyes glued to Banjo, they afforded not a glance to anyone else. One blonde and one brunette, they instantly looked at Jack. Now, the young detective could hear the Pitt's low, guttural growl as he eyed the blonde. It was his, sure statement—"Don't move."

"Do something," said a nervous waitress, edging closer to the young detective. "He's gonna bite one of them."

For the first time, the still groggy detective noted the several customers that haven't left. Most, even though they had quit eating, were still at their own tables. A few others were now standing near the far wall of the room.

"Keep your seats," said Jack. "No one will get hurt. This is official police business."

Only then did Jack notice that his tone had changed. But the flush, tingling feeling was only around his ears. Jack looked away from the approaching waitress and then walked toward those Banjo had 'treed' at their table. Avoiding eye contact with the two girls, he looked at Bubba. His shocked expression told it all.

"Lord Jack," managed Bubba. He instantly took a pair of sunglasses from his shirt pocket and handed them to the young detective. "Put those on for now," he all but whispered. "That blow to your head made your eyes a bit sensitive to this bright light."

Jack slipped them on and looked back at the girls at the table. They were still eying the big orange and black Pitt.

"Back away," said Jack.

As Jack kept his right hand upon the Pitt's head he sat down beside the blonde.

"Who are you?" asked Jack, looking toward her.

"Dory Berry," answered the pretty, short-haired blonde with blue eyes.

Jack instantly looked at the long-haired brunette.

"Erline Foster," added the tall brunette.

Jack then noted they were wearing black sweatshirts with Three Musketeers printed on them in red letters. Looking a bit uncomfortable, Earline slowly closed and zipped up her jacket.

"Do you mind?" Bubba leaned over the table and slowly unzipped the Brunette's jacket. "Yawl in in some kind o' club or something?"

Both girls sat silent and wide-eyed and just stared at the deputy.

"Who hit me?" asked Jack as he rubbed the back of his head again.

Not a word.

Bubba rolled his eyes. "All right, let's try this—Who was the person in the green Apache. She had red hair and I didn't have time ta get her name."

Silence.

Jack slowly got up, stepped back, and then looked down at the big Pitt. "Watch them, Banjo," he said just above a whisper.

Immediately, the Pitt moved to the left side of the table and eyed the blonde.

"He's not gonna bite me, is he?" asked Dory as both girls backed as close to the wall as they could.

Jack glared at the blonde. "You were followed from where I was struck at the pickup."

Dory nodded. "The girl just thought you were trying to steal the truck," she said with her eyes still glued to Banjo.

"Then. . ." Bubba raised his eyebrows, "who is the girl that hit Jack and drove away in the green Apache?"

More silence.

Bubba laughed as he looked at Jack. "Maybe we should just let Banjo have 'em for a little while. We can take a table on the far side o' the room and order a burger or somethin'."

Jack paused, noting the customers still in the dining area. Some had started back eating, but all were watching the happening very closely.

"Don't mind us," said one of the customers. "This is much better than the movie I saw last night."

Most laughed, but not a one got up to leave.

Jack smiled. "I'm Jack Shoultz of the Munford Sheriff's Office. We take car theft very serious." He looked back at the girls. "Assaulting an officer isn't high on our favorites list either."

"We didn't hit you," said Erline with Dory shaking her head in agreement.

"So. . ." Bubba smiled at Jack. "just who is the third Musketeer?"

127

"Ohhh. . ." Dory rolled her eyes. "I knew she was gonna get us all into trouble eventually."

"Don't do it," warned Erline. "Her boyfriend and his pals will get both of us and you know it."

"Well-well," said Bubba through a slight chuckle. "Why don't you both tell us what you know and let Jack and me handle the bad guys?"

"Enough talk right here," decided Jack. "Let's go to the office and continue this little conversation. I'll bet the High Sheriff can loosen their tongues a little."

Dory's eyes grew wide. "Are we under arrest? My Dad's gonna kill me."

Jack looked at her. "Perhaps if you two come quietly and tell the Sheriff what he wants to know, he'll only consider you two as material witnesses. Both of you can ride in Bubba's black and white. That is, unless you want to ride in the back seat of my unmarked with Banjo."

"We'll ride with Bubba," said both of them in unison.

*   *   *

It was past 6:30PM when Jack walked back into the office. He immediately knew something was afoot. The blank look from Lucy's at the dispatcher's desk, the silence stare from James at the Sergeant's Desk, and the sudden appearance of his grandfather at his office door to watch them all come in screamed 'you're in it again'.

"Over here," mouthed Fred, motioning for Jack to join him.

Jack glanced at Bubba. "I guess Will's chat with the Colonel was a bomb shell." He looked to James. "Don't book them yet. Put them in the interrogation room. If I make it out of Fred's office in one piece, I'll have a chat with them in a minute or two."

"In here," said Fred, a little louder.

Fred held his office door open until Jack entered and then closed it and took a seat behind his desk.

"Just a word or two," he started. "This business card you gave Will earlier was a time bomb."

Jack slowly sat down in front of Fred's desk. "Is Will still here? His office door is closed."

Fred nodded. "We're all here except for Dianne and Andy. They have a relief. I contacted Eddie Miles at MUFON and told him he was on his own." Fred smiled. "He said he was used to it."

Jack's eye roll ended up on his grandfather. "On his own? Used to it? What have I started?"

"Nothing that wouldn't have already happened," replied Fred. "Charles Davidson is on his way over here right now."

"What?" Jack slowly sat up on the edge of his chair. "The DA?"

"In-the-flesh," answered Fred. "Seems he got a call from that Army Colonel on the card you gave Will. Now, the Sheriff's in a pickle."

"He was told, in no few words, to ignore those cattle mutilations, wasn't he?" guessed Jack.

No sooner had Jack asked that, than the office door opened and in walked the High Sheriff. "Mind if I join you?" asked Will. He closed the door and took a seat across from Jack, looking at Fred. "You brief 'em?"

"Yep," came Fred's the one-word answer. "You look like someone pulled the stick out of your popsicle. What's going on here Will?"

Will stared silently for a moment at Fred. "What would you say 'bout runnin' this place for me for a week or two?"

Completely void of words, Fred's chin slowly lowered to this chest. "Are you taking a vacation in winter, Will?"

"Maybe." Will glanced at Jack. "I objected to that Special Ops Colonel fella a little too strongly, I think. He wanted, no, he insisted that I call off the investigation into Doc Hall's cattle theft and mutilations. I told 'em I couldn't and I wouldn't because we had an obligation to our citizens to protect life and property."

Fred slowly sat back in his chair. "And he wasn't pleased."

"Nope," managed Will. "I think I just touched off his short fuse and he hung up on me. The next thing I knew, I was gettin' a call from Charles Davidson. He reminded me just who I worked for and that he would see me in an hour or so." Will glanced at his wrist watch. "It's about

7:15PM now and that was over an hour ago. So. . .would you--"

Will's question was cut short by a weak knock on the door. With not a word from anyone, they all watched it slowly open.

"Will?" whispered Lucy. "Mr. Davidson is here. I showed him to your office."

"Thank you, Lucy," replied the old Sheriff. He slowly got up with Fred and Jack. "I put in a call to Doc Hall and told 'em my situation. He said he didn't give a damn about the Army and had always supported Davidson's campaign." He smiled nervously at Jack. "Maybe it'll help our situation."

"I'm sorry, Will," started Jack. "I didn't expect to--"

"You stop right there," snapped Will with a stiff finger on Jack's chest. "You did nothin' wrong here, son. What we got here is a bad case o' politics. Now, I got ta go and see who's pullin' the strings right now. If I get burned, it won't be you that struck the match."

Reluctantly, Will left Fred's office and walked the short distance to his. The door was still open and he could see Mr. Davidson sitting in the first chair in front of the desk.

"Mr. Davidson," said Will cheerfully as he entered the room and shut the door.

Slightly bald with thinning, light brown hair, the portly man of fifty or so stood and offered his hand to Will. He slipped off his dark blue suit coat and draped it on the back of a chair in front of Will's desk.

"You got a problem here, Will, and it's landed square on the top of my desk. I'm here to help you right now. One of your deputies has just opened a can of worms--one that has prompted a Colonel from the DOD to call me personally."

"Interesting," said Will as he stepped past Mr. Davidson and took a seat behind his desk. "Have a seat," he said, noting the DA was still standing. "First of all, every time a politician tells me he's gonna help me, I start ta itch where I can't scratch. We got a job to do here, Mr. Davidson, and that responsibility dictates that we are to serve and protect the lives and property of every citizen in

Tipton County and not just part of them. That 'deputy' you referred to is Detective Jack Shoultz, and he's not only a good one, he's a damn good one. Last night, while he and Deputy Watkins were investigating a car theft in Covington, they were approached by an unidentified individual and warned off of another investigation that Jack is involved in." Will slowly leaned back in his swivel rocker and smiled at the District Attorney. "Seems ta me, as long as all of us do our jobs, we wouldn't have, or shouldn't have trouble from anyone. That bein' said, you shouldn't have calls from such folks as Doc Hall and Doc Weatherington."

The DA slowly leaned forward, glancing back at the door. "I did get a call from Doc Hall just before I came over here. He was a big contributor to my last campaign." He paused, scratching the back of his head. "Will. . ." He paused, looking at the old sheriff. "I'll take care of Colonel Withers if you'll get a hold on that eager, young detective of yours. Shooting down government property is not going to help matters at all."

Will's eyebrows slowly rose. "Government property?" Will slowly leaned to his desk, resting his elbows on its top. "I got a glimpse o' that 'government property' while Kotts had the Grey Man in his cooler. It was stolen. While we are on that subject, you can tell your Colonel Withers that I take extreme exception to his other 'government property' breaking into our coroner's office, scaring the bageebers out o' my detective's family, and even warning him off of what I had assigned him ta do. I've put in a request for a case of M-16 assault rifles for my deputies. I don't play favorites here, Sir. Wrong is wrong in my book, no matter where it comes from."

The DA took a deep breath. "I see," he finally got out as he slowly shook his head as he stood. "We'll try that approach and see how far it takes us. The military should not be telling us what to do on our own property no matter who they're trying to appease."

Will stood and followed him out of the office. When they got to the front door, he turned to Will.

"I was supposed to take a harder approach with you on this thing, Will," he all but whispered. "But I just can't do it. I'll approve your request. You'll get your weapons in about a week."

*   *   *

Back in the interrogation room, Jack joined Bubba, Dory, and Erline at the table. Both the girls were wording a statement they both could agree on.

Bubba smiled at the young detective. "I think these young ladies are gonna do the right thing here, Jack. We already have five names: Cindy Gant is your speed demon redhead, Thomas Broker is her boyfriend and the leader of the crew. We also have Thomas Broker and Jackie Khan, and Chuck Neighbors to add to the list. I think they are just local tuff guys from this area."

"Be careful with that Khan fellow," warned Dory. "He's some kind of martial arts freak."

"Have we got a way to get a hold of these bad boys?" asked Jack, looking straight at Dory.

Dory rolled her eyes, ending up on Erline. "Tom has a house with a shop on the property not that far from here. That's where he works on the cars and trucks." She forced a smile at Jack. "You weren't far from it when you lost her on Highway 54 at the intersection. If you go on past where Highway 14 joins it, you'll see Estes Lane on the left. Just past that on the right is Terry Lane. Broker Cove is on the right about a mile farther. His driveway goes past his house and on into the woods where the shop is located."

"Put that down exactly like you just give it to me," said Jack.

Dora put her fingertips to her mouth. "We just ordered parts and made appointments. Erline was the cook for the whole group," she added as her eyes welled up with tears. "We didn't steal anything."

Erline, as scared as she was silent, watched Jack's expression closely.

"Wad-da-ya think?" asked Bubba, looking at Jack.

Jack shrugged. "Turning state's evidence goes a long way with the High Sheriff," answered the young detective.

"If this pans out like I hope, I'm sure he'll go to bat with the DA for these two girls, especially since they weren't active participants." Jack checked his wrist watch. "It's after eight right now," he said, quickly looking at the girls. "You both have one call, but if you don't mind, I would ask you to make that tomorrow morning. We'll spring for you a good supper if you will."

"That's fine," agreed Dora with a nod from Erline.

He looked to Bubba. "If Fred signs off on it, we'll make the raid on this place early in the morning.

*   *   *

The next morning, a Friday and shortly before 7:00AM, Jack pulled into the Munford office to see Virgil Forsythe's maroon 1962 Oldsmobile 88 parked close to the front door. With several perps involved, he thought it best to leave Banjo with Shelley's brother, Donnie. His airedale, Shadow, should keep him occupied. Besides, her being pregnant seemed to be a constant, but pleasant, distraction to him. Eager to get started, Jack headed right for the front door. As he entered the lobby, he spotted Charlie Two Shirts talking to Virgil in front of Fred's office. Instantly spotted by the Constable, he was pointed out to the old Apache.

"I see you, young Jack." Charlie's smile widened. "One is known by his enemies, I think. You are on the right track, I think."

Jack squinted and then looked to Virgil, who only offered a slight shrug.

"We will speak of this later," added Charlie. "I believe your Grandfather has a chore for you. Besides, I have help on the way."

"Help?" Jack looked at Virgil, but only got the same reply.

Although the smile on the old Indian's face piqued his curiosity, the young detective nodded his approval and continued past him to his Grandfather's partially open door. Easing it open a little wider, he could see Fred was on the phone. But upon seeing Jack, he quickly said his goodbyes and hung up.

"Busy?" Jack returned his smile.

"You bet," answered Fred as he nodded toward the first chair in front of his desk. "This Silver Streak case you and I have is going in more directions that Will and I can keep up with. But we gotta handle this car theft ring first. Then, perhaps, we can tackle Charlie's surprise."

"Charlie's surprise?" Jack slowly sat down in front of the desk. "He mentioned help on the way, but he didn't take the time to explain."

"That's me as well, Jack, but we gotta take care of business right now."

*   *   *

About half an hour later, and in plain clothes, Jack, Fred, and Deputy Williams, one of the newest officers, were following Virgil's maroon Olds in Jack's unmarked Ford. The latter was transferred from Lauderdale County to replace Deputy Hobbs, an officer who had been previously arrested for helping burglary suspects. As Virgil turned east off of Highway 51 and onto Highway 54, the Chief of Detectives explained his plan. First, was to have Jack and Virgil approach the house, secure that, and then prevent any alarm from reaching the shop a ways back in the woods. Once that was done, they should be joined by Fred and Deputy Williams and then proceed toward the shop. At just before 9:00AM, and with a mild and clear start of the day, Virgil made the turn onto Terry Lane and then slowed as he neared Broker Cove. Seeing the Olds slow to a stop, Jack pulled up beside him and rolled down the driver's side window.

"I cased this place out," said Fred, glancing at Jack. "It's the only house in the cove and the shop is a good piece away in the woods. Why don't you get with Virgil and go and secure the house. The ruse is you two are looking for a good, used car. I set it up with the girls. They already know a buyer is coming. When that's done, we'll join you and head to the shop."

Jack got out, looking at Virgil as he walked toward the Olds. "Remember, if that redhead is there, she might spot us and we'll go straight to the arrest."

"Got it," said Virgil. "Dory Berry sent us here to look for a 57 Chevy. She told us they were working on one right now."

"Good," agreed Fred. "Let's start this thing."

Jack and Virgil promptly pulled away in the Olds and eased on into the cove. With woods on both sides as well as in the rear of the house, the only thing that was kept up was the half acre or so the home sat on. One story fieldstone, easily four bedrooms, by the looks of the split cedar roof, it sported two fireplaces. Virgil pulled into the circle drive and parked next to a baby blue Cadillac. Stalling like they had all the time in the world, Virgil waited until someone opened the front door.

"Safe so far," he whispered as out stepped a young girl. Trim and blonde she was, about sixteen years old, she was dressed in blue jeans and a light brown blouse. She stood there holding the screen door open and looked at Jack as he checked out the Fleetwood.

"That's really not for sale," she said, smiling at him.

Virgil stepped out of the Olds. "We're here to have a look at a '57 Chevy. Do you know Dory Berry?"

"Yes, but she's not here right now. I think she's got a cold or somethin." answered the young girl, eying Jack as the tall detective walked back to join Virgil.

At that exact time, an older lady in her mid-thirties stepped up behind the girl and coaxed her out onto the porch. "Did Dory send you?" she asked, tying her long, brown hair back in a ponytail.

Jack nodded. "How far along are they on the Chevy?"

The older lady shrugged. "I don't really know. You'll have to talk to one of the others and they're all at the shop right now."

"So. . ." Virgil stepped around the front of the Olds and closer to the porch steps. "No one is here to talk about it right now?"

"Just us," replied the young girl. "I'll have to get Thomas here to talk to you. I can call him. He's in the shop at the end of the road that leads into the woods. Nobody's allowed back there."

135

"Then do me a favor." The Constable reached into this pocket and produced a badge and ID. "I'm the Constable of this county and with me is Detective Shoultz of the Munford Sheriff's Department."

Seemingly frozen in place, the older woman pulled the young girl close to her.

"Please step away from the house," said Jack.

Virgil turned and waved at Fred, now at the cove's entrance. As the Constable put the two in the back of his Oldsmobile, Fred came up fast in his unmarked with Deputy Jim Williams.

"Let's check the house," suggested Virgil, looking at Fred. "The ladies told us they were alone, but let's make sure."

Finding no one else there, Fred, Jack, and Jim joined Virgil at his Olds, still in front of the house.

"I need some time," said Jack. "Two of these guys are heavy into the martial arts. If they're working, today, they should be back there right now. Give me twenty minutes. By then, I should be able to get into the back door of the shop if it's got one." He looked to the girls. The older one nodded a silent 'yes'.

The Chief of Detectives shrugged. "Let's hope it's not locked."

Jack chuckled. "Well, we'll soon find out. When they see you come up, they may try to arm themselves. I'll already be in place, I hope."

"Where is the redhead," asked Jack, smiling at Fred.

Fred shrugged. "Perhaps you'll run into her back there. Now, get going and be careful. The clock is ticking."

*   *   *

Now, with twenty minutes to figure out how to keep anyone from being hurt, Jack ran around the house and entered the woods. As it was well before noon, a thick canopy of dark clouds held the morning's light at bay for the young detective. Keeping the long drive in sight, he soon spotted a flash of white through the trees up ahead. And then, as he slowed, there it was--a shop large enough to sport four, pull-down doors and what looked to be an

136

office as well. Two of the pull-downs were open. With a parking area on the far side of the building, he could see a Mustang, a Buick, and a Ford Falcon as he circled to the rear.

Sixteen minutes, he thought, glancing at his wrist watch.

Easing to the edge of the woods, and a bit closer to the back, he noted only one door and two windows. There was not a fence. He checked his watch again.

Twelve minutes.

Seeing no movement at the windows, he headed for the back door. All too quickly, he found himself gripping its knob.

"Now or never," whispered Jack as he gingerly twisted the knob. Jack held his breath as the door slowly opened into a dimly lit hallway leading into what looked to be the maintenance area in the front of the building. In the hallway, there were only two doors. The far one was marked office and the nearest read restroom. Jack paused, listening to those working in the front of the building. Suddenly, the office door opened causing Jack to almost shut his. Fortunately, the door opened toward him so he couldn't see the one standing behind it.

"Jackie, you and Chuck make room in the fourth bay. Cindy's spotted a new Ford four-wheel-drive 250, but she can't get it now," said the man standing in the office doorway.

Then, the man went back into the office and shut the door. Now, the young detective knew there were at least two in the maintenance area and one in the office. Easing inside, he slowly shut the door and glanced at his watch.

Nine minutes.

Watching the work area closely, he walked to the office door, slowly opened it, and then peeped inside. A young man, seemingly in his thirties, was sitting in a corner desk on the far side of the room. Easing the door shut, Jack crept up behind him. Feeling no flush at all, Jack pulled his .357 Smith and Wesson from its holster and slipped the cold, steel barrel behind the man's right ear. He instantly froze.

"Don't move a muscle," whispered Jack. "What you do now, will determine how many will get hurt--you being the first."

Jack glanced at his watch. *Four minutes.*

Grabbing the man by the back of the collar, the young detective pulled him from his chair and pushed him face down on the floor. After a quick pat down, he was cuffed and gagged.

"One and a half minutes," whispered Jack.

Jack turned for the door, but just as he did, a young oriental-looking man opened the door and stepped in. Immediately grasping the situation, the oriental man spun to his left. The kick that followed was so quick, the young detective barely had time to react. Trapping the man's foot between his rib cage and his left arm, Jack grabbed him by the throat and lifted him from the floor. Only then, did Jack realize he was in the 'Beast'. With no flush warning at all, the shocked Nephilim eased the still struggling man to the closest chair and all but crammed him into it.

Now, with a well taloned hand upon his chest, the man looked up into the face of something he had never seen before. The frown on its glowing, green eyes screamed "Stay Put!", and so he did.

"Make not a sound," said the Nephilim, his voice clearly in the Beast.

With a cord he pulled from the nearest table lamp, Jack tied the man to the chair. As he was finishing, he could hear a struggle coming from the maintenance area and it sounded like Fred, Jim, and Virgil had their hands full. As he ran from the still open office door, he dodged a pistol as it flew through the air and bounced past him. Right behind it stumbled Constable Forsythe, heading in the same general direction. Jack quickly grabbed him as he looked toward what he could see of the maintenance area. His grandfather, and another man, were rolling around on the floor. Just past them, Deputy Jim Williams, a good-sized man himself, seemed to be struggling to get up off of the floor.

"I got this," said Jack as he propped Virgil up against the wall behind him.

As Deputy Williams gained his feet, he stood frozen in his shoes as he watched the tall, dark-skinned, glowing eyed creature bound from the darkened hallway. Only then, did he come to the realization that the one called Horned Jack in Sergeant Andy Jackson stories was real. The imposing figure quickly knelt beside the two still struggling on the floor. Grabbing the crook's head with his right hand, the Nephilim pulled him atop his grandfather and shoved Fred toward Deputy Williams.

Jack looked at the man's face peering back at him through his taloned fingers. "If you continue to struggle, you'll only get hurt," he said softly with a deep and rattling tone.

The man instantly stopped struggling. "What the Hell are you?" he managed. His voice quaking.

Jack eased his face close to the man's. "One who is allowed to watch," he answered and then rolled the man to his stomach, face down upon the floor. With a firm hand on the man's back, the Nephilim looked up at Deputy Williams. "He's yours now. Cuff him."

As Deputy Williams took charge of the prisoner, the man Jack slowly stood and watched Virgil limp toward him, examining his pistol.

"Just got this thing repaired," grumbled Virgil. "And now, I've got a busted grip."

Jack smiled. "Is that all that's busted, Virgil?" he asked, nodding toward the Constable's right leg.

Genuinely favoring his right leg, the Constable was about to answer when his gaze went past Jack and to a still astonished looking Deputy Williams.

"Seems our prisoner was right," managed Jim as he slowly looked to Jack. "What tha Hell indeed?"

Virgil's smile widened as he held out his hand toward Jack. "Deputy James Williams, I'd like you to meet our Horned Jack. The High Sheriff will brief and warn you about that information when we get back to the office."

Book 3
Into the Darkness

Those who survived the battlefield
And escaped the Reaper's scythe,
Left out there a part of their soul,
Which oft returns when day becomes night.

Part 1
The Dark Forest

Saturday morning, January 11th, Jack rolled over and looked out of the bedroom window by his bed. A light snow had gifted the back yard with a white, powdery haze.

About 7:30AM, he thought, noting the Big Ben alarm clock on the nightstand. He slowly rolled to his back, glancing up at the ceiling, and then down to his exposed feet. As he noted the aroma of fresh coffee laced with frying ham, a smile gradually shaped his otherwise drowsy expression. Looking toward the ceiling once more, he had just shut his eyes again when a little hand gently touched his right arm.

"Yes, Pico?" replied Jack, without opening his eyes.

"Mrs. Shelley said you have fifteen minutes to get up, get shaved, and get dressed or we could eat your biscuits."

Jack slowly opened his right eye to see the eight-year-old's smiling face. "In that order?" he asked softly.

Pico's smile widened as she nodded a silent "Yes."

"I'm up! I'm up!" he exclaimed as he quickly sat up and reached for her.

But the littlest member of the Shoultz household was much too quick. Squealing, she fled the room for the hallway and disappeared toward the dining area.

"Got a call from Will about ten minutes ago, Jack," said Shelley from the kitchen.

"Uhhh. . ." Jack plopped back down on the side of the bed. "But this is Saturday."

"I believe he knows that, but he said it is something you would want to know. It's about old Yopp. The Stewarts on the corner called Will and said he wasn't in his hold and they couldn't find him anywhere."

Jack immediately stood and made his way to the open, bedroom door and the hallway. "Couldn't find him?" he repeated a little louder.

"That's right," replied Shelley. "Will said that James was watching the area right now. He also said that his little cave roof is pretty tore up and pushed back away from the opening."

Jack rushed up the hallway struggling with his jeans and tee shirt.

"Teresa," called Shelley, grabbing Jack's arm. "Get his boots, a heavy shirt, and a warm jacket." She looked back at him. "You can't go out there in your slippers."

"Got 'em," said Teresa as she ran up the hallway to join them.

"Geeze," complained Shelley as Banjo muscled by them both, stopped at the door, and then looked back at them both.

"I'll just be a minute," said Jack. "This tee will be just fine for now."

Snatching his black toboggan from the hat rack by the door, he and the Pitt were out the door and heading across the neighbor's yard in less than half a minute. The morning was well on its way but the light dusting of snow was holding with no sign of a thaw anywhere. Jack slowed as he approached what the old veteran called his 'hold'. The top was not only pulled back, it was leaning on its back side. As he neared the entrance, he could see that what snow had fell that night had also covered the entrance as well as down inside the cave-like structure itself.

"Jack, is that you?" called someone from the Stewart house within the same yard.

"It's just me and Banjo, James. How's the wife?"

"Judy's fine, but we're all a little worried about old Yopp. Judy woke me up at daybreak. Told me it was snowing and to try to get him into the house," he explained from the porch. "But when I checked, I found it just like you see it now. I haven't touched a thing."

Jack looked at the street, just past the curb. There were three sets of tracks. Two were motorcycles and the third some kind of vehicle.

James walked up and patted Banjo. "I got down into the hold but didn't move from the ladder. He's not there, Jack. The place was pretty torn up as well. They were looking for money I believe. Can you imagine trying to steal from an old man who lives in a hole? They must have done it sometime before midnight. The last time I saw him was when I checked on him at 8:00PM or so."

Quickly sketching the tread designs of the bikes and the vehicle, Jack glanced up at his neighbor. "You wouldn't know what time it snowed last night would you?"

James shrugged. "Not really, I was out at a little after 10:00PM."

"Motorcycles huh?" James eased closer to the tracks. Looking back to check the front porch, he eased closer to Jack. "If you keep this under your hat, I'll share something with you."

Jack smiled. "I'll do my best."

"Very well. . ." He checked the porch again. "Sometimes when I got off of work, I stop in at the Willow Road Inn for a quick beer with the boys. On occasion, I've noticed motorcycles parked there also. Once inside, it's not hard to pick them out—black, leather jackets, long hair, tattoos, and attitudes grandma."

"I see." Jack walked a slow, circle around the front of the 'hold' and where the tracks were closest to the curb.

There were footprints all over the place and leading up to where the vehicle tracks were. But look as he did, Jack couldn't find any leaving the immediate area.

Jack glanced back at James. "Did they have a club name on the jackets?"

James nodded. "Scorpions. The picture of the thing was on the backs of their jackets as well as tattoos of it on their arms. While I was with the guys at the club, I didn't hear but one name mentioned--Roger. He's a big, heavyset, dark haired fellow with a scruffy beard. Looked like he called the shots while they were there."

Jack nodded, rubbing his bare arms. At that exact time, someone bumped a siren and up drove Deputy Jim Williams in his black and white. Stopping his cruiser about ten paces from the 'hold', he got out staring at the two.

"Dianne said to meet you just east of your house, Jack," said Jim with a nod to James. "She said something about an old hermit was missing."

145

"Alec Yopp," answered Jack with a slight nod. "He's old, long, white hair with a beard, and about eighty-five or so." Jack nodded toward the tracks. "The boys were pretty sloppy. Two cycles and a vehicle were here. They tore the place up and took him I think."

James walked closer to the vehicle tracks. "Heavy duty tires, Jack. Some kind of truck--a pickup I believe. I'll get on the horn and have Dianne get Kotts over here with his fingerprint kit." He eased to the entrance of the 'hold'. "Maybe he can lift something from down in that hole-of-a-place." He glanced back at Jack. "Did he really live down there?"

"He did," answered James, glancing back at Judy now standing on the front porch. "He said World War Two taught him to live in a fox hole and he never got over it."

The Deputy smiled at Jack. "Aren't you cold? It's in the low thirties right now."

Jack nodded. "Just wondering how cold old Yopp is," replied Jack as he leaned over and looked down inside the man cave. "Somebody ripped his mattress from one end to the other."

"They would have," replied James, slowly shaking his head. "I think that's where he kept his money. Didn't trust banks at all after Wall Street fell."

"Are you going in?" asked Jim. "If you are, Will's there with Charlie's 'help'."

Jack rolled his eyes. "There's that word again," he grumbled. "What's this 'help' thing and what do we need help with?"

Jim shrugged. "The old Indian didn't say and I didn't ask. When I reported in this morning, there were two, dark blue four-wheel drive Fords in front of Charlie's Airstream. They both had Native American tags. I heard Charlie talking to Will before I left. The old fellow referred to them as Shadow Wolves, whatever that means."

Jack rubbed his arms again. "I guess I'll find out when I get there."

*　　　*　　　*

After checking with Will on permission to come in, Jack rolled Uncle Bill's '55 Ford into the Munford lot at

146

9:15AM sharp. Just as Deputy Williams had said, there were two Ford, dark blue F150 pickups still parked in front of the Airstream. They were both equipped with campers. Thinking of his old friend, he wasted little time outside.

As soon as he walked in the lobby, Lucy stood, looking at Banjo. "Sorry, sweetie," she said apologetically, "I'm fresh out of donuts. Andy and Charlie ate them all."

Jack gestured with his right thumb toward the front door. "What's going on. There's two big Ford trucks outside and they both have Native American Nation plates on them."

Lucy shrugged, glancing at Will's partially open office door. "Charlie referred to them as Shadow Wolves. Will said they were some kind of Tribal Law Enforcement Border Agents. Better check in with Will right now. He said today's liable to be very busy." She nodded toward Will's office. There all in there right now, Jack.

"Ohhh boy." The young detective looked toward Will's office. "As if I don't have enough on my mind to worry about right now.

"Well. . ." Lucy paused, looking at Jack. "You better go in there. Will knows you're coming in for your friend's disappearance."

Jack nodded. "Guess it's time to find out about Charlie's 'help'.

Without further hesitation, the young detective walked straight to Will's door, knocked, and then opened it a little wider. But the big Pitt knew little of waiting for OK's. He muscled by Jack for a look at the strange scents that were greeting him at the moment.

"Geeze!" and "What the devil!" greeted the Pitt as well as the sound of furniture being scooted around on the wooden floor.

But as Jack stepped closer to the doorway, he could see that what now had Banjo's attention was Will's peppermint bowl.

Will stood, laughing at the expressions on the Indian's faces. "Well, give 'em one before he eats one of Charlie's

147

friends," said Will to Jack. "He'll stare a hole in my bowl if you don't."

Charlie laughed, glancing at Jack standing just inside the doorway. "I got this," said the old Apache as he fished out a mind, unwrapped it, and then held it down to Banjo. The Pitt, after glancing at the newcomers on the far side of the room again, quickly took the treat. "I told you he was big," chuckled Charlie, glancing at his friends.

"Did the one you spoke of come with him?" asked a trim, black-haired man of fifty or so.

Jack peeped through the crack by the door hinges. They were all dressed in Levis, plaid shirts, and faded denim jackets and looking straight at Charlie.

Charlie's smile widened as he looked at the partially open doorway. "Come, join us, Jack," he said, motioning with his hands. "This is the 'help' I spoke of earlier. They are all Border Patrol Agents and now have permission to pursue and arrest outside of our Nation."

Jack, ducking under the door frame, stepped inside looking at Charlie. "Did you speak of the 'Beast', Charlie?"

Charlie nodded. "These are good men, Jack. They are called Shadow Wolves by our people. You can trust them as fellow officers."

Without a word, all four eased closer to Jack, looking him over from his eyes to his boots.

Charlie smiled at their interest. "The tall, thin fellow here is Stephen Two Bears," he explained. "He's their leader. The youngest fellow here is Chee Hatman. He's kind of a Shirtman. That is to say, he keeps the peace between God and man. The older fellow still wearing his hair long, is Thomas Greene."

"He keeps our spirits safe," laughed the fourth man in his thirties.

Thomas frowned, looking sternly at the young man. "The wise ass means liquor," he grumbled. "His name is Jason Black Eyes."

"Iron Eyes," corrected Jason as the others laughed.

"They're here for the Black Chopper, Jack," added Will.

"They hunt the Greys," said Charlie. "The Chopper will lead 'em to them, I think."

148

Jack slowly raised his eyebrows as he turned to Will. "Aren't we poking the hornet's nest again?"

Will leaned back in his swivel chair and smiled. "We're not. But these fellows have a runnin' feud with that little fellow who flies that Silver Streak. Since they can pursue across borders, let's just call this a professional courtesy. They would like ta see where you shot that thing down."

"Uhhh. . ." Jack glanced at Charlie, and then looked back at Will. "Am I still on the Yopp kidnapping?"

Will stopped rocking. "You think he was kidnapped? These guys can track 'em if he's in the woods."

"No need," replied Jack. "We had a light snow last night and his tracks stopped at a vehicle of some kind. There were no tracks leaving his 'hold'. I got a tip from a neighbor about a motorcycle gang called Scorpions and there were cycle tracks around the hold as well."

Will slowly stood, glancing at Charlie. "Well, since you got a jump on this case, why don't you take these fellas out to your place and show 'em where that thing went down? Then, you can chase your hunch on the Yopp case."

Chee stepped closer, looking at Jack. "When you shot the ship down, did it blow apart?"

"You bet," answered the young detective. "Sparks went all over the place and set off more little fires than you could count on both hands."

Chee grinned, glancing at the other Shadow Wolves. "Would you mind us collecting some of the metal?"

"Why would you want the metal?" asked Will.

"Better ammo," replied Thomas. "The lead you shoot in those big pistols damages too much of the ship, and as you know, can destroy it as well. Their Silver Streak ships are made of some kind of metal that's resilient, strong as steel yet as light as plastic. Bullets made from it will damage the outer skin of the vessel without destroying the whole ship. That's the secret—the outer skin. That's where the ship gets its main power."

"And you've fought these beings before?" asked Andy.

Chee smiled. "Our ancestors have recorded encounters with these ones—the Star People. When they

149

started taking their children, we started fighting them. Now, it seems, they are taking our cattle as well as yours." He looked back at Jack. "Will you take us to the ship you shot down?"

"Come with me," said Jack. "Shelley's working on a big pot of beef soup. We'll ask her to cook an extra pone of corn bread while you are searching for the metal and then we'll have lunch if that's all right with you all."

"Already sounds good to me," agreed Thomas as the others nodded in agreement.

*   *   *

After speaking to Shelley, Jack took the Shadow Wolves to where the alien ship blew apart and then headed toward the Willow Road Inn about two miles or so west on Willow View.

"On the table at 12:30PM," said Shelley as he backed down the driveway.

*   *   *

Sitting on the east side of Getwell Road and at the north-east corner of Willow View, the redwood front gave a rustic look to the little pub. Serving both bar beverages as well as grilled items, the Inn was a popular hangout for many who lived and worked in that community.

At 11:15PM sharp, Jack pulled his unmarked Fort Galaxy into the parking lot of the Inn. With eight cars already there, he noticed three Harley Davidson motorcycles parked right at the front door. The young detective smiled, quite pleased with his luck so far. Pulling his detective cap snug on his head, he got out and walked toward the front door. Upon entering the Pub, he paused just inside, staring at the pretty, little blond now working behind the counter located past the tables and at the back of the room. Upon quickly catching his stare, her chin dropped at the sight of the tall stranger dressed in an English, hounds tooth jacket and light brown pants.

"Can I help you?" she asked. Her tone hopeful.

Smiling at her eagerness, the three motorcyclists occupying a table at the back left side of the room, turned to hear his reply.

150

"In which direction?" asked Jack as he slowly walked toward her.

The blonde's smile widened. Looking very fit in her thirties, her big, blue eyes seemed glued to his smile. "Anywhere you'd like," she answered.

The bikers laughed as they looked back at Jack.

"How about a good bottle of wine?" countered the young detective.

"My place or yours?" she queried.

With a genuine grin, Jack held up his left hand to show his wedding band.

"Now there's a show stopper," quipped one of the long-haired, black leather clad bikers on his left.

Jack took a seat at the bar, right across from where she was working. "I'm Jack Shoultz."

"Can't blame a girl for trying," she poked. "I'm Maryland. How about Yellow Tail?" she asked.

The Biker table exploded with laughter as all three scooted back and turned their chairs to better see the two at the bar.

"Make it a double, straight up, and no rocks," ordered Jack, now getting amused himself.

Only then, did Jack notice the scorpions on the back of the biker's jackets.

"I'm looking for a friend of mine," started Jack, looking straight at them. "He took a ride with some others last night and he's not back yet."

"And you are. . ." A heavy-set, biker with long, black hair scooted his chair to face the tall stranger at the bar.

"Jack Shoultz. I'm a friend of old Aleck Yopp." Jack turned on his stool to face the three at the table to his left. "Haven't seen him lately, have you?"

Plainly nervous, the other two bikers scooted back from the table but kept their seats. But the long hair closest to Jack never moved, looking almost amused.

"What's your name?" asked Jack, not breaking eye contact with the biker.

"Roger Dorry," answered the young man, still smiling.

Looking back over his right shoulder, he whispered something to the others. Eying Jack closely, the two got up and walked toward the door, leaving their beer glasses still full on the table. After the two had left the Pub, the one called Dorry slowly stood, watching Jack closely.

"Just who the Hell are you, Mr. Shoultz?" he asked. His smile quickly faded as he noticed Jack's black cap.

"Now, Dorry," said Maryland as she walked around the end of the bar, looking at the big biker. "Don't you start something in here, Roger Dorry. If you're feeling froggy, you take it right outside. Do you hear me, Mr. Moped?"

Now laughing, Dorry started toward the front door. But as he walked past Jack, he noticed something in the tall, dark stranger's eyes, something that you couldn't readily put a name to. It was a feeling that took him all the way back to when he was a kid, when his father would catch him in a lie. He stopped but a reach from the young detective.

"Just who the Hell are you?" he asked again.

"Many things," answered Jack, now staring into the young man's dark brown eyes.

Once again, a storm broke in Jack's head. Visions of strangers, a crying mother holding a child, a red brick building on a road called Cherry, and all separated by fast passing scenes over the handle bars of a big motorcycle. But then there came a fleeting vision of what he was after--a glimpse of his old friend sitting in a chair next to a window. His face was bruised and bloodied and he looked bewildered at best.

Jack slowly got up from his stool, still looking at Dorry. The biker's expression was one of amazement with a touch of horror. Feeling his anger build and the flush now creeping up his neck toward his face, Jack pushed the man back to arm's length.

"Where is the house on Cherry Road where you're keeping Old Yopp?" he asked, noting he was almost in the 'Beast'.

Dorry looked as if he could hardly find words. And with the flush now in his face, Jack knew what he was probably seeing. The biker backed from the Nephilim, almost falling over one of the table chairs.

"Forty-two nineteen Cherry," he finally got out.

152

Jack cupped his hands, trying to hide his talons as he turned and started toward the front door.

"Are you all right, Roger?" asked Maryland, noting Dorry's expression.

"Call an ambulance," managed the big biker, looking like his feet were frozen to the floor.

Maryland stared at the big biker. "But you're not--"

At that instant, the barmaid's comment was interrupted by the noise of a confrontation outside.

"Get an ambulance!" screamed Dorry as he quickly kicked the chair away from the back of his legs.

But he never made a move from the table where the chair had stood. He just stared at the door as the crashing, shouting, and screaming got louder and louder. And then, the struggle stopped just a quick as it started.

Maryland turned to see Gene peering through the serving window. Throwing his apron aside the owner and cook came through the swinging door of the kitchen and looked at Maryland.

"What the devil's goin' on, Maryland?" he asked, glancing at Dorry.

The barmaid slowly shook her head. "The ruckus is over, Gene. Go and see if we need to call the police."

"Great," grumbled Gene as he headed toward the front door. "Every time those Scorpions come in here something like this happens. Gonna sell this place. . ."

Gene's words lost the breath to support them as he opened the front door. Two of the three cycles in front lay scattered in pieces all around the two bikers who had just left Dorry's table. One of the men lay motionless under the main body of one of the cycles and the other was in a heap farther out in the parking lot.

"Call an ambulance and the police!" shouted Gene as he stepped outside.

"I seen it! I seen it!" exclaimed a man now getting out of an old, light green '50 Chevrolet car. "Those two cycle punks jumped 'em when he came out o' the bar. One had a knife and the other a section of chain. Mindin' his own business the tall man was when he came out."

153

Gene looked down at the one under the cycle. "This one's clothes are cut to ribbons. What did he use?"

Still holding to the open door of the old Chevy, the man shook his head. "Didn't see a weapon, Gene. He just kind o' slapped at him. Threw the one with the knife way over there where he is now and hit the one with the chain with his own motorcycle."

"Great Gods," said Gene, almost in a whisper. "I ain't payin' for none of this."

*   *   *

Jack slowed his unmarked Ford to a stop about half a block from the house in question. It looked to be the exact house he had seen in Dorry's head. Having already called for backup, he expected to see Jim Williams pull up at any minute. In less than ten minutes, Jim pulled his marked cruiser behind Jack and quickly got out. The young detective reached across and opened the passenger side door.

"What the devil," said the young deputy, looking at Jack's blood-splattered shirt as he got in. "I just left James at the Willow Road Inn. The owner said that a man was jumped outside by some bikers. The paramedics were loading the attackers in the ambulance when I left. Jack, the bartender gave him your name as the one who was jumped." He stared at Jack's shirt again. "Are you all right?"

Jack smiled, as he pulled his jacket more over the blood stains. "I'm fine Jim. Just a shallow cut here and there is all. We need to go into that red brick house, two houses from here on the left."

Jim looked at the six-inch cut in Jack's right, jacket sleeve. "Are you sure you can do this?"

Jack nodded. "There's an old, white-haired man in there, Jim and he can't wait for me to see a doctor. Now, you go first and cover the back door. I'll bring up the rear and hit the front."

Jim shrugged. "Let's do it then."

Giving the Deputy Williams a thirty second head start toward the house, Jack headed toward the front door at a

154

dead run. In but seconds, the young detective was on the porch and pounding on the door.

"Munford Sheriff's Office!" he announced loudly. "Open the door!"

Hearing what sounded like one person running from the living room, he took half a step backwards, pulled his pistol, and then kicked in the door, sending splintered pine all over the room. As he entered, he could already hear Jim yelling at the man fleeing the house. Quickly checking the first two bedrooms, the third stopped Jack cold. His old friend was lying in the bed, mouth open, eyes closed, and not moving at all.

"Yopp!" exclaimed Jack as he rushed to the old fellow's side. "Can you hear me?" Jack patted the old fellow's shoulder.

Yopp didn't move at all.

"Jim! Get an ambulance here fast," shouted Jack.

"Got him!" shouted Jim from the living room. "I'll call it in!"

Turning back to the bed, Jack knelt by his old friend. "Yopp?" he said loudly again with a gentle shake of his arm. "It's me, Jack. Can you hear me?"

With his right eye batting wildly, the old man tried to wipe the blood from his left. "Don't need a thing, Jack," he managed weakly. "Still got some oranges Shelley gave me and two cans o' tuna." He then managed a glassy-eyed stare in the young detective's direction and tried to smile. "The forest is dark and deep, Jack. . .miles ta go afore I can sleep."

With that, his stare lifted to the ceiling and he closed his one, good eye.

"Jim!" called Jack again.

"Right here," said the deputy, now standing at the doorway. "Dianne's got the ambulance on the way." He looked to old Yopp. "How is he?"

Jack wiped the tears from his eyes and lowered himself to the floor by the bed. "Barely here," he said weakly.

"What did he mean by what he just said about the forest?" asked Jim. "He quoted Robert Frost, I believe."

Jack shrugged, looking at his old friend. "He probably didn't know the poet. But he loved that quote. Him and his buddies used to say that when they were in the Battle for Argonne Forrest. He was speaking of France in World War Two." He glanced at Jim and then checked the old fellow's pulse. "He never made it out of those fox holes."

Wiping his wet face again with his right jacket sleeve, Jack slowly stood and looked past Jim toward the still open bedroom door. Little by little, Jim noticed what Jack called the 'Beast' begin to doff the human.

"Now, Jack." Jim drew his weapon, backed toward the door, and watched as blood spots began to form below each of the deputy's hands. "Now, Jack!" Jim planted himself in the doorway. "He's in my cruiser and he'll get what's coming to him."

Jack lowered his eyes to the floor between them.

Now, watching his own weapon shake, Jim added, "You've got to think of your family, Jack. If you do something horrible to that scumbag out there, they'll put you in jail for sure and where will that leave them?"

Then Jim watched the thing he was seeing look toward the ceiling. The sound that started out with a low groan, ended up in a breath-taking, window shaking growl-of-a-howl.

"Don't do it, Jack," shouted Jim again. "If I have to shoot you, it'll not only ruin my year but your family's as well."

The Nephilim gradually sunk to his knees and buried his face into his taloned hands. Gradually lowering his hands to his knees, he looked back at Jim. "Can you find me something to clean up this blood? That can't be here when the Kotts gets here."

Jim nodded nervously as he lowered his pistol. "I will if you promise you'll not go near my cruiser."

Jack nodded. "Old Yopp's gone now. Nothing I can do will bring him back." Sitting flat on the floor again, he looked back up at the deputy. "You go and call Dianne for the coroner. I'll find a pail and some water and clean up my own mess."

156

Part 2
The Alien Map

Bright and early the next Monday morning, Shelley, Teresa and Pico headed to Munford with Jack to start Jack's shift. The news that Will had hired Shelley's best friend, Betty Lewis, pleased Shelley very much. So much so, that she wanted to be there when Betty got off her first night shift. . . .

Just as soon as Jack pulled Uncle Bill's Ford into the Munford lot, Pico stood from the back seat and pointed at two, dark blue Ford pickups parked at Charlie's Airstream. "The Indians are still here!" she exclaimed excitedly.

"Maybe they want some more of Shelley's beef soup. They all had two bowls a piece," Quipped Teresa as Jack opted for a spot by the front door.

"The one called Thomas said he would bring me a Story Teller doll. Do you think he remembered?"

As Jack opened the door, Pico pushed the seat forward trying to get out.

"Wait a minute," said Teresa, laughing as the little one followed her out. "We can all go in together."

But the excited eight-year-old didn't wait and scooted right past Jack with Teresa in hot pursuit.

"Whoa!" said Betty, laughing at Teresa.

"What's got you so excited?" asked Dianne as she walked from behind the dispatcher's desk. "Where is Banjo?"

"I'm sure he'll miss your donuts," explained Shelley, "but Jack took him to be with my brother's Airedale, Shadow." She glanced back at Pico. "The Indians are here and she has made a new friend in Thomas."

Pico nodded excitedly. "He's got a Story Teller Doll for me."

"Well good for you," said Dianne. "I'm sure they'll be out in a minute. She smiled at Pico as she picked up a plain, brown cardboard box about ten inches square. "I think Thomas left this for you," she added as she handed the box to Pico. "It's got your name on it."

With wide eyes, the little girl slowly reached for the box. "He didn't forget," she added weakly, looking at the words 'To Pico from Thomas'.

"Well open it," prompted Teresa.

Slowly opening the box, she pulled back what looked to be a miniature Native American blanket to reveal a young Indian maid with a child on each side of her.

"Do you like it?" spoke someone from across the room and behind her.

Pico immediately wheeled to see Thomas, Will and the others walking out of the Sheriff's office.

Gently holding the box, Pico ran to Thomas. "It's too pretty to play with," she said. "Thank you very much."

Thomas knelt and hugged her. As he did, his eyes grew wide, looking at Charlie. Gently pushing her back to arm's length, he smiled as he glanced back at Chee. "My young friend. . ." He paused looking at her face. "There is more to you than greets the eyes I think."

Pico smiled. "One watches you also," she added softly.

Thomas's eyes grew big again as he slowly stood.

"Are you all right?" asked Betty.

Thomas nodded, glancing at Chee.

"Be careful what you ask for, Thomas," warned Chee with a half-smile himself.

Thomas's gaze found its way back to Pico. "Tell me, little one, what did you see?"

"Someone was standing behind you, but I only saw her face."

"Be careful," warned Chee again.

With a half step back, Thomas continued to look down at the little eight-year-old. "This one you saw is not a demon, is it?"

Pico shrugged. "Not sure what a demon looks like. She was old and had long white hair. She was smiling at me and had a green, butterfly thing in her hair."

Thomas's expression slowly changed, now with a smile of his own. "My grandmother," he finally said as he turned and walked toward Dianne's desk. "She raised me," he added as he pulled a half-pint of Old Crow from his jacket pocket and dropped it in the waste can by the desk. Looking down at the half-full bottle, he added, "I gave her the hair comb. She never liked to see me drink. Always said there was a bad spirit inside each bottle and one must drink to feel him." He looked back at Pico. "Thank you, Little One, for that," he added softly.

"Thomas! We must go," said Stephen Two Bears. "The Sheriff has given us the alien maps. The Hall farm is not far from here. We will speak with the good doctor and show them to him and the written approval from the sheriff to investigate and set up camp wherever we find his cattle."

"Where in there is the time to eat?" asked Jason Iron Eyes, drawing laughter from the others.

"Hold on a minute," spoke Will, still at the office door. He looked at Stephen Two Bears. "Would you mind if I, unofficially mind you, send my detective with you? He knows Doc Hall's place as well as the man himself. He also knows where the last mutilation was."

"That would be good," agreed Two Bears.

Will looked at Jack. "The DA didn't exactly pull us off of Doc Hall's problem, so I would like for you to go with the Shadow Wolves as an advisor so to speak. Mind you, this is their investigation as well so help them as much as you can. If luck is with you, and you run across that Silver Streak thing, be careful. If it makes any kind of offensive gesture, you let the Shadow Wolves handle it. Charlie says they can shoot it down without making it explode."

Jack looked back at Charlie. "Are you going on this hunt with us?"

"You bet," replied the old Apache. "To hunt with a Nephilim is a blessing to an Apache. Bring Banjo. The Grey Men hate dogs."

Shelley looked at Betty. "Come and sit with us for a little bit. We've got some catching up to do."

*　　　*　　　*

About two hours later, and after clearing things with the good doctor, Jack left the Shadow Wolves with a copy

159

of Will's alien maps. Having agreed to meet up with them at Sparkey's Bar-B-Que at 7:30PM, the young detective was now well on his way there at 6:30PM. As per their agreement, their blue Fords were parked right in front when the young detective pulled into the parking lot. . . .

As Jack walked in with Banjo, he spotted them--all five at a table that could barely accommodate four. Taking a table next to them, he smiled at Charlie. "Did the maps work for you?"

"They did," answered Charlie. "We looked at the field at Prior's Road and the area where you last saw the glowing ship. The cattle have been let into the pasture just north of that intersection."

"We'll watch that one tonight," said Jack. "Do you have a short-wave radio?"

"One in both trucks," answered Two Bears. "We're on the police band."

*   *   *

That Monday night proved fruitless, as did the next three. The only one who enjoyed it was Banjo, who seemed to sleep through the whole thing. But on the next Friday, their patience was rewarded. . .

Leaving his unmarked Ford at Sparkey's, Jack opted to ride with Two Bears, Charlie, and Chee Hatman. They hid their vehicle in a dry creek bed just north of where Ruleman intersected the Richardson Landing Road. Thomas Green and Jason Iron eyes hid their truck in a stand of trees about three hundred yards east of them and with a good view of the intersection. With at least one hundred head of Black Angus between them, it looked to be the best set-up of the week. Banjo, on the other hand, was content to chew on the big, cow bone Charlie had bought him.

Crouched by a wild plum thicket, Jack watched as the young one called Iron Eyes left their truck and walked toward the Black Angus with two, metal containers in his hands. Slowly easing in and among the cattle, he stopped several times to pour what looked to be a dark liquid upon the ground.

160

Seeing this, Jack eased closer to Two Bears, the one who seemed to be the leader of the Wolves. "What is Iron Eyes doing?" he asked.

Two Bears eyed the big Pitt, but didn't seem nervous. "He's baiting the one without a soul," answered the Apache with a bit of a smile. "Two Bears thinks these demons use the blood somehow--to exist probably."

Jack squinted. "They drink it?"

Two Bears shrugged his shoulders. "I do not know. But Two Bears thinks this. Once, when he came upon where the Silver Streak had slaughtered one of our cattle, he found the Grey Man's scat. He said it was loose, dark crimson, and very sticky."

"And this will bring the Grey Man?" asked Jack.

"Perhaps." Two Bears smiled. "Time will tell, I think. He has baited two other places very near here. If the demon comes to one of them, he will surely see the cattle."

"You might be right," said Jack. "He seldom takes meat. Sometimes kidneys or udders, and others eyes, gums, and lips."

Two bears shrugged again. "I have never seen the people who send them, only Clones and the Grey Men."

"Perhaps there are no others," replied Jack. "Cloning may be the only way they can survive. Charlie has told me that at times they have taken your people, children even."

"This is true." Two Bears looked to the north, toward the road and the field beyond. "But unlike the white man, we will not tolerate it. If we can get close enough, we have ten-gauge shotguns with number three buckshot made of the bright ship's metal. At your place, we found a good number of pieces with the help of your Pico and her strange, little friend."

Jack smiled. "Did she have wings?"

"Indeed," answered Two Bears weakly. "I trust she is not a demon, Jack."

Jack's smile widened. "Her name is Woo. She is as much a demon as I am. She is my friend as well. You would do well to trust her."

161

Two Bear's gaze slowly moved from the road to Jack, and then a smile slowly erased the cautious look. "Sometimes, I don't understand exactly what I know of you, Jack Shoultz. All this Nephilim and Horned Jack thing is new to me. Charlie said you were a 'Watcher'—one who is allowed to work the good among us." He paused as a confused look slowly marred his expression. "He said not to shoot you when the 'Beast' came. I have tried to understand his words, but I have failed in my efforts I think."

Jack smiled as he looked about the heavily shaded area where they were hiding. "Shall I show you?" he asked softly.

Two Bears' eyes widened, his mouth opened slightly, and then he backed up two steps. "You will call the 'Beast' now?"

Jack nodded. "He has always been but a short reach from you all along."

Bowing his head, Jack thought of those who kidnapped the girls not long ago. Almost instantly, his hands began to tingle as his face grew hot. When his fingertips started to sting, he raised his eyes to the one close to him. Even before their eyes could meet, Jack could hear the breaking of limbs and scrub as Two Bears fled the small stand of trees. Jack looked through the trees to see him standing out in the open, looking back at him.

"Charlie was right!" exclaimed the Apache loudly. "The others must know this. If Iron Eyes sees what you call the Beast, he will surely shoot what he calls a demon. I must tell them what I have seen is not a demon but a good thing." He walked cautiously a bit closer to the stand of trees, stooped, and then looked in toward Jack. "This thing is gone now?"

"It is," answered Jack with a chuckle. "You can come back in."

Doing just that, Two Bears knelt on one knee a respectful distance from Jack and the Pitt. "This one is always with you?" he asked confusedly.

Jack smiled. "Like a bad cold."

162

The Apache nodded and then checked his watch. "It's getting close to nine and it can't get any darker. "If this trick of Iron Eyes works, I'll buy breakfast at Sparky's in the morning."

Then, just as Iron Eyes rejoined them, the radio in the truck sounded off. "Two Bears! Two Bears! Thomas here! Can you hear me!"

Banjo jumped, dropped his bone, and then looked back toward the truck.

"Damn thing too loud," grumbled Two Bears as he scrambled for the truck. Grabbing the mic, he quickly turned down the volume. "We're here, Thomas. You see anything?"

"You bet," came the excited reply. "Look south across the Landing Road, and about two hundred yards into the field where Iron Eyes dumped the first batch. The Silver craft is with us again."

Chee Hatman immediately went into the truck camper. Jack watched him come out with a ten-gauge pump. The barrel looked at least forty inches long.

"Goose gun?" asked Jack, noting the smile on Chee's face.

"Silver goose," quipped the young Apache.

Quickly turning to where Two Bears was now looking, he immediately spotted their glowing target. It was hovering silently about fifty feet over the pasture and about two hundred yards south of the Landing road.

"It needs to be much closer," complained Chee. "How can we get it within range of this gun?"

"Damn!" said Charlie, trying to be as quiet as his excitement would allow. "What tha Hell is Iron Eyes up to?"

Quickly looking through the tree toward the second truck, Jack could see the young Shadow Wolf cross the Landing Road and run toward a section of woods on the far side. He looked to have another shotgun with him.

"Just-just-just hold tight," said Two Bears. "The demon can't see him from where he is at. "He's across the road and into the woods at a dead run with the other Mossberg."

163

"Damn it!" grumbled Charlie, smacking the ground with his closed fist. "If he scares the demon off, I'll have his feathers." He glanced at Jack. "He lost a nephew some years back to the Sky People. The ten-year-old was never found."

*   *   *

Now, one hundred yards into the woods, Iron Eyes continued as fast as he was able on the east side of the alien ship. Dramatically slowing, he shifted the weapon's sling to the other shoulder and looked through the trees at the still hovering ship about forty yards from him. But now, it was starting to move slowly toward where the cattle were grazing.

"No-no-no," said the young Apache as he hurried toward the edge of the woods.

*   *   *

Hearing the crunch of ice crystals on frozen grass, Jack eased to the edge of their thicket and peered out across a perfectly, moonlit field. The clouds had parted and gifted the area with what looked to be a perfect picture from one of Edgar Rice Borrows novels, space craft and all.

"See 'em?" asked Charlie as he eased up beside Jack.

"I do," replied the young detective. "He just ran out of the woods and is now about thirty yards behind the ship." He glanced at Charlie. "That thing is armed. Won't the alien see him?"

"No!" Two Bears took hold of Jack's forearm. "This craft has a window you cannot see. It is only a single, big one and in the front of the ship."

"He's gaining," said Chee, "and the demon is almost at the road."

But suddenly, everything changed. The calm night was shattered by three blasts from the Mossberg. Completely surprised by what just happened, all four joined Jack still crouching behind the old oak.

"Look," said Chee. "Bless his feathers, he got it good."

Sure enough, Jack watched the craft's glow start to flicker in some spots and completely go out in others. It was now trying to cross the road, but was having trouble maintaining enough altitude to even clear the fences.

Chee eased up closer to Jack. "Their science is much greater than ours. Somehow, the skin of the ship powers the vehicle. The pellets from the shotgun have somehow disrupted the flow of energy on the surface of the ship. Look!" He pointed toward the ship. "It barely cleared the fences and now can only slide across the grass."

"Stay put!" said Charlie. "It's coming in our direction."

Now, everything started to happen so fast, Jack could hardly figure out what to do. Two Bears bolted from where they were hiding and ran toward Iron Eyes, who was now aiming his weapon again.

"Enough!" shouted Two Bears as the strange ship slid within thirty yards from where the others were still hiding.

Completely forgetting the bone, Banjo ran from Jack's side, but stopped as he entered the pasture. Eying the strange craft, he stood his ground, constantly looking back at the others. Now, with only a small flicker of light here and there, the ship was the color of a ripe olive, about the size of a sports car, and the shape of an almond.

Still reluctant to move, Jack watched Two Bears walk back toward the ship with Iron Eyes. "Thomas!" he called loudly. "This one is yours, I think!"

Jack looked past the ship to see the big Ford burst from the dry creek bed and head straight for the alien's ship. Sliding to a stop about thirty feet from the far side of the still struggling ship, Thomas Greene jumped from the truck and ran to within fifteen feet of the front of the craft, smiling at Charlie like he had just received a Christmas present.

Charlie tugged on Jack's arm. "Come, my Nephilim friend, and bring your dog. We will now let him extract the demon from this flying apparition."

Slowly following Charlie toward the ship with Banjo at his side, Jack now could only see a sparkle here and there upon the surface of what was now, an almost black ship. "What kind of ship has no seams at all. . .and where is the window?"

165

"Do you remember where I said it was?" asked Two Bears.

Jack looked to the front of the craft. "It looks like the rest of the ship. I don't see it."

Thomas smiled at Jack's amazed expression. "Feel it, but watch the little, flickering flashes. It can shock the crap out of you."

Because they sounded like bacon frying, Jack was extremely leery of the flashes popping on and off here and there. The young detective eased his hand to the craft's fuselage. "It's soft—not metal at all, is it?"

Charlie smiled. "It is metal, young Jack, but a kind I am not familiar with." He looked at Thomas. "We must do this thing before the black chopper is alerted."

Thomas nodded, pulled his Bowie knife, and then slowly stepped to the front of the ship. Seeing the knife, Jack glanced at Chee. He and the others had already pulled their handguns.

"Chee, what's happening here," whispered Jack.

"He's making the demon show himself," explained the young Apache. "He will threaten the ship with the knife. It's like the demons protect their ships as we do our horses." Chee smiled at Jack. "It's like they think the damned things are alive or something, I think."

Then, sure enough and just as Chee had explained, when Thomas held the point of the big Bowie closer and closer to the window, its black color slowly faded to grey and then became perfectly clear. The wrap-around window instantly revealed the Greyish-green Man sitting beneath it. It had no expression at all and remained perfectly still, with its solid black, almond shaped eyes trained on Thomas.

"Watch," whispered Chee. "The demon fears for the ship as one would a living thing."

Then, as Thomas moved the knife closer to the skin of the ship, the alien quickly held his hands out, palms up, for the Indian to see.

"He says he has no weapon," whispered Chee.

Now seeing the Grey Man fumble with something just under the collar of his tight-fitting shirt, Jack leaned close to Chee. "What's he doing?"

Chee smiled. "Revealing his true self."

Evidently releasing a snap near the back of his neck, the alien pulled at what looked to be a flexible helmet from his head. The boyish face Jack was now looking at was that of a fourteen or fifteen-year-old, American boy, with brown eyes and darker brown hair.

"What tha Hell," whispered Jack.

"Shhh!" scorned Charlie. He then nodded for Thomas to continue.

Thomas tapped on the window with the tip of his knife and motioned the blade toward the sky.

Not saying a word, the Gray Man nodded and then tripped something on the dash of the craft. Ever so slowly the window made a snapping sound as it rose slightly and then slid back to into the top of the craft.

Ever so slowly, and with his eyes glued on the Indian with the knife, the young-looking alien slowly stood up in the cockpit. Only then, did he notice the tall man on his left, standing with the Shadow Wolves. Staring at the big Pitt, he quickly looked to Jack.

"*Nay-flam,*" spoke the gray man with a voice and tone of a teenager. "*Naish qua nahgo,*" it added. Lowering its hands, it made a slight bow to Jack, looked back to Thomas, and then held them out again in the same gesture.

Only then, did Jack note that the young face strangely resembled that of a Native American, darker skin and all. "What did he say?" whispered Jack.

Chee shrugged. "Not sure. But Nah Ish means thank you and I think he called you a Nephilim."

"He said 'Thank you for being with me,'" replied Charlie.

Jack looked toward Thomas, still right in front of the ship. "Don't hurt him."

"He's right," said Charlie, looking as disappointed as Thomas. "Jack doesn't think we need to slap the 'bear' twice."

167

Slowly shaking his head, Thomas lowered his knife and motioned toward something on the dash of the ship. Reluctantly, the young-looking alien unplugged something and handed the Apache a small black box, its wires and headset still attached.

"We're wasting time," said Two Bears. "Let us go from here. It's a blue-eyed wonder that black chopper isn't already here."

"Go!" Thomas motioned to the alien with his right hand quickly pointing toward the sky.

Jack looked to Chee. "What did he hand Thomas?"

"The radio and the box that talks to the government, I think. It proves they know of these demons."

As they quickly got in the trucks, Jack kept an eye peeled toward the south, but noticed not a light in the sky.

*   *   *

Jack being scheduled to work the weekend, Saturday, the seventeenth of January, quickly presented itself with more problems than usual. With the mysterious alien craft being solved, a larger problem arose--how to write up a believable report that would satisfy Will. Jack pulled Uncle Bill's Ford into the Munford lot at a quarter to seven. It never looked so deserted. Betty Lewis' green Chevy Nova was there. He noted James' Camaro. He was probably working the Sergeant's Desk for Andy. Charlie's old truck was parked beside his trailer as usual. Resembling a lot from Christmas Day past, Jack got out of the Ford and hoped for a slow day to match it. Stopping just inside the lobby doorway, he looked toward what he always considered Dianne's desk. Betty was now sitting there and smiling back at him.

"What?" Jack cocked his head to the right. "A dispatcher's morning desk with no donut box in sight."

"Where's Banjo?" she asked.

Jack smiled. "He's with Shadow, Donnie's dog. He's spending more time with her than me these days."

"Coffee's fresh," tempted James. "Two Bears called in a touch base with Will last night." He paused, looking at Jack. "Will's wondering what happened to your call."

168

James paused again, silently laughing. "He grumbled something about you shooting down another aircraft."

"It's some kind of aircraft these people fly when they watch us--exactly like the one I shot down." answered the young detective. "Besides, the Apache called Iron Eyes got this one and the demon in it."

James froze, dropping his paperwork to the top of the desk. "Demon?" A blank stare now graced James' face.

Jack smiled at his confused expression. "Perhaps that's a bit too drastic. That's what the Shadow Wolves call the Grey Men."

James stepped around the desk and walked closer to Jack.

"Go ahead," prompted Betty, quickly walking toward him from her desk. "You can't just leave us hanging. Will hardly allows us see anything you and James write up now-a-days. What's this 'Grey Man' thing?"

"You saw the alien this time didn't you?" James, now standing right in front of the young detective, stared straight at him.

Jack nodded with, "Face to face. If I hadn't been there, they would've killed him, I believe."

"I see," said James.

"Well, I don't see," said Betty. "Dianne and I have been dying to find out what you've been chasing. Now, what does this alien look like?"

"A kid," answered Jack. "He had a strange helmet on that certainly gave him an alien look, but he was nothing but a fifteen-year-old kid, or looked like one at least."

"Do you think you could fill out your report in Jim Williams' black and white?"

Jack looked to James. "What happened to Jim? Where is he?"

"The hospital," answered James. "His wife, Nancy, is having her child, or at least soon will be shortly." He raised his eyebrows. "Will said if you objected, you could have the desk."

Jack smiled. "Are you comfortable wearing Andy's shoes?"

James grinned, nodding silently.

169

"Done then," decided Jack. "I've got his cruiser for the weekend. Do we have anything pending?"

"Cindy Gant," answered Betty. "Redhead, twenty-six years old, green eyes, and about five feet-seven."

Jack rubbed the back of his neck and glanced at James. "Help me out here. That name sounds familiar."

James grinned. "She's your nemesis, Jack. Or, I should say, Fred's really. She's the one who outran both of you the other day in a stolen vehicle each time."

Jack's gaze slowly made it to the ceiling. "Great God of Benjamin," he groaned. "I've got it now. She's the pretty redhead who frequents the Covington area."

"That's where you'll be," replied Betty. "We don't have a thing on her save the name and description."

*   *   *

Three hours later, fairly close to 11:30AM, Jack made his third drive down the main highway as it passed through Covington. Saturday never seemed so slow. Seeing Frosties Hamburger Restaurant up ahead, he quickly decided to beat the crowd. He knew a cool root bear and a cheeseburger would go a long way in brightening up his day. With tables readily available, he had no problem ordering. In less than five minutes, the little waitress sat his 'Brown Cow' ice cream float in front of him.

"I'll have your burger and fries here in a jiffy," she said, smiling warmly at him.

"That's fine. No hurry," replied Jack.

But just as soon as his lips touched the straw, he noticed something outside. Maybe it was the beautiful red paint job on the 1958 Chevrolet Corvette that caught his eye as it pulled into the parking spot directly in front of his window. Or perhaps it was the smile on the face of the beautiful, green-eyed girl behind the wheel that did the trick. At any rate, he pulled his attention from her eyes and looked at her beautiful, wavy, shoulder length, red hair.

"Red! Damn!" Jack jumped up, all but knocking the burger from the waitress's hands. "Keep it warm for me. I'll be back," he managed as he made a dash for the door.

But the redhead didn't waste a second. Still smiling, she peeled out of the parking place backwards and shot across the lot like a bat straight out of Hades. Waving at the blue smoke from her tires, Jack jumped in his cruiser and started it up.

"Are you pulling out?" asked a man, almost directly behind him.

The young detective glanced at the man, and then looked for the red Vette. It was nowhere in sight. Looking back at the main highway offered no help either and the man was still blocking him.

"I say, buddy," said the man loudly. "Are you backing out or what?"

Jack slowly shook his head as he turned the cruiser off. "I may be down, but I'm certainly not out," he answered loudly.

Part 3
Momma Rose

Scheduled to work the weekdays once more, Jack was given the next day off. As luck would have it, a troubled Thomas Greene asked if he could visit the family that Sunday. Shelley responded by extending the invitation to all the Shadow Wolves, but Iron Eyes, Two Bears, and Charlie had other plans. But, as it were, Chee Hatman accepted with Thomas. Being a Shirtman and a Peacekeeper, he knew Thomas was troubled and was more than just a little interested in what he was going to ask Pico.

At eight that morning, Jack had managed only one roll-over toward consciousness. Pico eased to the partially open bedroom door and peeped inside. The aroma of fresh-perked coffee and baking biscuits filled the room.

"Get him up, Pico."

Jack heard Shelley's voice from down the hallway, but his mind didn't quite grasp the situation. Pico, on the other hand, wasted not a second. Running the short distance across the room, she jumped to the middle of the bed and straddled its comatose inhabitant.

"Wake up! Wake up!" said Pico loudly. "Mrs. Shelley said the Indians are gonna be here for supper and she's got the soup beef in the pressure cooker and the sausage and biscuits ready for breakfast."

"Got-cha," replied Jack as he slowly rubbed the sleep from his eyes.

*   *   *

Thirty minutes later, he was standing in the living room entrance way with a cup of coffee in one hand and a sausage and biscuit in the other. Just as he took the second bite of his biscuit, a flash of color through the living room picture window caught his eye. It was the same, dark blue as Chee's Ford 250. Easing inside the living room for a better look, he quickly knew his first guess was right.

172

"Ohhh boy, Shelley," he groaned. "I hope you've got more of those Jimmy Dean biscuits."

"What?" Shelley walked from the kitchen and into the dining area. "Why would you say that?"

Jack smiled back at her. "Your company's here."

"What?" Shelley trotted on toward the living room with Teresa right behind her. "It's hardly nine in the morning and they're here already?"

"Is Chee one of them?" asked Teresa excitedly as she joined Shelley at the window.

Shelley glanced at Jack. "What's wrong with Thomas? Chee's the only one getting out."

Teresa opened the front door, pushing at the screen door as well. "Isn't Thomas coming in?" she asked.

Chee smiled, glancing back at the truck. "He is searching for something and only now he is afraid he'll find it." He looked back at Thomas again. "You can't get your answers from inside the truck," he said, adding a silent chuckle.

Shelley watched Thomas reluctantly drag himself out of the passenger seat and slowly walk toward the porch steps. The aroma of the coffee greeted the two as they followed Shelley and Teresa into the living room. Once there, Thomas stopped abruptly and eyed Pico, now rocking in Bill's old chair. Her smile with raised eyebrows was of one awaiting an easy question.

"I'll get you two some coffee," said Shelley as she coaxed Teresa from the living room to help her.

Thomas nodded and then looked back to Pico. "I've been having dreams, little one," he started. "My grandmother calls to me."

"Are you by yourself in the dream?" asked Pico as she stood from the rocker.

"Does she talk to you?" asked Chee.

Jack looked to see that Chee's question was directed to Pico and not Tomas, and she was slowly nodding. Jack looked at Thomas. "What are you looking for?"

"Answers," replied the Apache. He looked back to Pico. "Momma Rose, my grandmother, came to me in a dream two nights ago. She told me Rosa Little Bird was coming."

173

"Who is she?" asked Teresa.

"My cousin," answered Thomas. "She left Fort Apache Reservation with a half-white man last year. His name is Blue Boy Roberts. He is good for nothing but trouble this one."

"And this Little Bird is coming here?" asked Chee."

Thomas nodded. "Coming to Munford I think." He looked to Jack. "I don't mean to bring my troubles to your people, my Nephilim friend, but I fear she is already in trouble and that is your business."

"Well. . ." Jack paused, scratching his head under his black, detective cap. Glancing at Shelley, he added, "Let's just enjoy the day and I'll brief Will with this information come Monday morning. That way, if I pull off of my assignment to help with your problem, he'll at least know what's going on."

"Agreed," said Chee, not waiting for Thomas to answer.

The older Apache just nodded silently.

*   *   *

Later that afternoon, closer to three than not, found the little group all gathered around the dinner table. Shelley had just brought Thomas his second bowl of beef soup and was heading back toward the kitchen when the phone rang.

"I'll get it," said Teresa.

She popped up from the seat beside Chee and headed toward the living room. Quickly setting down her bowl of peach cobbler and vanilla ice cream on the coffee table, she picked up the phone. Jack listened to the traditional 'Hello' but the 'yes' and strained 'really' got his full attention. He watched her place her hand over the mouthpiece and look toward him.

"Trouble?" asked Jack as he slowly stood from the table.

Teresa shrugged. "It's Betty Lewis, the dispatcher at the Sheriff's Office," she replied. "She said Bubba just brought in a young girl who broke down in Munford."

"Broke down?" queried Jack. "When does the Sheriff's Department provide taxi service for someone who has car trouble?"

174

"Well. . ." Teresa glanced at Chee, and then looked at Thomas. "She kind of hit a utility pole. When Bubba got there, she said she knew the Shadow Wolves and was looking for Thomas."

"Little Bird," said Thomas. Quickly standing, he fumbled with his large glass of iced tea, making Jack flinch as it hit the floor.

"I'll get it," said Shelley as she hustled back from the kitchen with a dish rag. "You'll cut yourself."

"I'm terribly sorry," apologized Thomas, stepping out of the way. "I must of lost my grip on the glass. I will replace it for you."

"Nonsense. Don't worry about it," smiled Shelley. "We have plenty of others. Shall I get you some more tea?"

"No thank you," replied Thomas, now looking at Jack. "Can we follow you to the office?"

"Uhhh. . ." Jack glanced at Shelley. "Yes," replied Jack as he watched the older Apache leave for Chee's truck.

Once Chee was on the front porch, he quickly turned to Jack. "He used to be a Shaman until he lost his wife and little girl to a house fire. He tried to continue with that, but the nightmares destroyed his efforts. He had always been a good tracker, so Two Bears gave him a chance with the Shadow Wolves. As you can see, the Shaman is still in him. The spirits still seek him." He looked toward Shelley, standing at the open, front door. "Thanks for the invite. The soup and cornbread was great. We need to go now and help his cousin." Chee paused again at the steps and looked back at Jack. "When the spirit of Thomas's grandmother contacted him, I'm sure it was not about some car accident. We will have to pull Two Shirts out of retirement again."

*   *   *

The next morning, the 20th of January and a cold and frosty Monday, Jack pulled Uncle Bill's '55 Ford Custom into the Munford Sheriff's parking lot at 6:45AM sharp. Even though he didn't know the Shadow Wolves that well, he felt a strange connection with what Thomas was going through.

"Jack!" spoke someone just as he got out of the Ford.

The young detective turned to see Charlie waving at him from the open door of his trailer. His 'come here' wave and expression didn't translate as one who was pleased with what was going on.

"With me, Banjo," said Jack as he walked briskly toward Charlie.

"The others are inside with Fred," said the old, Clear Water Apache. Sitting down hard on the porch steps, he looked back up as Jack and Banjo walked up. "We need your help, Jack. I need one who walks in two worlds right now."

"That's fine, Charlie," said Jack. "How can I help you?"

Charlie glanced at Banjo and then dropped his gaze to the grass between him and Jack. "Do you remember the one, William Brown?" he asked without looking up.

"Sure I do," answered Jack. "That's my Uncle Bill. I told you of him not long ago."

Charlie slowly nodded with, "He mentored you into the world of the Nephilim. Do you still remember how strange that was?"

"Yes, and still is sometimes. What does that have to do with what's going on right now?"

Charlie slowly looked up at him. "If you agree to help us, you will have to deal with the one called Blue Boy. He is about twice your age, heavyset, not as tall, long, black hair, and dark eyes. He has a bad scar on his left jaw, from below his ear to the top of his chin. He is half Chiricahua and half Navajo. Like you, he lives in two worlds as well. But unlike you, his other world is evil."

"Evil, Charlie?" asked Jack. "Just how is he evil?"

Charlie looked back down at the grass. "He is a witch —a Navajo witch." Looking back up at Jack, he added, "He will not fight you as a human. When he comes, he will be in the wolf—one who walks on two legs."

Jack paused, looking at Charlie. "You mean he's some kind of werewolf?"

"No," replied Charlie abruptly. "He is a skin walker--a witch and a fooler. If you agree to help us, you will have to face him soon."

"Just how does this Blue Boy person fit into this picture?" asked Jack.

With a slight shrug, the old Apache added, "I have seen this in a vision. So has Thomas, but he will not speak of it to you for fear he will bring the witch to himself. He asked me to do this thing for his cousin, Little Bird. She flees from this one and his evil ways. The hold he had over her has made her old before her time." Charlie stood and nodded toward the front door of the Sheriff's Office. "Little Bird is in there. She waits in Will's Office for the one who walks in two worlds. Will you help her? Will you help us?"

"Certainly," replied the young detective as he turned and looked toward the front door.

As he did, a feeling washed over his whole body like a cold shower, but cold showers don't bring visions. Now standing in a well-worn path that came out of a very dark woods, he could make out Thomas walking from the darkness and into the light. The young detective froze, trying to focus on what was following him. As Thomas drew closer, Jack could see the yellow eyes of the creature behind him and it was every bit as tall as the Apache.

"Jack. . ." Charlie took hold of his right forearm and shook it. "Jack!"

"I'm here-I'm here," managed Jack, rubbing the feeling back into his face.

Charlie stepped in front of him, looking closely at his face. "Where did you go?"

"Go?" Jack glanced at the old Indian. "I've been right here, Charlie."

"That is true," replied Charlie, "but for fifteen minutes you stood there, eyes wide open, and froze like a pumpkin in a blizzard. What did you see?"

Jack slowly shook his head. "Not real sure just what to make of what I saw. I was standing in a path that led out of a deep and dark woods. Thomas was walking toward me and there was something following him in the darkness. I couldn't see it that well, but it was as tall as Thomas and had the darnedest, yellow eyes."

"And not human," added Charlie. "This thing you saw was the witch, Blue Boy." Charlie looked away and rubbed his long, grey hair back from his face. "He has touched you. He knows you are with us now. Unfortunate this is. I had hoped for more time." Facing Jack again, Charlie reached into his pocket, pulled out a small leather pouch, and then handed it to Jack. There are six .357 hollow point cartridges in that pouch. A drop of water and an ashen powder was placed in hole of each bullet causing the powder to stick as the water dried."

Jack jiggled the leather pouch, judging the weight of its contents. "I get it," he finally said. "This is kind of a werewolf silver bullet thing."

Charlie rolled his eyes, his gaze ending back up on the young detective. "You've been watching too much Lon Chaney movies. Get your head out of the TV and into the real world, Jack. What I'm tryin' ta say is if you're not in what you call the 'Beast' when this witch comes, you may never see your family again. Now go inside and speak to Little Bird. She needs to know you will help us. I hope I was not wrong."

Jack smiled at Charlie's troubled look. "A Shaman, wrong?" he added with a bit of a grin.

"Retired, Jack. Retired," corrected Charlie.

"I will be there," assured Jack. "If I can't help, it won't be because I didn't try."

Jack turned from the old Indian and walked straight toward the front door with Banjo right behind him. As he entered the lobby, he nodded to Dianne at her desk and then looked to Andy at the Sergeant's Desk.

"Where is the young lady Bubba brought in?" he asked.

"That would be Little Bird," answered Andy. "Her car's a mess, but the pole is fine. I had it towed and Thomas took care of the bill. She's in--"

"Are you Jack?" asked someone from across the lobby.

Jack looked toward the Sheriff's office to see a young, girl of Teresa's age standing in front of Will's open door. Very trim and pretty, she had long, black hair, and was about five feet-eight inches tall.

Rubbing the bruises on her forearms, she added, "Thomas said I should trust you. The old Holy Man said the same. I have something someone wants and he's willing to kill me to get it. The Holy Man said he would ask for your help."

"He has asked and I will help," replied Jack. "What do you have that has kindled this man's anger?"

Little Bird looked down at the handkerchief she was wadding up in her hands.

"A ton of money," interrupted Will, not standing in the doorway right behind Little Bird. "It was stolen from a developer who owns land bordering the White Mountain Apache Reservation in New Mexico. His name is Bob Radford. The money's in the bank right now, awaiting Mr. Radford to sign for it."

"Blue Boy will still come for me," managed Little Bird, still twisting the handkerchief tightly. "I took the money from him while he slept about three days ago."

"You can stay here with us," said Will. "We'll move a bed and chest into the first cell and give you a key. I know it's not the Ritz, but it comes with free meals and no rent." He looked at Jack. "This is Two Bear's case, Jack. This Blue Boy fella is wanted by the Nations." He scratched his head as he seemed to study Jack's expression. "I know you are scheduled ta work days now, Jack. But I'll pay you two hours for comin' in and then, if you will, report back here at 4:00PM to keep an eye on this place while Little Bird is here."

Jack smiled, glancing at Little Bird. "I'll be back at four."

*   *   *

That afternoon, about thirty minutes till four, Jack rolled into the Munford Lot. He noted right off that the place wasn't exactly void of vehicles. Will's Ford was there, with the two Shadow Wolves trucks and Charlie's old truck. Also with them were Dianne's and Lucy's vehicles. Once inside the lobby, he paused, noting Dianne's blank stare. Officer James Williams was sitting in a chair very close to her desk.

"Over here," she mouthed with a quick, 'come here' gesture with her right hand.

Easing in that direction, Jack could see that Andy was too busy with paperwork to note anything.

"What's up?" whispered Jack. "We got wolf trouble already?"

Dianne frowned. "Jack Shoultz, you get serious this very minute," she snapped. "If Charlie heard that, he'd give you another lecture I'm sure. Will briefed us just as soon as Lucy got here and all this weird stuff has got her plum beside herself. She's in the bathroom with Little Bird right now, trying to pull herself together."

"Werewolves," quipped James, now trying to hold back a most obvious grin.

Jack's gaze finally made it to Lucy as she and Little Bird walked out of the ladies' room. But Lucy wasn't grinning at all.

"Are you working here tonight?" asked Lucy, looking straight at Jack.

"I've got the desk," added James.

"I'll be here," replied Jack.

"Where's Banjo?" asked Lucy. Looking about the lobby, she added, "He certainly wouldn't be afraid of that wolf thing."

"Don't think he would," replied Jack, "but he's with Shelley's brother Donnie. He's taken with the family pet, Shadow, and spends more time with the Airedale now-a-days."

"Will said I could use one of the couches in his office," said Little Bird. "There's already someone in the lockup."

"Jonathan Smith," explained Dianne. "He's in the third cell for drunk and disorderly at the Western Auto Store. Will's holding his old white Dodge truck until he pays for the window. Bubba and Will had to almost carry him in just after he brought Little Bird to us and he's been out and under the blanket the whole time.

Jack nodded as he watched Fred and Charlie walk into the lobby and continue on toward Will, now standing at his office door with Little Bird and Lucy.

180

"You here tonight?" asked Will, looking straight at Jack.

Jack nodded silently.

"Good then," replied Will. "Don't rightly know how much stock ta put in Charlie's wolf thing, but given his battin' average, I'd stick close ta here if I were you, Jack. Bubba will be back here ta relieve you at midnight.

Lucy quickly looked at Jack. "You're gonna stay right here with us aren't you?" she asked with no little concern.

Jack nodded. "Right here or on the grounds close outside with my silver bullets."

Charlie immediately mumbled something that Jack couldn't hear. Although it made Little Bird and Will laugh, Lucy wasn't at all amused.

"Well then," replied Will as he walked toward the front door. "We're outta here." Pausing at the door, he looked back at James. "Got a box o' soda crackers on my desk for that old grey in the third cell. Keep an eye on him tonight."

"We got this," replied James half-heartedly.

*   *   *

But Lucy's phone was silent that afternoon, save for the occasional speeder or sign runner. But at 7:10PM, Jack give up on the Press Scimitar's cross-word puzzle, glanced at James, and then looked to Lucy.

"Slow night," groaned Lucy, smiling at his board expression.

"You know. . ." Jack pushed his fingers under his black, detective's cap and scratched his head. "Pauline's Restaurant has a great sausage and mushroom pizza. I'll pay for it if someone will order and fetch it for us."

Little Bird sat up from the closest lobby couch, but said not a word.

"I got this," said James, adding, "Black olives, onions, and bell peppers?"

"Sounds good," agreed Lucy with a nod from Jack. "Can I go?" she asked. "I'll spring for a gallon of her sweet tea with lemon."

"Sure," replied Jack, pulling his wallet out. "Make it two extra-large with extra cheese. I could eat a horse right now."

Watching the two leave the lobby, Jack sat down in Lucy's chair, glanced at the radio, and then leaned back against the wall. "Are you hungry?" he asked, looking at Little Bird.

She smiled with a silent nod.

Jack smiled, leaning back once more against the wall. No sooner had he done that, than he thought he heard a weak "Hello" from somewhere in the room.

Jack looked at Little Bird. "Did you hear that?"

She shrugged with, "I left Mr. Brumley's FM radio on in his office. He said I could listen to it. I hope it's not too loud."

"That's fine," replied Jack. Sitting up once more, he looked toward the partially open cell block door. "I thought I heard something and I don't think it came from Will's office."

Little Bird shrugged her shoulders as Jack walked toward the cell block. Then, as he got within a reach of the door, the weak "Hello" came again and this time it was from inside the block. Looking down the block hallway, he could see a pair of arms extended out between the bars. They were slowly drawn back in the cell and out of sight.

Jack stepped inside, took the keys from the wooden peg just

right of the door, and then proceeded down the hallway toward cell number three. "Are you all right?" he asked as he came closer. "I've got soda crackers if you feel queasy."

The man sat down hard on his cot and glanced up at Jack. Heavy set, in his fifties, grey hair, and about six feet tall, he bowed his head again and groaned softly.

"Take this," the man said weakly. He held out something gold and shiny in the palm of his right hand toward Jack and quite near the bars.

Glancing back toward the still open cell block door, Jack could still hear Will's radio.

182

Jack cautiously watched the man with his head still bowed, and then looked at what appeared to be a gold double eagle in the man's right hand.

"Take it," he said again, gently shaking his hand. "It will pay for my fine."

But, as the young detective reached for the coin, Smith dropped it, grabbed the detective's left hand, and then jerked it so hard, Jack's shoulder became wedged between the bars. With one, strong puff into Smith's left hand, a russet-colored dust engulfed Jack's face and head. Smith immediately released Jack's hand, sat back down on the cot, and then watched the detective free his shoulder and stumble back from the bars to the wall behind him. Finding it with the back of his head and shoulders first, Jack slowly slid down to the floor.

"Breath it in," whispered a deep and guttural voice from somewhere in front of him. But Jack found it hard to focus on anything. Everything was a blurry mess and kept tilting to the left, causing him to constantly push himself back up and away the floor. What's more, now he couldn't see where Smith was.

"Couldn't be easier," said the rough voice as Jack heard the cell keys jingle.

Now, realizing he had dropped them when the stinging dust hit his face, Jack could do nothing but try to focus on the perfectly blurry, black figure now stepping through the door of the cell right in front of him. The snap-popping sound it was making with its teeth was quickly becoming as real as the yellow-eyed creature that was starting to kneel right in front of him.

Ohhh God. . . thought Jack, *it's the thing that followed Thomas from the woods.*

Charlie's warning, "You'll never see your family again," kept running through the young detective's head. With a thump, Jack felt the creature grab his jacket and start to lift him from the floor. The awful stench of the horrible apparition was that of decaying man flesh. With no ability to resist, Jack awaited the blow that was bound to come.

"Get away from him!" shouted someone, seemingly from the cell block doorway.

The voice was strangely familiar—a young girl perhaps. "Little Bird!" said Jack. "Get out of here!"

Try as he did, the young detective couldn't get enough volume for a proper warning. Jack batted his eyes wildly, trying to focus on the beast that was still holding his head and shoulders off the floor. But now the lycanthrope was no longer looking at him. It seemed to be concentrating on the one near the doorway.

"Shut the door!" tried Jack once more. But he could barely get the words out.

Suddenly, something violently shook the right pocket of his jacket, causing Charlie's leather pouch to fall directly into his right hand. Jack could now feel at least four of the .357 cartridges in the palm of his hand. Not only that, but the open pouch, now on the floor right below his right hand, seemed to be shaking wildly, causing a grey dust to rise from it. Releasing Jack's jacket, the wolf creature fell back hard against the bars directly behind him. Coughing and sneezing, he grasped the bars and pulled himself up to a standing position.

"Reload your gun, Jack!" said yet another familiar voice, but this one seemed to be to his right and quite near the back door.

As Jack pulled his Smith and Wesson from its holster, he could see the creature holding to the bars as he worked his way away from Jack and toward Little Bird still at the cell block doorway. As he ejected the shells from the pistol he watched in horror as the young girl seemingly stepped toward the wolf creature and then stumble into the open door of the first cell. Shoving two of the shells into his pistol, Jack fumbled with the third and fourth. As he did, he watch in puzzlement as the cell door seemed to shut itself.

"What the. . ." Jack quickly loaded the other two shells.

Even though the wolf creature glanced back at Jack's remark, his attention was drawn to a shadowy form standing between him and the cell Little Bird was in. Quickly rubbing his eyes, Jack could now make out the infamous walking cane belonging to William Brown. His old but polished western boots and the worn, brown Stetson quickly took form now only a reach from the creature.

"Uncle Bill!" shouted Jack at the smiling face now leaning against the first cell's door.

"Hurry, Jack!" shouted his old mentor. "Time you haven't got, my boy!"

As Jack raised his pistol toward the creature, he quickly realized what the old ghost was talking about. The series of events that happened then were so quick, the young detective could hardly keep up. The cell block door flew open again and in stepped Shelley with Banjo at her side. Seeing the creature between her and Jack, she screamed and fell back against Teresa. Banjo, however, was hardly jaded. Barely flinching from the two blasts toward the creature from Jack's Smith and Wesson, the big Pitt Bull plowed headlong into the lycanthrope, sinking his teeth soundly in his upper, right thigh. Jack instantly put two more rounds into the wolf man's already bleeding back, causing him to grasp the bars of Little Bird's cell. But Banjo was still on him. With a steel trap grip still on his thigh, the big Pit Bull jerked him from the bars. But now with Shelley, Teresa, Donnie and Pico all standing at the Cell Block doorway, Jack couldn't get another safe shot.

"Watch him, Jack!" shouted Shelley as the creature literally ripped his way free of the Pitt, turned, and then ran down the hallway toward him. Pushing himself back against the wall, the young detective fired two more times as the black, yellow-eyed creature bounded past him toward the back door. With black fir and blue smoke in the air, all watched as the wolf man burst through the wooden, back door, fleeing into the darkness with Banjo right behind him.

"Banjo!" screamed Jack as he struggled to gain his footing. "Banjo, come back here," he shouted again.

But the huge Pit Bull had already drawn blood and there was no stopping him now.

"I'll get him!" exclaimed Teresa as she and Donnie brushed by Jack before he could stop them.

"Don't go out there!" shouted Jack as he stopped Shelley and Pico before they could get by them.

But before Teresa and Donnie could get to the shattered, back doorway, three shots rang out in the alleyway, stopping them just outside the doorway. Half staggering and half trotting, Jack quickly worked his way toward the two at the door. But as he did, a smiling face stepped into the light of the room.

"Did the 'Beast' fail you this time, Jack Shoultz?" said Charlie Two Shirts, holding a .44 Colt Magnum in his right hand.

Jack paused beside the girls and cast a relieved look at his old friend.

"Come and get your dog," said Charlie. "He doesn't seem to know what to do right now."

Jack eased out of the doorway with the girls in tow, paused beside the old Apache, and then looked to his left. About twenty paces from where they were standing lay the darkened figure of a man, just past the corner of the building. Still growling, Banjo was slowly circling the lifeless figure, but refusing to attack what now looked to be a man.

Charlie, now laughing, turned to Jack. "You are a lucky bunch, Jack Shoultz, and your brave dog as well. Few who tangle with a shape-shifter will live to tell the tale." He looked back at Shelley, Teresa, Little Bird, and Pico now standing at the doorway. "You'll need a new door I think. Don't believe I can glue this one back together."

Smiling, Jack looked back toward the body of Mr. Smith, only to see Uncle Bill walking past it and out of the dim light of the street lamp. Never turning, he waved one time and then faded into the night.

Part 4
Faux Doppelganger

Old legends, like heroes, can fade away over the years, but urban legends may stay around much longer. Three days later, January 23rd and a Thursday, Jack walked into the lobby of the Munford Sheriff's Office at 7:30AM on the nose. Just as he did, Dianne motioned for him. . .

"What have we got?" asked Jack, grinning at her puzzled expression.

"I thought 'Horned Jack' was on a permanent sabbatical," she quipped. "Will was under the same impression I believe."

Jack slowly raised his eyebrows. "You're both right," he finally replied. "I haven't been in the 'Beast' but a few times in the last month and most were at Will's approval."

Dianne moved a piece of paper to the far side of her desk. "We haven't told Will about this. Your grandfather wanted to speak to you first. Most of these dates Fred has placed you either at home or on duty somewhere else."

Jack picked up the paper. On it were almost a dozen dates from the middle of December to the present. All had notes posted next to them.

"They're sightings, Jack," explained Dianne. "Fred thinks someone is breathing life back into Horned Jack."

The young detective slowly shook his head. "This is definitely not me, Dianne. That is, at least most of them."

Dianne quickly checked Fred's and Will's door. Both were closed.

"I wouldn't lie to you," grumbled Jack. "If we have a copycat, this could get real sticky really quick."

"It already has," said Dianne. "That's why I'm letting you see this right now before you see Fred. He'll have to brief Will on this today." She slowly sat back in her chair, still looking at the young detective. "Do you know who Frank Monroe is?"

Jack look puzzled at the dispatcher. "Is he still here?"

Dianne nodded.

"He's the troublemaker James had to deal with at Hernando's Hideaway about a year ago."

"Well. . ." Dianne slowly shook her head. "Not far from there, at the Emporium in Munford, a young, eighteen-year-old Miss Dorothy Garland was attacked, by Monroe we think. But just about the time the altercation started, someone intervened and our Mr. Frank Monroe got sliced and diced by the one they are all calling Horned Jack. It was so violent that it put Mr. Monroe in Covington's Baptist Memorial. It seems that our Mr. Monroe was at his usual—disturbing the peace at the Hideaway again just before the attack went down."

"What has this to do with me?" asked Jack, with no little interest.

"Nothing with the young detective," said Dianne, "but Dorothy's white knight was very tall and was dressed just like Horned Jack--sharp claws and all."

"Is Fred putting me on this one?"

"I think so," answered Dianne. "But this time, Bubba is going with you. He'll be able to attest to where you go and what you might have to do. Besides, Fred said it might take Horned Jack to catch this fake." She smiled, looking toward the clock behind the Sergeant's Desk. "You might better go clock in and then check with Fred. If Will signs off on this, you and Bubba with be off toward the hospital I'm sure."

"And he said Go," spoke Fred, now walking across the lobby from his office. He looked at Jack. "Bubba's gonna be a tad late. He had a flat about a mile from here. Just as soon as he gets here, you two head for the hospital and check on our Mr. Monroe. Get his statement and get this damn doppelganger off our backs before Horned Jack gets famous all over again. And, if at all possible, you keep a check on the 'Beast'." He then handed a piece of paper to Jack. "This is information on one, Miss Dorothy Garland. She lives in Munford, just this side of the Camp Grounds. She's the young lady that our Mr. Monroe attacked behind the Emporium. Get her statement as well."

*   *   *

188

Now, with Jack's mind was spinning not only about the imposter, but also the trouble he could create for Horned Jack. At almost 9:00AM, Jack and Bubba pulled into the hospital parking lot in Jack's unmarked.

"Troubled?" asked Bubba. "You haven't talked much since we left. Will brief you?"

The young detective slowly nodded. "It seems that someone is imitating Horned Jack," replied the young detective as he parked his cruiser.

Bubba rolled his eyes. "What if this guy kills someone, Jack? He'd go from something mysterious and good to something to be feared on Halloween."

"Well. . ." Jack got out with Bubba. "Let's go and see what this Monroe has to add to our puzzle."

As the two walked into the Baptist Memorial, the young, desk clerk recognized the tall detective immediately. Thumbing through the registration book, she quickly turned it toward them as they walked up.

"Remember me?" She smiled at Jack. "I'll bet you're gonna want to see that Mr. Monroe fella. He's the only one here with a police guard at his door." She smiled warmly at Bubba.

Jack returned her smile. "You bet I remember you, and we're here to see that very man."

"This is gonna be a quiet visit, isn't it?" asked the receptionist. "The last time you were here you caused quite a stir with that ghost or person you were after. Did you catch him? The paper said it was a man, but security called it a ghost."

Jack nodded. "I believe we got to the bottom of it. What room is our Mr. Monroe in?"

"Room two-twelve," answered the receptionist. "Please be a little quieter this time if at all possible."

"Lord help us," groaned Bubba, rolling his eyes. "That's our lucky floor all right." He glanced at Jack as they walked toward the elevator. "James said every time he works with you, he gets thrown in the stew."

Jack laughed silently as he pushed the 'up' button. "I can smell the carrots and potatoes starting to simmer right now."

Stepping out of the elevator and onto the second floor, Jack instantly spotted Head Nurse Goodwell behind the desk.

"Lord save us," she said weakly as her eyes grew big. "Should I call security right now, or wait 'till someone dies?"

"Neither I hope," laughed Jack. "We're here to see Mr. Monroe."

Mrs. Goodwell nodded down the hallway. "Can't miss 'em. His room's the one with a policeman at the door. He claims he was attacked at the Emporium by that one they've been callin' Horned Jack. Looks like somebody got after him with a Weed Eater. The doc on duty worked with him over three hours and a hundred or more stitches. Please try to hold it down this time if you can."

Jack nodded as he and Bubba walked from the desk. As he did, he noticed that Bubba kept looking back toward the desk.

"What is it?" asked Jack, glancing toward the desk also.

"Awww nothin' I suppose," answered the big deputy. "Just can't get over the last splutterment we had here."

The Covington policeman at the door nodded toward the two as they walked up. "Chief said you would be here today. Something about a connected case you had going."

"Yep," answered Bubba. "Hope we get a lead or two right here."

Jack tapped on the door to two-twelve as he slowly eased it open.

"Come right in," said a middle-aged man, eying Bubba as he stepped in. Sitting up in his bed with a robe on, he looked to be dark-haired and in his early thirties. "I expected. . ."

Monroe's voice quickly trailed off as Jack ducked under the door molding and walked in behind Bubba. Pushing himself back upon his pillows, he watched as Jack walked to the foot of his bed.

"Why. . .you're as tall as that Horned Jack fella who attacked me," he complained loudly.

"Everything all right in here?" asked the guard, now standing in the doorway.

"I guess," answered Bubba. "He seems to be afraid of our Detective." Bubba looked back to Mr. Monroe. "We're from the Sheriff's office, Mr. Monroe. Detective Shoultz here would like to ask you a few questions if you feel up to it."

"Fine," replied Mr. Monroe, still eying Jack.

"The one who attacked you, what did he look like?" asked Jack.

"Very tall. Just like you. Had on an old, red plaid shirt faded jeans, and a faded, denim jacket. His skin was dark tanned. He had black gloves on but his claws stuck our right through them."

"What about his eyes," asked Jack.

"Eyes?" The man squinted, as he looked at Bubba.

"Did they glow?" asked the big Deputy.

"Didn't notice," answered Mr. Monroe. "I was too busy dodging those damned claws."

"Did he say anything to you?" asked Jack.

"Yes," answered Mr. Monroe just as Mrs. Goodwell walked in. Adjusting the IV bottle, she looked back at Jack.

"Don't mind me," said the nurse. "This'll just take a second or two."

"The voice," prompted Bubba, looking at Monroe. "Did it sound high-pitched, deep, or normal?"

"Average I guess," replied Mr. Monroe. "No deeper than any other man I suppose. Kept calling me knucklehead."

Nurse Goodwell walked by Jack and Bubba and paused at the door, looking back. "This fella's a wanna-be, Jack. I've patched up what some say this Horned Jack had at. The wounds were like that of a big cat. Mr. Monroe here has ultra-thin slashes just like a razor makes." She smiled at jack. "If this is your case, old Will Brumley has given you another dandy. This guy's Looney Tunes and he's not gonna stop unless you stop 'em. The police say this is the third one he's attacked, but first, real blood."

"Third?" Jack looked at Bubba.

"Don't look at me," said Bubba. "I don't know where Dianne gets her information."

"From me," spoke someone behind them.

Jack turned to see the Munford Police sergeant standing in the doorway. "Wild Bill wasn't the least bit pleased."

Bubba noted at the sergeant's stripes. "Missed those stripes when we walked in. How do we get a sergeant pulling guard duty at a hospital room?"

Five feet, eight inches tall, about two hundred pounds, with sandy hair, the policeman smiled at Bubba. "Sergeant Dunn, Al to my friends." He glanced at Jack. "Didn't go by proper protocol this time Mr. . ." The Sergeant raised his eyebrows, looking at Jack.

"Sorry about that," started Jack, offering his hand. "I'm Detective Shoultz, and this is Sergeant Watkins."

"Bubba to my friends," added the Sergeant, offering his hand as well.

"Glad to meet you," said Sergeant Dunn. "Some time ago, I told Dianne that I would share any information that came across my desk about your Horned Jack." He smiled at them both. "Crazy about Dianne I am. Now it seems that Wild Bill's got a thing about proving whether this Horned Jack thing is real or not."

"Uhhh, Wild Bill?" queried Bubba.

Sergeant Dunn smiled. "That would be our Chief, William O. Gillespie--Oscar to his friends." He looked back to Jack. "He spoke several times last month to Sheriff Brumley about this character, but he would only change the subject." He motioned toward Monroe in the bed. "Now, we got this and Wild Bill's back in the saddle again."

Jack stepped closer to Sergeant Dunn. "Is there anything you can tell me about our Mr. Monroe?"

Sergeant Dunn shrugged. "Like the nurse said, he is the third one. Had a few other Horned Jack sightings between these assaults, but they proved only close encounters I think or just plain made up. But then, the claws came out." He stepped

192

inside the room, closed the door, and then looked back at Jack. "On the second assault, one of our detectives found a Willow Road Inn napkin at the scene. The alcohol on it smelled fresh. You need to get the old Sheriff to share more information than he's doing right now."

Jack's gaze dropped to the floor and then slowly made its way to Bubba. "I guess this puts me back at the Willow Road Inn again."

"Yep," agreed Bubba. "But you ain't after a motorcycle gang now. This time it's just one man."

Jack nodded. "We need to go and have a little talk with Miss. Garland before we tackle the Inn. She lives at 4219 Drummonds Road, right across from the high school."

*   *   *

At 11:30AM that same morning, Jack and Bubba pulled into the driveway at the Garland home. A young brunette in her late teens opened the front door and peered through the screen. Her big, hazel eyes seemed to be glued on Jack as the two got
out of the unmarked Ford.

Pushing the screen door open, she stepped out on the front porch as the two approached the steps. "My parents will be back soon," she said, still holding to the screen door.

Pausing at the steps, Jack smiled at her. "Are you Dorothy Garland?"

She nodded silently. Dressed in a thin, blue blouse and Levis, her petite frame looked to be barely five and a half feet tall.

Jack tipped his cap at her. "I'm Detective Shoultz from the Munford Sheriff's department and the big fellow here is Sergeant Watkins."

"Bubba," corrected the Deputy. With a broad smile, he tipped his hat as well.

"I guess you're here about that fella who attacked me last night, aren't you?" she asked, returning the Deputy's smile.

"Not really, no Ma'am," replied Bubba. "You see, we got him. We would like ta know what you saw of the one who pulled him off you."

Miss. Garland's eyebrows slowly rose. "Scary," she finally managed weakly. "At least, from what I could see of him. It was kind of dark back there. I was taking out the trash last night and left the back door open for more light. Just when I put the two bags I had in the dumpster, the light from the doorway went out. I just froze, staring at the closed, back door. I didn't even see this Monroe guy until he grabbed me and started tearing my blouse off. I screamed, but not a soul inside the Emporium heard me. The next thing I knew, he had ripped off my bra and was forcing me to bend over the hand rail next to the dumpster. In little time, he had my jeans down to my knees." She glanced at jack, and then looked back to Bubba.

"That's when Horned Jack came. He jerked the man off me like he was a baby."

Bubba glanced at Jack with raised eyebrows and then looked back to Dorothy. "Did you see any part of this fella who came to your rescue?"

"Kind of." The young girl forced a smile. "When this Monroe fella was pulled off of me, I pulled up my jeans, grabbed my bra, and then ran back and opened the back door." She glanced at Jack. "Knowing that now I had more light, I just had to look back. This tall thing-of-a-creature was holding him up like a rag doll and slashing him with claws like some kind of werewolf or something." She looked at Jack with a half-smile. "I was told it was Horned Jack 'cause that's what he does." She shrugged, holding the smile. "I've never seen him before, but I'm sure glad he came to help me last night."

"Well. . ." Bubba looked to Jack and then back to Miss. Garland. "Do remember anything else—eyes, hat, skin color?

"I suppose so," started Miss. Garland. "When he pulled that Monroe fella off of me, I got a whiff of his breath."

"Horned Jack's breath?" asked Bubba.

194

Miss. Garland nodded. "I got a strong whiff of hard liquor laced with a strong, tobacco odor."

"Well that's somethin'," replied Bubba, glancing back at Jack. "You ready to tackle Willow Road Inn again?"

Jack nodded without a word.

*   *   *

About two hours later, around 2:30PM, put the two finishing their meal at Nat's BBQ On Getwell, just a block from the Inn. Jack eased his unmarked down the street and then pulled it into the Willow Road Inn parking lot.

Bubba nodded toward the three, Harley bikes that were already there. "Are those the same group that gave you a fit tryin' ta find Old Yopp?"

"Some of the same I think," replied Jack as he pulled in three spaces from the bikes. He glanced at Bubba as they got out. "Watch them, Bubba. If they get up to leave, they might mess with the car."

Opening the front door, Jack stepped just inside the doorway and stopped. The blonde bartender spotted him right away. Bubba instantly caught the smile on her face.

"Wow," said the big deputy just under his breath. "That's a bit more than friendly, Jack--petite, blonde, blue-eyed and thirtyish. She looks truly glad to see you."

"Snap out of it," grumbled Jack as they slowly walked toward the bar. "Watch our friends at the table on the left and run interference with the barmaid."

"Sorry about your old friend," said the barmaid. As she wiped at a spot on the bar, she gave a quick nod toward the three bikers at the table close to the wall on her right. "Tall Sheriff's detectives aren't exactly popular right now."

The bikers slowly got up with their eyes glued to Jack. Stepping between Jack and their table, Bubba watched them closely as they headed toward the front door.

Jack returned her smile. "Maryland, isn't it?" he asked.

She nodded as she leaned across the bar, close to the two. "You better watch your car from the table at one of the front windows," she whispered.

195

"I got this," said Bubba as he instantly made his way to the table just left of the front door.

Maryland leaned back, winking at Jack. "I know you didn't come just to see me, Jack Shoultz. What's going on now?"

Jack returned her smile as he slipped up on the swivel, stool seat. "Have you ever heard of the urban legend called Horned Jack?"

She shrugged, wiping at the bar top again. "Only what I've read in the paper, mainly last year. He kind of gave the bad people a fit, didn't he?"

"That he did," said Jack. "But now, someone is cashing in on his reputation." He paused, looking at Maryland. "This fella would have to be really tall."

"Do you mean a copycat?" she asked.

Jack nodded.

"Gene!" she said loudly as she looked back toward the kitchen through the service window.

"Trouble?" came the voice from the kitchen. A middle-aged man with a white, chef's hat looked through the window at the two.

"No trouble so far," said Maryland. "Do you remember the name of the delivery guy from Whole Foods?"

"Sure. That would be Bill Pierce." Gene glanced at Jack. "Is he in some kind of trouble?"

Maryland shrugged, looking back to Jack. "Besides you, Bill is the only other really tall fella I know." She smiled at Bubba, holding it until he did the same. "Why don't you join him? I just made a fresh pot of coffee and I'll bring you two some."

Bubba raised his eyebrows, looking at Jack.

"Well. . ." Jack slipped from the stool. "Sounds good to me. It's not far from getting off time anyway," he added, as he walked toward, Bubba's table.

In less than five minutes, Maryland was filling their cups, adding two slices of pecan pie. "On the house," she said, winking at Bubba. But just as she walked away, the front door opened and along with it came a familiar voice.

"Sweet Maryland Roe," said the man boldly as he walked through the door. "How's my favorite barmaid?"

"Shhh," hissed Jack. "That's Wild Bill, Munford's Chief," he whispered. Noting that the front door opened toward them and blocked the Chief's view, the two sat quiet and listened.

About the same age as the Sheriff, the old fellow stepped in, smiling broadly at Maryland, who knew full well the game was afoot with the three. Thinning, white hair, an inch or two shy of six feet tall with a medium build, he turned away from Jack and Bubba to ease the door shut.

"You look sharp today," said Maryland. "Khaki pants, blue shirt and jacket and even a new, beige Stetson."

The old Chief smiled. "Tell me, Sweetie, has Bill made his run for Whole Foods yet?"

Bubba's eyebrows slowly rose.

"You missed him, Oscar," answered Maryland. "He was here about five hours ago." Her smile widened. "You after more free dinner rolls?"

"Awww no, Maryland," chuckled the Chief. "He does odd jobs for me sometimes and I got a hum--"

The old fellow's words froze in his mouth as he spotted the barmaid's quick glance back at Jack and Bubba.

Slowly turning, he spotted the two. "Well-well, Officer Watkins. The last time I saw you, you were with Memphis."

"Moved to Atoka," replied Bubba as he and Jack stood.

The Chief slowly looked to Jack. "And you must be Will's new Detective."

"Jack Shoultz, Sir. Glad to meet you," replied the young detective with a slight nod.

The old Chief glanced back at Maryland and then looked to Jack. "What's the Sheriff's Detective doing these days?"

Jack forced a half-smile. "Chasing my tail right now it seems. But I usually end up with both hands on it before the game's over."

Holding his smile, Chief Gillespie turned and continued toward the bar where Maryland was stocking the rear shelves with liquor. When he got close to the bar, he whispered something to her. She nodded a 'yes',

197

causing him to turn and make his way back toward the front door.

Tipping his hat, he said, "Have a good day, boys, and tell old William that the game is still afoot."

Bubba, with his eyes locked on the old Chief, watched him until he shut the front door. "What's this 'game' thing?" he asked with his eyes still on the door.

Jack slowly shook his head. "I'm afraid to ask. Will's gonna have to put a handle on that one."

"Yep," replied Bubba, rubbing his face. "He was silently laughing when he left." He glanced back at Jack. "Sounds like there's some history goin' on between those two."

*   *   *

Shortly after 4:00PM, and back at the station, Jack and Bubba wasted little time getting inside. Seeing Will's door closed, the two proceeded toward Dianne's desk.

"Is Will here?" asked Jack. "I see his cruiser outside."

"Ohhh my," groaned Dianne. "I'm afraid to ask what's going on."

"We need your help," whispered Bubba.

"What now?" She glanced cross-eyed at Jack.

"Just a little history lesson," replied Jack. "I know you're a lot more connected to the grapevine than any of us. About an hour ago, Bubba and I were at the Willow Road Inn looking for a suspect in this Horned Jack copycat thing when who should walk in but Wild Bill himself."

"Oscar?" Dianne's chin slowly dropped as Jack and Bubba nodded.

"What's the connection between him and Will right now? When he left, he said to tell Will that the game is still afoot."

Dianne slowly sat back in her chair. "Great Caesar's ghost," she groaned weakly. She slowly stood from her chair and glanced at Will's still closed door. "There is no connection," whispered Dianne. Some time ago, when they were both in the Memphis Police Academy, Will caught Oscar and two others smoking pot and going over hot transcripts of the next two tests. Somehow, and I

198

don't know how, that news got back to one of the head instructors. The transcripts and pot were found in Oscar's room the next day. All three were given a chance to bow out gracefully. Oscar went on to Jackson, Tennessee to finish at the Academy. Will graduated at the top of his class and came here. Oscar eventually came to Munford and ended up where you see him now. The air stayed tepid, to say the least, between the two. About ten years or so ago, Oscar went on a vendetta against the bootleggers from Drummonds and Guilt Edge. One of Will's deputy's stepped in to stop a senseless beating of one of the haulers and was arrested by Oscar himself. Will quickly questioned a member of the hauler's family and found out that he was giving someone a cut to haul to Munford. Thinking it was probably Oscar, Will went straight to the Munford Police office to get his man. Both him and Oscar had a heated, closed door discussion. I don't know just what proof Will had, but he walked out in less than thirty minutes with his deputy."

Jack nodded, glancing at Bubba. "Then I really need to give that message to Will right now, Dianne."

"What message?" asked a familiar voice from across the lobby.

All three turned to see Will standing at his open door.

"How much did you hear?" asked Jack.

"I heard that Oscar said 'The game is still afoot.'" He looked over his reading glasses at Dianne. "I can only surmise that you know the rest of the story."

"Yes, Sir," admitted Jack with a silent nod from Bubba.

"And he gave you that message?" asked Will.

"That's about the size of it," replied Bubba.

Will's gaze slowly made its way to Dianne. "Your history goes back about as far as mine, Dianne. What do you think Oscar's got on his mind now?"

"Ohhh boy," said Dianne as she eased around the desk and stopped beside Jack. "You know, I'm just guessing here, but would revenge about that school thing be out of the question? We hardly work with Munford unless we have to. Some time ago you forced him to turn your

199

deputy loose when he stopped a bootlegger from being beaten. Maybe his game now is getting even."

"Even?" Will looked at Jack and Bubba. "Will you two please help me get a handle on this before it comes to a pimple-poppin' head? I know you two got your hands full with this imposter thing, but this is important to me."

"Well. . ." Bubba glanced at Jack. "He did whisper somethin' to Maryland before he left."

"And Maryland is. . ." Will looked over his glasses again.

"The barmaid at Willow Road Inn," answered Jack. "Before we left, I asked her about it and she said she was asked to tell Bill Pierce, our suspect, that he had another job for him."

"Well-well," said Will, now smiling at Dianne. "It seems that the game is indeed afoot and it seems old Oscar has made the first move." He looked straight at James. "The first thing tomorrow morning, you two get together again and find our mister Pierce. Press 'em. Perhaps he can provide a piece or two for our puzzle as well as this Horned Jack imposter."

Book 4
Running on Empty

Part 1. The Impostor

Evil is oft times hard to see--
Masked by those with friendly faces.
But the test of Time oft brings to thee
The truth as it finally escapes its traces.

Part 1
The Imposter

Working in a small town like Munford and the surrounding area can, at times, be a love-hate situation for policemen. Being able to help the people you know is definitely the upside. But having to deal harshly with some of those same people can also be a slippery slope leading to the other direction. In the latter case, a person might need a good compass and a strong anchor when the weather turns foul and the dark clouds began to form. Acting upon the Sheriff's orders, Friday morning on the 23rd of January, Jack and Bubba headed away from Munford at 7:30AM sharp. Knowing that Bill Pierce's run would get him to Willow Road Inn between nine and ten that morning, Jack let up on the gas and tried to enjoy the beautifully crisp and clear Friday. Not much more than forty-five minutes later, they were pulling into the Willow Creek Community and eying the Inn, not that far down the street. . .

"Jack. . ." Bubba checked his watch. "They serve breakfast here from eight till eleven or so. Have you eaten?"

Jack smiled. "If you call a Jimmy Dean sausage and biscuit and a cup of coffee breakfast, I guess I have." He smiled at Bubba.

Bubba grinned with, "Sausage gravy and biscuits, country fried potatoes with onions, scrambled eggs with cheese, and--"

"All right already," said Jack as his white flag went up. "We can watch from one of the front tables I guess."

Once inside, the barmaid spotted them. Smiling broadly, she walked from behind the bar and straight to their table. "Just can't get enough of me, can you fellas?" she said, eying Bubba particularly.

"Nooo Ma'am," grinned the big sergeant. "I heard you had a great breakfast."

"Yep," replied Maryland, her smile widening. "Everything here is good to eat.'

"Uhhh, Yes. Well. . ." Bubba glanced at Jack. "Two eggs scrambled with cheese beside and order of biscuits and gravy and bacon for me."

"That's me as well," agreed the young detective. "Has your Whole Foods man been here yet?"

"Bill?" Maryland shook her head, glancing at her watch. "It's not quite 9:00AM yet. He usually gets here about 9:15AM or so.

"How much do you know about him? What kind of guy is he?" asked Jack.

Maryland shrugged. "I don't date him if that's what you mean. When he started this run over a year ago, he wore khaki pants and a solid color Polo shirt. But for the last few months, he's been dressing like Paul Bunyan or something."

"Paul Bunyan?" Bubba's stare was blank at best.

"Yes. You know--that fella who chops down big trees and runs around with a blue ox. Always wears those lumber jack shirts and jeans." She smiled at Jack, "I'll get your order in right away and bring your coffee in a jiffy." Looking at Bubba, she added, "I'm free this Saturday, you know." and then walked back toward the bar.

Jack glanced at Bubba. "Couldn't be this easy could it?"

Bubba slowly shook his head. "She could, but this case wouldn't. Stranger things have happened, I guess. But remember what the Sheriff said, if this guy gets froggy, don't go Horned Jack on him. I'll take care of him."

Making short work of breakfast, the two sat back, nursing their third cup of coffee when Bubba noticed a white, delivery truck turn into the lot and head around toward the back of the restaurant. The big, black letters spelling out Whole Foods was hard to miss.

"Steady," said Jack, noting that Bubba was about to get up.

"Maryland," called Gene from the kitchen. "Bill's here. Come and check him in if you're not busy."

204

"I got him," answered Maryland as she walked down the short hallway toward the back door.

Jack slowly stood, looking at Bubba. "Go and check out his truck while I keep him busy in here."

*   *   *

Once outside, Bubba eased around the north side of the restaurant to the drive that led to the back of the Inn. There he waited until Bill rolled his loaded dolly into the back door. Drifting closer to the truck, he could hear Maryland and Jack talking to him. Their tone sounded calm.

"Well. . ." Bubba looked toward the open, back doors of the big bread truck, but opted for the passenger side door instead. As luck would have it, there was an opening between the seats that led straight to the back of the truck. Besides the usual wares of one delivering in the baking and fresh food business, nothing looked out of place. But then he spotted a small, black suitcase neatly stuck behind the passenger's seat. Pulling it out, he quickly opened it.

"Awww, it can't be this easy," he whispered, looking at a black toboggan lying over what looked to be leather gloves with razor-like, three inch claws made into the tips of the fingers. Neatly folded beneath them, was a faded, red plaid shirt and a pair of faded, blue Levis. Slowly pulling his pistol, Bubba eased to the still open back and peeped around toward the back door of the Inn. Seeing all were still inside, he stepped from the van and proceeded to the back door of the Inn. Looking through the screen door, he could readily see his suspect as he handed Maryland some of the things he had brought inside. Jack, only about six inches taller than Bill, was on the far side talking to him as he worked. Bubba eased the door open, crept down the short hallway, and then paused by the open kitchen doorway.

"Good Lord," whispered Gene, noting that the deputy had already drawn his pistol.

"Shhh," hissed Bubba softly and then mouthed, "Stay right there."

205

Seeing Bubba had drawn his pistol, Jack eased back a half step, keeping his eyes on Pierce as he handed her a case of napkins.

"Don't move," said Bubba, now about five feet from Pierce. "Keep your hands where I can see 'em."

Pierce froze, looking at Maryland, and then slowly moved his gaze to check Jack. The look upon his face was that of a ten-year-old who had just been caught in a lie by his father. Seeing Jack had pulled his weapon also, he slowly turned toward Bubba. "What's goin' on?" he asked. "I'm answering the detective's questions. Why the gun?"

"Well it's my turn," said Bubba, quickly glancing at Jack. "You tell me what's in the little, black suitcase tucked behind the driver's seat in your van."

Pierce's chin dropped. "You don't understand." He quickly turned to Jack. "Neither of you understand!" he repeated, louder. "I'm only doing good. Horned Jack's hardly heard from anymore. Besides, I'm only doing what I'm told."

Bubba backed up a half step. "Someone told you to impersonate this Horned Jack fella?"

"Told you he was way out there," said Maryland, slowly backing to the far side of the bar.

Jack glanced at Maryland. "You just stay right there and listen to what he says. I'm gonna need a witness to this."

"Goood Lord, what next," groaned the barmaid.

Pierce slowly raised his hands and backed up against his dolly. "I'm not afraid. I got the Munford Police on my side."

"Munford Police?" echoed Jack.

"Well, Sheriff," quipped Bubba. "Looks like Christmas ain't over yet."

"I'm not saying anything else," grumbled Pierce. "When I get my call, it's going straight to the Chief of Police."

"Good," agreed Jack. "Call your boss right now and tell him to send someone to take care of your truck. You're going with us. I also have someone who would just love to talk to you. Gonna give him a buzz on the radio just as soon as we get you comfortable in the back seat."

*   *   *

Back at the office, Will was waiting for them at Dianne's desk. Fred Shoultz, the Chief of Detectives, followed the four into Will's office, all taking seats near Will's desk. Jack placed the black suitcase next to Will's chair.

The old Sheriff opened the suitcase and looked down at the contents. "Well. . ." He smiled at Pierce. "You're certainly tall enough to pull off a good Horned Jack. Why did you do it?"

"I want that call," grumbled Pierce, glancing at Jack.

"Make it so, Jack," said Will. "He can do it in Fred's office."

Fred followed him into his office and pointed out the phone. Partially closing the door from the outside, he quickly looked to Dianne and then mouthed, "Monitor that call." Dianne immediately put Fred's line on the speaker, turned it down a little, and then grabbed a pad and pen. When Pierce had finished, Fred led him back to the Sheriff's office where he was seated right in front of Will's desk. As Fred took a seat on the couch next to Jack, Dianne walked in, handed her pad to Will, and then paused at the doorway. The old Sheriff immediately put his reading glasses on, sat back in his chair, and then looked over the dispatcher's notes.

"Mr. Pierce. . ." Will paused, looking up from the pad at the man. "Do you know what you can get for scaring the bageebers out o' five of our citizens and puttin' one in the hospital?"

"I never hurt her," said Pierce. "I only saved her from getting hurt."

"Not talkin' 'bout the girl," said Will. "I'm particularly speakin' 'bout the one you sent to the hospital with these." Will tossed the razor gloves to his desk top and slowly sat back in his swivel rocker. "I know what shape you left Miss Garland's attacker in. Just what do you think would happen if the real Horned Jack got a hold of you?"

207

Pierce, remaining silent, slowly slumped down in his chair.

"He's not real--just a fable," he managed weakly. "He's an urban legend that folks talk about and make up stories and such." He looked up at the old Sheriff. "You don't expect me to believe he's real, do you?"

Smiling, Will looked through Dianne's notes again. "I see you made a call to Oscar Gillespie, Munford's Chief of Police." He looked up at Pierce. "You left him a message —'I did what you wanted, now come and get me out of jail.' you said." Will sat up, took off his reading glasses, and then sat them on his desk. "Just what did old Wild Bill ask you to do for him?"

Pierce grew dark and sullen. "I want a lawyer. I don't have to say a word to you."

"That's fine," said Will, "and we want you to have one. But I'm afraid it's a bit too late for that right now. You've already admitted to the assault as well as the copycat thing. I'll bet our lab can get blood samples off of these gloves as well. The only thing you need to do right now is to help yourself and you can start doin' that by answerin' my last question--What did Chief Gillespie ask you to do?"

"Will. . ." spoke Andy with a soft knock on the still open door.

"Yes, Sir, Andy," said Will as all looked toward the door at the Desk Sergeant.

"We just got a call from Chief Gillespie," said Andy with raised eyebrows. "He'll be here in five minutes. He said that Mr. Pierce is an informant and an operative in an ongoing case."

"Ohhh boy," groaned Dianne as she left the doorway and walked briskly toward her desk.

"Good," chuckled the old Sheriff, glancing at Jack. "Maybe we can get to the bottom of your Horned Jack copycat today." He looked at Bubba. "Sir, will you please put Mr. Pierce in our very best cell."

*   *   *

Fifteen minutes later, Chief William O. Gillespie marched into the lobby. Hitting heavy on his heels and hardly afforded Dianne a glance, he glared at Andy behind

208

the Sergeant's Desk and then walked straight toward Will's office. Seeing the door partially open, he continued inside and then shut it.

"Come right in," said Will as he got up from behind his desk. "Have a seat right there on the couch, Oscar, and I'll join you. Perhaps you can shed some light on the rather strange goings on around here."

Oscar glanced at Fred and Bubba, and then glared at Jack as he took a seat across from them, on the couch with Will.

Will's gaze went to Oscar, then back at Jack. "This is my new Detective Jack Shoultz, Oscar. I believe you two have already met." He then looked at Jack. "This is your case, Jack. Go ahead and start this thing."

The young detective slowly looked to the Chief of Munford's Police Department. "How is it that a man impersonating a popular, urban myth is working for you?"

"How do you know that?" asked the Chief, now glaring again at Jack. "I didn't come here to be questioned by a green detective like a common suspect," he snapped. "Did he make some kind of statement? If he did, I hope you got witnesses."

"He made an outright statement in a message to you that said he did what you wanted," said Jack. "He also stated that he had the Munford Police on his side."

"I got no such statement," snapped Oscar. "I don't know what you're talking about."

"Now-now boys, play nicely," chuckled the old Sheriff. "He's just askin' a viable question, Oscar. Were you havin' our prisoner impersonate Horned Jack, and for what reason?"

The Chief slowly sat back, his eyes locked on Jack.

"Don't dance around this thing with me, Oscar," snapped Will. "I heard the one call and he nailed you with it."

Oscar rolled his eyes, slowly sat up on the edge of the couch, and then looked straight at the old Sheriff. "You're not the only one with access to the CIA investigations and MUFON files as well. I think there's more to this urban legend thing than you or MUFON would have any us to

209

know." He glared at Will. "If this alien thing is a threat, in any way, to the people of Munford or even Tipton County, they have a right to know."

"Alien?" said Will weakly.

Bubba slowly got up, tried to rub the smile off of his face, and left the office. Although he didn't outright laugh, he was certainly struggling with it.

Will got up as well and returned to the swivel chair behind his desk. "Tell me. . ." The old Sheriff slowly sat down, "just who did you talk to at MUFON?"

"Larry Noles," replied Oscar, leaning forward a bit. "He works with Eddie Miles on investigations and such. He said he saw the weapon you gave Eddie and described it as 'other worldly'. He also said that one of your deputies actually shot down the alien's craft. Was it killed?"

"Killed?" Will glanced at Jack and then slowly sat back in his chair.

"Yes, killed," snapped Oscar. "Is Noles speaking of this Horned Jack fella—eyes that glow green, eight feet tall with horns and dark skin. Is this the alien that was shot down? Was he killed?"

"You can't kill an Urban Legend, Oscar," said Fred as Bubba's laughter could now be heard outside. "Most of 'em only live in the minds of novelists and Hollywood movie producers."

Oscar, now looking a bit indignant, slowly stood from the couch. "William Brumley, I'm the Chief of Munford's Police. When you decide to quit sweeping this under the carpet, give me a buzz. Maybe then, I can help you." Walking toward the office door, he paused and looked back at Will. "I would like to speak to this Pierce fellow who said he worked for me."

"In due time, Oscar, in due time," agreed Will.

Oscar nodded slowly. "In the meanwhile, if this alien thing harms anyone, you'll see more of me than you would want. You know more that you're tellin', Will Brumley. Mark my words, the truth will eventually seep through the cracks."

Spinning around, the Chief of Munford's Police stomped out of the Sheriff's office, continued on through

210

the lobby, and then left without another word. Andy stepped from behind the Sergeant's Desk and looked puzzled at those now gathering at Will's door.

"What?" said Will, looking at Andy. "I tried to be polite. He was lookin' for Horned Jack the alien. I don't think he could deal with the little Grey who flew that glowin' thing that Jack shot down."

"But he didn't fess up to hiring that Horned Jack impersonator," said Bubba.

"Sure he did." Will winked at Jack. "Didn't you hear him say he would like to speak to that Pierce fella? Not a one of us give him his name. Now, just how did he know who he was?"

Jack slowly copied Bubba's smile. "There's another piece of the puzzle, I guess."

*   *   *

Now, with the old sheriff and MUFON having exposed a Black Ops connection in the wrongful conviction of Larry Call, things still were still not exactly as usual. The back of his neck still had that 'someone's watching' itch. Old Charlie's referral to the 'Deep State' still weighed heavy on his mind. He had given them a big black eye and MUFON was now publicizing the event almost every week. But for the Sheriff's Office, the new week started and continued calmly right on into the morning of Wednesday, January 25th. That morning, just as soon as Dianne had stepped into the lobby for her day shift, Oscar Gillespie walked right in behind her. . .

"Can I help you?" asked Dianne, quickly stepping to one side.

"Yes Ma'am," replied the Chief of Munford's Police as he slowly removed his light brown Stetson.

Dressed in khaki pants, light brown shirt, and russet-colored hounds tooth sport jacket, he rather looked more like he was going to church.

Smiling at Dianne, he added, "I see Will's Ford is already here. Could you see if he can spare a minute with me?"

"Sure, Oscar. He's in his office by himself. Probably reading the morning paper," replied the receptionist. "Just come with me."

Dianne watched him smooth back his thinning, grayish-blond hair from what looked to be a troubled brow. Catching her staring, he forced an uncomfortable smile.

"Well. . ." Dianne knocked on the partially open door just hard enough to open it a little wider.

"Yes, Dianne. You here already?" The old Sheriff lowered the paper and then looked past her to the Police Chief. "Oscar?" He promptly got up and walked toward the two at the door. "I got this," he added, nodding to Dianne. He looked back to Oscar as he closed the door. "Well, I must say, I didn't expect you back so soon. Found your alien yet?"

Oscar slowly shook his head as he sat down on the nearest couch. "Wish that was my only problem, Will," he replied, looking down at his hat in his hand.

"Well, Oscar. . ." Will sat sown on the couch directly across from him. "I've got the time. What's on your mind?"

Fiddling with his hat, he looked back up at the old Sheriff. "We've come a long way William, you and I," he started just above a whisper. "I know we've had our differences in the past. But, all in all, we're still walkin' the same road, aren't we?"

"I'd say that," answered Will with a slight nod. "I'm not really used to seeing you worried like this. Is there something I can help you with?"

A slight smile slowly graced Oscar's face. "Thank you for that, William. For about the last six months or so, from about August of last year 'till now, we've been workin' around the Gin House Lake and Park. We've been tryin' ta catch somebody who is assaulting women in that area. We really have no usable description—average build, average height, and wears a dark ski mask. They were all tied up, gagged, and beaten. The assailant then cuts off a lock of their hair—for a trophy I suppose." He slowly shook his head. "I've had my best detective on this since day one and still haven't found a viable lead." Oscar leaned back, deep in the couch, still making eye contact with Will. "Lord only knows you have your own problems, Will, but if you could spare that young detective of yours, say for a week, I'd certainly be in your dept."

Will smiled, leaning back in his couch also. "Actually, Oscar, Jack's just finished up a case. He's just idling along right now. If you like, I can coast him in your direction right now."

"Please," replied Oscar, quickly sitting up at the edge of the couch.

Will got up, walked to and then opened the office door. "Dianne," he called loudly.

"Coming," replied the dispatcher, now walking toward the two standing at the doorway. "What can I do for you?"

Will chuckled, looking over his glasses at her. "Be careful what you ask for, young lady," he quipped.

Oscar's smile widened as he looked at Dianne. "Blonde, blue eyes, very pretty, and could easily pass for younger with that ponytail she wears sometimes."

"You've noticed," smiled Dianne. "Am I to be worried about what you two are drumming up?"

Oscar raised his eyebrows. "Well, I'm crowdin' retirement but ain't near dead yet, young lady," he quipped as he turned to Will. "Are you talkin' trap here?"

"Yep," answered Will.

Holding his smile, Oscar added, "Does your boy, Jack, go along with this deal?"

Will nodded. "Wouldn't think I'd send her in harm's way without him watchin' from the trees, would you?" Will looked over his reading glasses at the Munford Chief. "Don't separate them. Wherever she goes, he goes."

"Deal," replied Oscar.

Will looked to the dispatcher. "Where is Jack now?"

"I've signed him in. He's picking up some medical supplies for me at Walgreens. You wanted us to equip all cruisers with medical kits. Remember?"

Will nodded. "Have 'em come to my office with you just as soon as he comes in." The old Sheriff stopped as if studying her expression.

213

"What?" asked Dianne.

"You always wanted to work the field," said Will. "Are you sure this is all right with you?"

"Perfect," answered Dianne excitedly.

"Good," replied Will. "Have one of the girls fill in for you for a few days or so. If not, I'm sure Andy can double up somehow."

"I'll cover the expense," said Oscar. "If I can get this monkey off my back, it'll sure be worth it. The City Council's givin' me a fit."

*   *   *

Leaving the details up to Jack, the Chief assigned Detective Joseph Tibbs to help in the investigation. Dressed like a college student-sweats with low-cut top, Dianne made her presence known at the park around 7:30PM. Detective Tibbs, a trim, six foot, thirty-five-year-old black Chief of Detectives, posted himself at the first covered pavilion at the park entranceway. Looking homeless and down on his luck, he fashioned his 'nest' with a small pop-up tent complete with blankets, pillows, and a big cooler next to the pavilion's fire place. Jack, on the other hand, remained aloof--arriving on his own and always out of sight of the other two. He constantly watched Dianne as she did her stretches, jogged, and then talked with the occasional park visitors. The only vehicle within easy reach was Detective Tibbs' BSA Black Shadow motorcycle, always just a touch from the fireplace. Then, as Fate would have it, on the third day, a Friday the 27th at 5:30PM, their efforts seemed to start paying off. . .

Still enjoying the unfamiliar stretch of woods around the huge Gin House Lake, Jack didn't pay close attention to the green Gator cart that was running about the park. The young, sandy-haired man in it was dressed in maintenance grey pants and shirt with a park jacket to match. But after making several, very slow passes by where Dianne was jogging, Jack noted that the young man's attention wasn't exactly on his work.

"Jack, Joe? Can you hear me?" said Dianne.

"Jack here, Dianne. I see him. He's working maintenance and has been here ever since I've started."

"I know," replied Dianne. "but now, he's looking really hard and I don't see a smile anymore. Do you think my outfit's a bit too telling?" The double snicker on the other end did little to calm the young dispatcher. "Guys?"

"You're fine, Dianne," answered Jack. "I've got my eye on him. Let's just be patient and see what he's up to."

"Use both eyes, Jack," countered Dianne. "This guy's starting to freak me out."

Just as she said that, the man in the green Gator pulled from the road and headed across the grass field toward the part of the jogging trail where Dianne was headed. Slowing to a stop, he looked to be blocking the trail just thirty yards from where the young dispatcher was running.

Dianne slowed. "Do you see that?" said Dianne. Her tone sounding stressed. "He's just blocked the trail and now he's out and waiting for me. I don't see anybody anywhere and he's got something in his right hand."

"On my way," said Joe.

Dianne could hear the big BSA echo through the park trees as she slowed even more. What's more, she couldn't see Jack anywhere at all as she got closer and closer to the Gator.

"Jack! Jack! Please be there," said Dianne. Her tone at a panic high.

Having seen the chrome-like reflection off the object in the man's hand, Jack was off like a shot. Feeling the flush hit his face and the tingling in his hands, he was out of the woods immediately. Now on the paved trail and about twenty yards behind Dianne, he passed her before she knew he was there. With his eyes on the metal object in the man's hand, Jack watched him drop what looked like a tin cup to the grass and then fall back heavily to the seat of the Gator. Completely innervated by what he was quickly approaching, the young man pushed himself back upon the Gator's seat and braced himself. Never missing a step, Jack picked up speed, passed the Gator, and then took a quick turn from the trail and toward the woods.

"Stay there!" shouted Joe, as the BSA roared past her and continued on toward the Gator.

"Stand down! Stand down!" shouted Jack on the earbuds. "No weapon! He has no weapon!"

Sliding to a stop about fifteen feet from the Gator, Joe looked at the startled young man and the birdseed all over the ground beside the Gator. About two feet from the left front wheel lay a silvery metal cup in the grass. Above it, was a pole-mounted birdfeeder.

Joe kicked the bike stand down, eased off the motorcycle, and then pondered just what to say.

"Did you see him? Did you see him?" exclaimed the young man, seemingly reluctant to exit the Gator.

"Uhhh. . ." Joe looked back at Dianne as she trotted up.

"See who?" she asked.

"The tall man!" exclaimed the maintenance man. "Black cap, new blue jeans, and a navy blue sport coat." He looked at Joe. "He ran out of the woods and passed her like she was running backwards."

"Another jogger, I guess," replied Joe, glancing back at a now quiet Dianne. "He was just using the trail."

"No! No!" exclaimed the maintenance man. "He came out of the woods back there, ran like a deer right passed her and me, and then went right back into the woods. He was over seven-feet-tall with dark skin, and his eyes--I saw his eyes."

"Calm down a little," said Joe.

"No! No!" exclaimed the young man. "He looked away from me when he passed, but not before I saw his glowing red eyes."

Joe looked back at Dianne, but only got a shrug for his effort. "This ain't our boy," he said softly. "He's barely twenty and works here at the park." He looked back at the maintenance man. "What's your name?"

"Rodney Gant, Sir. I work maintenance and ground duties here and for the City. Been here for almost five years." He glanced back to where Jack had entered the woods. "I'm also a big Science Fiction fan and go to all their conventions. Our Lon Cheney Fan Club has been gathering all the information we can get ahold of on the urban legend, Horned Jack, ever since the middle of last year." He glanced at Dianne, now standing beside Joe. "I thought folks had blown what they thought they saw out of proportion or exaggerated them somewhat, but now I don't think so at all. That was him. The one that passed you and then me was Horned Jack. Don't you see? He's real! The rumors are all true!"

"Ohhh Lord," groaned Dianne. "I'm sorry, but I really didn't get a good look."

"That's right," echoed Joe. "Sorry you spilled your bird food. Maybe you'll see your 'Horned Jack' jogger again sometime."

Part 2
Fanning the Flames
(of curiosity)

Putting the maintenance man incident behind them, Dianne was back at the park the next day at 4:00PM. Knowing that the assaults occurred around dusk, they hoped the assailant would try again. Although neither saw Jack, in her heart, Dianne knew the Nephilim in him would have him watching. . .

A typical day in January, the park looked almost deserted. When Dianne pulled up to the pavilion, she instantly spotted Joe, sitting in his lawn chair in front of the fireplace. Dressed in jeans and a sweatshirt this time, she got out with her 'care sack' and walked toward him.

"I see you've got a fire going," she said cheerfully.

He nodded without a word.

"You still look cold and uncomfortable," she added. "How long have you been here?"

Joe shrugged. "Twelvish I suppose," he replied, holding his hands close to the fire. "The weatherman said clear and forty-six degrees today. When I got here, there was still frost holding on in the shade."

His smile widened as she held out a large thermos to him.

"Thanks," he managed. Eagerly taking the thermos, he eyed the sack. "My McMuffin played out about an hour ago."

"There's two Black Forest ham and cheddar cheese sandwiches in there," explained Dianne as she sat the sack beside him. She eyed the 1955 Bellaire pulled up under the far side of the pavilion.

"That's my back up plan," he explained with a smile. "It's got a great heater and radio." He glanced back at the main part of the woods. "You think Jack's here?"

Dianne smiled with a slight nod. "Don't worry, Joe. When you don't see him, that's when he's watching you."

With a slightly one-sided grin, he looked up at Dianne. "I got a glimpse of that fellow who passed you and returned to the woods yesterday. You know, he scared the pants off that maintenance man yesterday. Didn't get a good look though. He was tall like Jack, but moved like he could outrun Tarzan. The maintenance man called him Horned Jack. I've heard of him—some kind of fable, hero thing. Why would he call him Horned Jack?"

Dianne shrugged. "I guess. . ."

Dianne's voice trailed off as she watched another vehicle pull up alongside of her Fiat.

"Speak of the Devil," said Joe as he slowly stood with Dianne. "That's Gant, the maintenance man right now."

"Who's with him?" asked Dianne.

Joe shrugged. "Don't know her," he answered, eying the '60 white, two-door Biscayne as the couple got out.

"I knew you two would be here," said Rodney, glancing back at the young lady as if pleased.

Looking in her late teens, the trim and almost six-foot blonde walked directly behind him, peeping now and then at the two at the fireplace.

"This is my girl, Drew Barry. I told her what I saw yesterday and she wanted to have a look. She's the secretary in our SciFi club."

"Have a look?" Joe squinted at Dianne.

"Yes," admitted Rodney. "We're members of the Lon Chaney Fan Club. In the last two years or so, Horned Jack has made this place come alive. We've logged in every sighting. But, for this year at least, his sightings have grown cold so to speak."

"Ohhh Lord," said Joe under his breath. "So, what has that got to do with the price of eggs in Tipton county?"

Drew smiled, stepping up beside Rodney. "You two are police. We figured you were investigating the assaults we've been having since the first of this year or so."

"Yep," agreed Rodney. "We've come here to tell you that Horned Jack is not your man. Other than the obvious criminals, he hasn't harmed a soul since his first sighting way back in 1955."

"What's goin' on here?" came a booming voice from where Dianne had parked her Fiat.

Joe and Dianne looked up to see Chief Gillespie in his cruiser. "Not that sure, Chief," replied Joe. "Just talking to the park maintenance man."

Drew looked back at the older gentleman in the black Fairlane 500. "We are the investigative branch of the Lon Chaney Fan Club."

The Chief glanced at Joe and then looked back at the young girl. "Investigative branch of the. . .what?"

"They are about to leave," said Dianne as she stepped up beside Drew. "I'm quite certain they don't want to interfere with our investigation."

The Chief looked at the two standing beside Dianne. "Then do it now and don't jinx this operation." he grumbled.

Drew rolled her eyes, her gaze ending up on the Chief. "Did you miss the investigative part?"

Dianne quickly put a hand on Drew's right shoulder. "We'll take care of this, Chief," she added. "Jack's in position right now and we are about to start."

"Good then," replied the Chief as he glanced at his watch. "It's already 5:30 and evening is approaching fast. Carry on."

As all four watched the Chief leave, an older black Chevrolet pulled passed him and continued on into the park.

"Tinted windows," noted Joe.

Dianne nodded, looking at Rodney. "Have you seen this vehicle lately?"

"Occasionally," answered Rodney.

"Want us to check it out?" asked Drew.

"Certainly not," replied Joe. "You heard the Chief. If you really want to help us out, take your girlfriend out of this park right now."

"Wait a minute," grumbled Drew. "This is a public park and we can jog if we want to"

"Ohhh Lord," groaned Dianne. "The Chief's not gonna be crazy about this."

"I know. I know," replied Joe, looking at the smile on Drew's face. "But I can't just order a citizen out of the park."

"Exactly," quipped Drew as she moved to Dianne's side.

Dianne glanced at her watch. "I've gotta go. It's going on six already. I'm not calling the Chief. So, I guess me and little miss persistence will go jogging. I wouldn't want her to go all by herself."

*   *   *

Fifteen minutes later and Dianne and Drew were on the Loop Road, north of the entrance and just west of the huge lake. All in all, it was part of a three and a half mile stretch of paved trails that wound through the park. It circled the lake and then cut through the picnic grounds and camp sights on the east side. . .

"Cold?" Dianne glanced at Drew. She seemed to be snugging the collar of her fuzzy, brown sweater much too often.

"Not too bad," answered Drew. "I. . . ."

Drew's comment was interrupted just as something whizzed past Dianne's ear and struck the young girl on the right side of her neck. Flinching, Drew grabbed the strange, dart-like projectile, looked puzzled at Dianne, and then slumped into the young Deputy's arms.

Instantly lowering her friend to the grass, Dianne looked back toward the woods. "Joe, Jack, we've been--"

But the second dart was already on its way, sending the young Deputy to the grass beside Drew. Dianne, lying on her left side, tried to reach into her pocket for her derringer, but could hardly move her right arm. The tranquilizer had left her so weak she could hardly keep her eyes open.

"You wanna do 'em now?"

Dianne heard the dreamy question, but could only see Drew's blurry, brown sweater in front of her.

"Later," spoke another voice, sounding much older. "That maintenance boy's on the far side of the loop. He's got that black bum with him. We can dart them also. That'll give us time to work on the girls."

221

Unable to move, Dianne could hear the Gator get closer and closer, but that faded into the darkness with everything else.

*   *   *

The flat tire on the cruiser dropped a monkey wrench right into Jack's plans. With a one-mile range at best with the earbuds, he knew contact with Dianne and Joe was impossible. But, as providence would dictate, he was very close to where he had parked the cruiser the day before.

"Five thirty," said Jack as he looked at his watch and then the flat tire.

But as he opened the trunk, a week sound on the breeze caught his attention. Jack stopped and slowly faced the breeze.

"Move Jack! Move now!" came the voice on the wind.

Jack dropped his jacket in the front seat, reached in the back seat of the Ford, and then grabbed his black coveralls. With his right leg in the garment, he struggled with its sleeves as he ran toward the lake and the loop road. The voice back at the Ford had not only panicked him, it had also summoned the Beast, claws and all. Now, dealing with the flush feeling that was flowing all over his body, he slowed to listen to another sound as he struggled with the zipper on the left leg of his coveralls. Looking through the trees, he could now see Gant's Gator as it moved west along the Loop Road. But there was yet another sound, a different vehicle perhaps. Jack continued, paralleling the Gator until it stopped. The other vehicle, a dark-colored Chevy station wagon, quickly closed in on the Gator and stopped right behind it. Still at a dead run, and a good fifty yards from the Gator, Jack watched two men get out of the Chevy. Not until the Nephilim heard the muffled pops and watch Joe and Rodney fall to the grass beside the two girls he notice that at least one of the men had a weapon. The young Nephilim screamed as loud as he could, watching the two men jump and then look toward the woods.

"Not a real gun. Not a real gun," said Jack as he continued toward the back of the black Chevy.

The two men had heard the sound of the Nephilim, but were now looking through the woods and toward the main road for whom or whatever had made the sound. Now, almost even with the back of the station wagon, Jack noticed the right-rear door open. The young red-headed man who got out never knew what hit him. As his pistol went off twice, Jack jerked him out and then bounced him off the Chevrolet as if he was a child.

*   *   *

Meanwhile, still lying very close to Joe, Rodney was jerked back into reality by the sharp report of the pistol. The dart that was directed at him had struck his collar and didn't fully penetrated the skin. Easing the collar away from his neck, the young maintenance man located the dripping projectile and tossed it to the grass. Still addled from the partial dose, Rodney rolled his head to the left. Through blurred vision, he could make out a very tall person rush from the black Chevrolet station wagon and attack the two men quite near him and the others. The attack was so quick and violent, he could hardly follow it. The first man was thrown over him like he weighed nothing at all. He looked at the second man just in time to see him pull a pistol, but it was promptly removed from his person along with three of his fingers. Both the weapon and fingers fell within reach from where Rodney was lying. Then, Rodney's dreamy gaze found the red and glowing eyes of the one who came to their aide. Dressed completely in black and with horns clearly visible through his black hair, the extremely tall creature seemed hardly out of breath. Looking at the girls and Joe, his gaze moved to Rodney, the pistol and then back to Rodney again.

"Friend. . ." managed Rodney as he held up his left hand in a sign of submission.

Resting his head back to the grass, Rodney watched the Nephilim's eyes change from red, to a brilliant green. The one he now considered to be the urban legend, quickly turned and took something from Joe and Dianne. Turning, he dragged the three criminals to the nearby oak they all were under and fastened them, in some way, around its trunk. After quickly checking Dianne and Drew, the strange being ran back into the woods without another look. With a deep breath, Rodney rested his head back in the grass and closed his eyes. . .

"Rodney! Rodney! Wake up!"

Recognizing Drew's voice right away, the young man rolled over to his side and pushed himself up to a sitting position. From there, he could see a black Fairlane 500, a Munford Police car, an ambulance, and a Sheriff's vehicle. There were so many flashing lights it looked like Christmas all over again.

"How are the girls?" asked Rodney, briskly rubbing his face.

"Drew and I are fine," answered Dianne. "The paramedics are working with two of the perpetrators and Deputy Ward of the Sheriff's Department has the third in his car. All are pretty banged up. One of them has actually lost some fingers. Someone handcuffed all three to the tree we are under."

With that, the maintenance man scrambled to his feet and then looked toward the woods. "He was here, Drew! He was right here! I saw him just as plain as I can see you two right now."

"Who was here?" asked Drew, glancing at Dianne.

"Horned Jack of course," answered Rodney. "I actually saw him beat the crap out of all three of those men before I went out."

Drew sat there, wide-eyed with her gaze on her boyfriend. "Then. . .it's true. Everything we heard and wrote down is true?"

"Ohhh-my-God!" exclaimed Rodney, scrambling to his feet. "I heard shots and more than one. Did anyone get hit?

"That's my question as well," said James as he walked up, looking at Rodney. "I found a pistol lying close to the front of the black station wagon. It had been fired three times."

Rodney slowly shook his head. "I don't own a gun, but I saw Horned Jack take the one that was lying close to me from the man who lost his fingers."

"That one wasn't fired," explained James.

"How are the prisoners," asked Dianne.

"They'll live," spoke the Chief of Munford's Police as he walked up. "The one with the neck brace and missing fingers keeps ranting about being attacked by some red-eyed demon. I suppose they all were smoking weed. I found a bag of it in the station wagon."

Dianne instantly glanced toward the woods and then looked to the Chief. "Jack was our back up. Have you seen him?"

"James, Dianne," said Will as he trotted toward them from his car. "I see everyone but Jack. Lucy tried ta hail him, but he won't answer his radio."

"He won't answer on the earbuds either," added Joe.

"The one who helped us had red eyes, but I swear, the last time he looked at me they were a bright green." Pointing toward the woods, he added, "He cuffed those men to the oak and ran right back in there just before I went out again."

"Uhhh. . ." Will glanced at Dianne. "I need to find my detective. He might of caught one of those bullets James said was fired. We'll tackle the red-eyed whatever later." He looked to James. "Take your cruiser and check the west side of the loop, and the camping area for Jack's Ford. Oscar and I'll check the west side and the entrance. Oscar's got a car coming from Munford for those three." Looking back at Dianne, he added, "It's just not like that boy to not be here when the dust settles. Get a hold of Shelley. Jack's always talkin' 'bout his 'help'. Maybe she can coax some of that in our direction."

"Help?" The Chief's gaze was locked on Will.

"Friends, Oscar. Just friends," answered the Sheriff.

Joe sat quietly on the back of the ambulance with Dianne, watching what was going on. Finally, when Gillespie and Will were on their way back into the park, he leaned a bit closer to her. "I don't know zip about this urban legend thing, but what the maintenance man described seems to fit the subject like a glove. Real or not, vigilante or whatever, he saved all of our bacon today." He

225

stopped, watching James trot toward them from his cruiser.

"Constable Forsythe has found Jack's cruiser on Highway 178 and just about two miles east of here. It was left with a flat tire. Will wants me to go and pick up Shelley, Banjo, and someone called Woo. "I'll be back as soon as possible."

*   *   *

Almost an hour had passed before James could get Shelley, the big Pitt, and Woo to where Jack was last seen. By that time, everyone was involved in search. But there was not a more hopeful sign of finding Jack, than the one Banjo delivered as soon as James let him out where Rodney last spotted the mysterious man who had helped them.

With no one at the spot when James pulled up, the young deputy stopped and pointed toward the woods. "I think Jack went in right there, Shelley," he said as they all got out.

Seeing the big Pitt leave so quickly, Shelley turned to Woo. "Please, Woo. We can't possibly keep up with him. Keep him in sight for us."

"Will try," replied the little batgirl as she quickly took to the air and disappeared into the trees.

Now, with evening upon them, dusk was devouring what little sunlight there was left. Shelley followed James well into the woods, closely watching as the young deputy's three-cell flashlight carefully swept the area in front of them.

"Wait a minute. I heard something." said James. Holding Shelley perfectly still, he directed his light into the trees ahead of them.

"Found him," shouted a little, girlish voice, seemingly in the knee-high scrub and brambles up ahead.

"That's the batgirl," noted James as he lowered the Everready's beam and looked to Shelley. "Jack's 'friends' never cease to amaze me."

"Woo!" shouted Shelley. Seeing James was seemingly frozen in place, she quickly stepped around him and ran toward where the deputy was shining his flashlight.

"About forty yards ahead," said James, now trying to keep up with her.

As the two ran up to Woo, now standing by herself in the two-foot tall grass, James noticed a dimly glowing object some twenty yards ahead of them.

"What is it?" asked Shelley.

Woo shrugged. "It looks like an old, black man. He's glowing all over." She glanced up at the two. "That's why I'm here and not there. I can't see what he's thinking."

"What?" James looked confusedly at Shelley.

"Ohhh-my-God. That's Uncle Bill," managed Shelley weakly. Tugging on James' arm, she pulled him gently behind her. "I'll explain later. Jack has got to be here somewhere."

"But he looks like a gho. . ." James' voice seemed to lose its strength as Shelley pulled him closer and closer to the glowing apparition.

"I know. I know," whispered Shelley. "He passed before Jack and I got married."

"That's it," said Woo, and back into the trees she shot.

"It must be safe," said James. "Banjo is sitting right beside him."

Then, looking where Banjo was sitting, Shelley got a glimpse of black fabric through the grass. "Ohhh God! He's down!" she screamed and then bolted toward the three up ahead.

Paying little attention to the glowing figure just a few steps away, Shelley fell to her knees in front of Banjo and her husband.

James, on the other hand, eyed the smiling face of the old black man closely as he eased up behind the Pitt.

"Jack! Jack!" shouted Shelley. Quickly unzipping the coveralls, she frantically looked for blood stains. Failing that, she pulled his head and shoulders into her lap and noticed he was no longer in the 'Beast'.

"Isn't love wonderful," said Uncle Bill as he continued to smile at James' astonished expression. "Leaning on his cane, he added, "He's fine, Shelley. Give 'em an hour or so. Right now, he's runnin' on empty; the strain of the 'Beast' shut his mortal side down, so to speak."

227

"You said Beast," managed James.

Uncle Bill nodded. "That's what my boy calls his alter self."

"Then. . .you are with him at times when he's in the 'Beast'--an Angel?" asked Shelley.

"All the time," corrected Uncle Bill so loudly it made Woo leave where she was hiding in the trees and drop soundly to the knee-high grass behind Shelley.

Laughing at the batgirl's antics, the old black man looked to Shelley. "I am what you might call a Familiar-- one who is allowed to direct in an Angel's stead. While I walk in these shoes, I do not hunger, tire, or get disappointed with my charge. It simply isn't in me."

"And your charge is Jack?" guessed a little, girlish voice from behind Shelley.

Genially tickled, Uncle Bill glanced up through the trees and into the dark skies. "The little one with wings and the Pitt do not lie. They do but love and serve. They are much similar to the 'Beast' side of Jack." He smiled at Shelley. "When the man, Jack, awakens, give him something to eat and drink—red meat, fruit, and plenty of water."

Then, as if on que, Jack began to move and awaken. In seeing that, the light around their old friend began to fade.

"Please don't go," said Shelley as she reached out to him.

But pinned to the ground by her husband, she could only watch as he smiled and faded from sight.

"Shelley?", managed Jack, now trying to sit up from Shelley's lap. "Is everything all right?"

"All is well," replied Shelley as she got up and brushed the grass from her jeans.

"Come," said James, glancing at Shelley. "I don't have earbuds and we need to tell the others that Jack is fine." He looked at Jack. "Can you walk?"

Jack struggled to his feet with Shelley supporting him. "Not that sure," he admitted. "The minute the 'Beast' left me, I got dizzy, the trees started to spin, and the ground rose up and smacked me. The next thing I knew, I was in Shelley's lap."

"Well. . ." James smiled at Shelley. "We've got what we wanted. Let's get back to the cruiser and I'll radio the others."

Part 3
The Knowing

It would be difficult for one to explain 'The Knowing'. Perhaps a glimpse of the future is close enough. The majority of us are not blessed with it until the end of our days. Over half of those left, simply dismiss the event as, perhaps, an overactive imagination. But some, a silent few, are convinced of the event and take to the blessings it sometimes affords us. . .

Jack sat in his swivel rocker in front of the big, picture window of his home and stared at the old rocker Uncle Bill had left him. The sounds of the morning were especially pleasant—Shelley frying bacon in the kitchen, the birds singing in the big Sycamore above the front porch, and Teresa playing with Pico somewhere in the back of the house. But that hardly distracted him from the old rocker. It was slowly, ever so slightly, moving back and forth. Jack looked down at Banjo. He was staring suspiciously at the old piece of furniture. Ever since it was brought into the house, he refused to lay on the left side of Jack's rocker. It was just too close to the old chair.

"Sit. . ."

Jack quickly sat up and looked toward the chair as did the Pitt with a low woof.

"Easy, boy," said Jack, patting Banjo's head. "That's not Uncle Bill's voice."

Jack checked the dining area and what he could see of the kitchen. There was no one in sight, but he could still hear Shelley move about. Positive the voice was familiar, Jack slowly stood, causing another warning 'woof' from Banjo. The rocker was still moving but without its usual pop creaking sounds. Then, just as soon as he stepped toward it, the old chair stopped moving as did Jack and the Pitt.

"Sit?" asked Jack just above a whisper.

"Sit!" came his answer, echoing as if it came from a huge and empty cavern. So loud was the noise it caused

Banjo leap from where he was, bound into the dining area, and then slide to a stop facing the living room. Jack quickly looked back toward the kitchen. Shelley was still unaware of what was happening.

"Very well," replied Jack. Covering the short distance, he promptly sat down in the old chair.

But just as soon as he did, a drowsiness swept over him like a cool and refreshing breeze, quickly pulling him into a dark place and away from his home. It seemed that only seconds had passed when the darkness gave way to an early morning sunrise. Jack found himself standing near a ridge that overlooked a beautiful woodland valley. Standing at the edge of the ridge with his back toward him was a man of fifty years or so and wearing a brown toga with matching pants with no pockets or cuffs. The leather sandals he had on looked worn and faded. His shoulder-length, brown hair gently moved with the morning breeze.

"So. . ." Jack stepped closer to the right to better see his face.

"Simjaza," spoke the man, his voice soft.

"I remember you," replied Jack. "Where have you been?"

"Following those in my charge," he answered. With a slight glance at Jack, he added, "You frustrate me, Jack Shoultz. Helping those lost in the forests and defending those in need are honorable things. I cannot stay by your side every day you face the evil side of the others you deal with. Filling your shoes when danger presents itself is becoming much too frequent, more especially now since another has come to your charge." He slowly turned to face Jack. "I have read everything from 'Lil' Abner' to "War and Peace'. Since when did you take up this 'Dick Tracy' attitude? Your mentor, Uncle Bill as you call him, was a constant blessing both to me and all who knew him." He slowly walked toward Jack and stopped so close, it made the young detective give ground. "You have a constant fear of becoming evil as was your father." With those words, Simjaza's countenance grew until Jack was forced to look up into his face. "I might have fanned the flames of that fear and for that, I apologize," he continued.

"When I stepped into the light to help you out of a dangerous spot, your recollection of me in the event was blocked and was only allowed my memories. Your father has had no control over you either in your past, your present, and certainly not your future. On the contrary however, your mother's love and that of her parents is a strong presence in your life and soul. That was quite evident in your stand against your father."

Then, as Simjaza stepped slightly back, his countenance diminished to about six feet or so causing Jack's chin to slowly drop.

"I will go now, Jack Shoultz," he continued. "But you must remember; you now live for your wife and those, two girls. The Nephilim trait is within the two young ones and especially strong with the little one." With that, Simjaza slowly backed away, stepping over the edge of the cliff as if it did not exist. As he did, his physical appearance began to fade and shimmer. "That's where Horned Jack must come into their lives," he added. "You must be here for the little one in eight years. Her training is essential. She is your relief."

"What?" Jack rushed to the edge of the cliff, watching what now looked like a thin, white cloud floating out over the valley. "Eight years? She is my relief? What?"

But the one who could provide his answers was no longer there. As he watched the cloud become thinner and thinner, Simjaza's words 'eight years' played over and over in his head with that same, hollow echoing sound.

*   *   *

"Jack. . .Jack!"

Jack slowly opened his eyes to see Shelley's smiling face looking down at him.

"Were you dreaming?" she asked.

Realizing he was still in the old rocker, he quickly stood and looked back at it.

"Something wrong?" she asked, still holding her smile. "You said something about eight years and it was fairly loud. Were you talking to someone?"

Truly amused, Jack shook his finger at the old rocker. "Pico's right. When you sit in that thing, sometimes you're not alone."

"Well, you said 'eight years' so loud it spooked Banjo right into the kitchen again," chuckled Shelley. "Did your Uncle Bill visit you again?"

Jack shrugged. "I wish," he grumbled. "The one I dreamed about, I don't see very often. I don't know that much about him and what I do know, I don't completely understand."

Shelley squinted at him with, "May I ask what it was about?"

"Not sure," admitted Jack. "When I figure it all out, I'll share it with you."

Shelley glanced back toward the kitchen and the hallway entrance to their bedrooms. "Woo and Teresa are in Pico's room. Banjo's with them, I think." Seeing they were still alone, she quickly turned back to Jack. "Fess up, Jack Shoultz. Lucy told me about the report James wrote up. The man you ran at had a gun and they said he fired three times. You could have been hurt or worse."

"Lord. . ." managed Jack, as he watched the tears track their way down her cheeks. "Shhh," he said softly as he took her in his arms. "The one who visited me in my dreams is called Simjaza. If I was to guess, he's a guardian angel for more that are just like me and Uncle Bill. He said I was taking too many chances as well. What's more, he told me that I was to be Pico's mentor."

Wiping her wet cheeks with the tips of her fingers, Shelley slowly looked up into his eyes. "Pico's mentor?" she said weakly.

Jack nodded. "She and Teresa are Nephilim, but Pico's trait is much stronger, but she won't have horns like me."

Shelley stepped back a little, still keeping eye contact with him. "Then. . .he must have arranged your meeting with the girls."

Jack shrugged. "That's a big leap considering all the things that happened leading up to when Pico first said 'I see you'."

Shelley forced a half smile. "Then you've got to be there for her. Jack, I can't help her like you can."

*   *   *

Still bothered by the strange dream that morning, Jack pulled into the Munford Sheriff's lot at 7:00AM sharp. The first thing he noticed was Charlie's old truck, but it was now hooked up with his camper. Banjo sat up, looking out of the front, passenger side window, but there was no sign of the Shadow Wolves. There was, however, a late model black Chevrolet station wagon parked on the right side of Will's Sheriff's car. Jack eased the '55 Ford Custom in the space to the left of Will's cruiser. Banjo, almost helping Jack get out, hit the pavement right behind the young detective. Just as soon as he started toward the front door, Jack heard someone tapping on one of the building's windows to his right. Turning toward the sound, he noticed Dianne and Lucy, waving excitedly for him to come inside in a hurry. Taking the hint, Jack quickened his step, opened the front door, and then let the excited Pitt inside.

"Over here," said Dianne as she sat Banjo's bowl down on the floor.

The two donuts were gone in but seconds.

"What's going on now?" asked Jack. His voice low.

"Closed door meeting," said Lucy. "They're all here in Will's office and been here since six this morning."

"Who's 'all'?" asked Jack.

"Eddie Miles from MUFON," answered Dianne. "Charlie's in there as well with Two Bears and his Shadow Wolves." She cast a suspicious eye at Jack. "What have you got into now?"

"Not guilty," quipped Jack with a little shrug.

Everyone paused, noting the laughter coming from Will's office.

Lucy stepped closer to Jack. "I heard Charlie say something about break-ins and close encounters," she whispered. "Will nodded and then said there were at least a dozen and most of them were close to the river between Richardson Landing and Randolph."

234

"Close encounters?" Jack glanced back toward Will's closed door. "Are the Grey Men now moving from cattle to humans?"

"Yep, but they've changed their tactics," spoke a familiar voice from across the lobby.

Jack turned to see Charlie standing with Two Bears at Will's now open office door. Eddie Miles was right behind them with Will and the rest of the Shadow Wolves. Every one of them were smiling at what seemed to be Charlie's lack of one.

Eddie nodded at Charlie. "He thinks you won't come with us. Having second thoughts about dangerous assignments."

Jack glanced at Dianne, looked at Charlie, and then walked over to join them. Charlie's stern expression didn't change. "How would you know I would have trouble getting involved again?"

Charlie shrugged. "I'm a --"

"I know-I know, Charlie," interrupted the young detective. "You're retired. Now tell me how-did-you-know?"

Charlie elbowed Two Bears for his silent chuckle. "I had a visitor last night. He was a Dream Walker, this one. New to me, but it seems he knows you. Told me to tell you to be in the 'Beast' when needs be. It was your callin'." Charlie finally smiled. "He is right, you know. Told you that I could."

Jack stopped but a short reach from the old Apache and looked down into his eyes. "This dream walker, what did he look like?"

Smiling a Banjo trying to get another donut out of Dianne, he looked back at Jack. "Just saw his face at first. He had long, light brown hair and about fifty or so I think. After he told me what I told you, he turned, walked back into the woods and out of my dream. 'You are what you are. Please be careful,' he said. He sounded regretful."

Jack then looked at Will. "Am I with whatever is going on here?"

Will nodded. "You'll be workin' under Two Bears for now, Jack. The Shadow Wolves will run the show. Eddie here will offer a little MUFON muscle if you attract the wrong somebodies."

Jack's eyes narrowed as he looked back at Charlie. "There's more to you than meets the eye, Charlie Two Shirts."

The old Apache laughed. "Bring your dog, Jack. He will be a help to us and perhaps loosen the Grey Man's tongue if we catch 'em. They don't like dogs much, you know."

*   *   *

Down Drummonds Road and on through Drummonds the Shadow Wolves went with Jack and Banjo in the truck with Charlie and the Shadow Wolves in the Airstream camper. Once through Drummonds, Charlie headed straight toward Richardson Landing on the Mississippi River. Jack sat there without a word until Charlie turned left, on Highway 59. Then, his curiosity could stand it no longer.

"I guess I'm working under you, Charlie," he started.

Charlie glanced at him with a smile. "Sounds like it," he said as if pleased.

"Good," replied Jack. "I would like to know a few things. Why do you have such a diehard interest in this UFO thing?

The old Apache smiled again at Jack. "This is a holy thing, young Jack. The demons that fly the bright ship have plagued our people for over a hundred years. Our people have went missing without a trace, found murdered without a believable clue, or caught wandering in the desert without a useful memory left to them. Now, there are those in the government who are working with them." He glanced at Jack with another, short smile. "But the dark clouds have moved and let the sun shine upon us once more. The Attorney General has given us cross borders permission to pursue, arrest, and confiscate evidence in crimes against our and your people as well." His smile widened as he stared at Jack.

"What?" the young detective finally asked.

"Now, we have hope, think the Shadow Wolves. 'We have an angel' they say."

Jack rolled his eyes with a deep breath. "Great God of Jerusalem," he grumbled. "How am I to keep a low profile and the 'Beast' out of this story with comments and expectations like that?"

"I have not your answer, young Jack," replied Charlie, enjoying Jack's situation. "Perhaps there will come a time when you won't have to."

Jack slowly looked to the old Indian. "And Just how will that come about?" he asked.

"Not sure." Charlie's smile waned. "The white man is too superstitious. Perhaps you'll have to move your family to the Nations."

*   *   *

It wasn't long before Charlie made a left turn on the Landing Road. Jack then could see two other trailers and the Ford trucks belonging to the Shadow wolves. Charlie pulled up within twenty feet of the nearest trailer. Banjo quickly sat up and checked Jack's disposition.

"How is your granddaughter?" asked Jack. "Wasn't she staying with you?"

"Marty?" Charlie smiled as he stopped the old truck. "She likes Munford. She is very resourceful I think. She and her girlfriend are sharing an apartment there. They both are working at Mrs. Pauline's Restaurant. The Sheriff has also given her a part-time job cleaning up around the office." His smile widened. "He looks on her as a daughter. I think that is a good thing."

When Charlie turned off the ignition, Jack laid a light hand on his forearm. "Do we have a plan?"

The old Apache glanced at him with a smile as he got out. "The best one yet, young Jack. Let's join the others in my trailer and we'll talk it over."

Jack got out with Banjo on his heels, eying Iron Eyes standing at the open door, nursing a small cigar.

"Rum Soaked Crooks," grumbled Charlie, staring at Iron Eyes. "I know you're not smokin' that thing in my

237

trailer. You know ever since I got the long face from the doctor, I no longer smoke the pipe."

Iron Eyes quickly thumped the fire from the end of the cigar.

With the frown quickly melting into a slight smile, Charlie added, "You got another one o' those on you?"

"You back to smokin'?" asked Two Bears, now standing at the door as well.

"Not really," answered Charlie as he stepped inside with Jack and Banjo. "I just wanna smell it now and again."

As everyone took a seat in the trailer, Iron Eyes handed him one still in its cellophane wrapper.

"Well. . ." Two Bears hesitated, looking at Jack. "We're here and Jack is here." He nodded at the new, shortwave radio in the corner of the trailer. I finally got that thing working. The Colonel is just a short dial away." He looked at Charlie. "Where is the man from MUFON?"

"We can catch him on the radio," answered Charlie. He looked to Jack. "We have Colonel Pete Castle with us as well. He's with Millington's Search and GCA Radar." Laughing, he raised his eyebrows at Jack. "I'm gettin' an education too. That's Ground Controlled Approach to some. Just after Chief Brumley was contacted by that whistle blower, he got the Colonel to sign on with help from his radar machines. He said he could track that Black Chopper when it got close enough."

Jack squinted. "What whistle blower? Will didn't brief me on that."

Charlie shrugged. "Will called him Billie. He works at where they keep that Black Chopper I think. He told Will not to be too worried when the Greys work on the cattle. Now, the Black Ops are turning a blind eye while they start the same thing on white folks."

Chee rolled his eyes. "They been doin' that to our people before I was born, Jack. You'll have people missing and some with amnesia so bad they won't even know their name or where they live."

"That's true," agreed Charlie as he looked at Thomas Greene, the oldest member of the Wolves. "Tell Jack,

Thomas, what to expect and show him the transmitter detector." He smiled, looking at Jack again. "I think all this, new knowledge is givin' me a headache."

"Well. . ." Thomas pulled from his Jacket pocket a metal box about the size of a box of kitchen matches. "Eddie Miles gave me this thing. It is very simple. It has an on and off switch, a sensitivity knob, and a meter that shows you when the signal is present and which direction it is coming from. That means you can move it around locate the strongest signal. Then, you'll know where the device is."

Jack's puzzled stare was back. "What device?"

"I got this one," said Two Bears as he looked at Jack. "Within one of the houses the Demon visited, was a young girl of sixteen or so. Her parents were at a neighbor's house cutting up meat from a big steer they had just slaughtered. That was only a hundred yards away. Then the black suits came in, they shot the girl with a dart gun and then stripped her. She passed out while they were taking her clothes off. Our old doctor, William Winters, checked her from head to toe. Said she was fine. But then he noticed a small, red scab high on her shoulder near her neck. Swabbing it with a numbing medicine, he removed a small, silver object not much bigger than a grain of wild rice and sharp on both ends." Two bears pulled something from his pocket wrapped in aluminum foil and handed it to Jack. "Hold this, remove the aluminum foil, and then watch," he instructed.

Doing as he was directed, Jack could see a small, box of matches. Within it were three, silver shards resting on a bed of white cotton. He quickly closed the box.

Two Bears turned the detector on, moved it about the room,

and then pointed it toward Jack. The needle instantly pegged.

"See that?" asked Two Bears.

Jack nodded.

"Wrap those things back up, Jack," said Charlie. "We don't want them to get a bead on them right now.

239

"Will they come to the signals these things create?" asked the young detective as he wrapped the aluminum foil back over the box.

Charlie nodded. "These beings impregnate the young girls with their own sperm I think. Maybe they can't have children anymore. This would explain why some of our young women have gone missing."

"You bet," agreed Eddie Miles as he stepped up beside Charlie. "Are we all set?" He looked to Jack. "Are you on board with us?"

Jack nodded. "I'm reporting to the Shadow Wolves according to Will."

"Then. . ." Charlie gaze dropped to Banjo. Lying at Jack's feet, he looked to be sound asleep. "You been lettin' him chase rabbits at night?"

Jack slowly shook his head. "I think the donuts did it."

Charlie laughed. "Then, most of us are all set, Eddie. Chee has set us up with a nice, three bedroom, completely furnished home just east of here where Needham Road turns off Highway 59. Just as soon as Marty's ready, you two can set up shop at--"

"Hold it right there," interrupted Jack. "Will never said a thing about your plan. What's this 'set up shop' thing and what does your granddaughter have to do with all of this?"

Charlie's smile slowly came back as he glanced at Two Bears and then looked toward the bedroom at the back of the trailer. "Marty, are you ready?"

"I am," came the answer from the bedroom.

The young girl stepped through the doorway and paused, looking at Jack. Trim, nineteen years old, long, dark brown hair, she looked exactly like what the aliens were after.

"I'm OK with this if you are, Mr. Shoultz," she said. "Two Bears put me on the Shadow Wolves payroll. I hope this doesn't scare Mrs. Shelley."

Jack rolled his eyes, his gaze ending up on Charlie. "Let me guess--Marty and I are in the house?"

Charlie nodded.

"Uh huh. . ." Jack's worried look deepened as Chee's smile widened. "And the Grey Man slips in the house at midnight and does what?"

Charlie shrugged, glancing at Chee. "He's just being cute. You'll be dealing with men in black suits really, I think. One o' those shards belongs to Rose White Horse. She looks very similar to Marty. Marty will be using that shard. They took tissue samples from her from ten different places--skin, blood, sexual, and internal organs, hair, and even eye lashes and fingernails." He paused, looking straight at Jack. "They cloned our people. Now, they are starting on yours."

"But we still don't know how these Demons pull this off," grumbled Jason Iron Eyes. The thirty-five-year-old, dark-haired Lakota Sioux glanced at Charlie and then looked back at Jack. "I have spoken to your wife. She thinks you have one who watches over you. We will be watching the house as well."

"From the barn," explained Chee. "We have set up two heaters and provisions for a week. If that Black Chopper comes, we are ready for that also."

"Tut-tut-tut," grumbled Charlie. "None of that," he scolded. "Jack and Marty will not part of that."

"Part of what?" Jack stared at Charlie.

"Never mind," answered Charlie. "The less you two know, the better. You two and your dog will ride with us. Don't want them to see that big, black Ford of yours. It might tip them off and spoil the whole thing. Just remember that you two will be the bait and we'll spring the trap."

*   *   *

That evening, as the old, mantle clock over the fireplace chimed the half-hour for 7:30PM, Jack sat on the couch, looking toward the television. Banjo, however, was close to the hearth, and once again, fast asleep. Even though the Sunday Matinee was playing 'Tarzan and his Mate', the young detective was paying little or no attention to it. All of his senses were now tuned to the woods and fields behind the old home and the small pasture between the house and the barn. Charlie had taken the metal

241

shard marked 'Rose' and placed it in a wad of bubble gum now clinging to the ceiling fan in the master bedroom. . .

"Jack?" called Marty from the kitchen.

The young detective sprung to his feet as did Banjo with a breathy woof.

"Are you all right?" he asked.

"Just fine, thanks," she answered, peeping from the kitchen doorway. "Hope you don't mind cold, ham sandwiches. I made one for Banjo as well as some chips and a fresh pot of coffee."

"Sounds good to me," replied Jack.

But just as he got up, the lights of a vehicle flashed through the living room windows as it pulled into the circle drive. Jack quickly knelt on the couch and peeped through the drapes of the nearest window. The burgundy, '64 Oldsmobile was a dead give-a-way. With another muffled woof, the big Pitt trotted to the door and placed his nose just under the handle.

Part 4
It Is What It Is

Jumping out of the frying pan and into the flames was something Jack was, once again, trying to avoid. He knew most of old Charlie's plan but was also painfully aware that the old Apache was trying to distance him and Marty from whatever else he had up his sleeve. But he was now to deal with, as Charlie put it, 'the government you don't know' and that was another concern altogether. Now, as he watched Constable Virgil Forsythe get out of his burgundy Oldsmobile, he was getting even more uncomfortable. . . .

"Jack!" called Virgil as he stepped up to the screened in front porch door.

The loud rap on the screen door all but put Banjo crowding the door with a low, growl.

"Shhh. . ." hissed Jack loudly as he pulled the big Pitt back from the front door.

"Jack!" spoke the voice once more, putting Banjo completely beside himself.

Gripping the Pitt's collar tightly, Jack glanced at Marty. "Hold him and I'll let Virgil in."

"Ohhh my," groaned Marty as she gripped the Pitt's collar and planted her feet.

"Jack! I know you're in there. I can hear Banjo."

"Coming," replied Jack as he fumbled with the lock.

Hearing his name, Banjo relaxed a bit, but still strained toward the now-opening front door. As the young detective opened it, he glanced at the shortwave radio Chee had set up on the couch end table. He knew that the old Apache wouldn't like another 'outsider' involved in his plans.

Virgil rattled the screen door. "It's hooked, Jack. Let me in," he complained.

"Hold your horses, Virgil." Jack stepped out onto the huge porch, glancing back at Marty. "Banjo looked as if he was about to drag her out of the living room."

243

Jack lifted the latch, trotted back into the living room, and then snatched up the shortwave's mic. "Chee, you there?" he asked loudly."

"You got comp'ny?"

"Charlie. . ." Jack scratched the back of his neck. "Virgil, the Constable, is here," explained Jack. "Guess he saw the lights on in this old farmhouse. It's been vacant for years."

"Ever since Mrs. Easley died over a year ago," added Virgil.

Jack glanced at the Constable. "I'll get rid of him, Charlie. He doesn't need to get involved it this."

"Involved it what?" asked Virgil, glancing at Marty, still struggling with the Pitt.

"You wouldn't believe me if I told you, Virgil," said Jack. "How about a cold ham and cheese sandwich with a cup of fresh-perked coffee to go with it? I'll try to explain while we eat."

Well into Jack's explanation and a starting on his second sandwich, the Constable laid the half-eaten sandwich down on his plate and looked puzzled at Jack. "How in Sam's Hill do you get involved in such cases as this? Is James in the stew with you right now?"

"Not exactly," answered the young detective. "This all started when one of Doc Hall's prize bulls got cut up by what old Charlie calls a Grey Man."

"And that glowing thing you shot down at your place was a part of this?" asked Virgil.

Jack nodded with a bit of a smile.

"Who's that in the barn?" asked Virgil. "I noticed a small light through the partially open front doors.

"Border Patrol Agents from the Nations," answered Jack.

Virgil paused, glancing back toward the kitchen, his gaze finally made it back to Jack. "Since when does Tennessee have the Indian Nations helping out with their borders?"

Jack shrugged. "They don't. These are Special Federal Agents called Shadow Wolves. I'm working under them right now according to Will."

"Goood Lord," groaned Virgil as he sat back hard in his chair and then handed Banjo his unfinished sandwich. "Why do I feel like I just stepped into another world?"

Marty's laughter now could be heard from the kitchen as she prepared another pot of coffee. "Welcome to the jungle," she quipped loudly.

"Just why are you here?" asked Jack. "I know you didn't come all the way out here to check up on Mrs. Easley's old home place."

"Nope," answered Virgil. Slowly shaking his head, he leaned forward, placed both elbows on the table, and then stared at Jack. "Will told me to keep you grounded. Whatever that means. And if things got weird out here, I am to take you and the girl away from this place. Then, he said something that really got my attention. He mentioned Black Ops. Is the government mixed up in all of this alien mutilating stuff?"

Jack shrugged. "To tell you the truth, Virgil, I really don't know where this case is going. Charlie can answer that better than I can, but that is certainly a possibility."

Virgil slowly shook his head. "Dianne said the Black Chopper would sometimes follow that glowing ship. Do you think that's Black Ops?"

Jack nodded without a word.

Just then, the sound of the back door opening brought the two men to their feet and sent Banjo charging toward the kitchen.

"Whoa-whoa-whoa, Banjo, it's me!" exclaimed a familiar voice.

"It's Chee," said Jack, easing his .357 back in its holster. "It's Chee Hatman," explained Jack, glancing at Virgil. "He's one of the 'Wolves'."

"Is it safe?" said Chee, peeping from the kitchen. "I almost got ate by your dog."

In his twenties, the dark-haired Lakota glanced at Jack and then stared at the Constable. "Too many hands spoil the stew, Jack," he said softly.

Jack nodded, glancing at Virgil. "Chee is one of our Federal Agents. They have tracked those responsible for crimes in the Nations into our world right here." Jack looked at Chee. "Will sent him to watch me," he added, almost as a joke.

Chee smiled, almost laughing. "Well, his red Oldsmobile will fit right in. I'll try to explain this to Charlie. He is not amused. He said contact tonight will be lucky, many nights will come if we're not." He looked back toward the kitchen. "Do you have catsup here? Charlie wants it with his fries."

*   *   *

True to Charlie's 'unlucky' guess, two days passed without a nibble. Then, on the afternoon of February 1st, the old Apache finally got his wish. Finding it unseasonably warm for February, Jack pushed his quilt down to his knees, leaving him with only a sheet and light blanket. A long and boring day coupled with trouble with their two-way radio had put two of the three in their own bedrooms at 8PM. Marty retreated with and unfinished novel and Jack with his half-read newspaper. This left Virgil fidgeting with the power cord connection on the two-way. The big, black and orange Pitt had given up on all of them and was now fast asleep on the foot of Jack's bed. . .

"Got it," said Virgil proudly as he gingerly put the works back into the black leather and chrome case and snapped the back side of the Motorola back together.

Cautiously plugging it in, he looked back at the six-band radio.

"Good. No smoke and sparks," he said softly.

But just as soon as he touched the big, tuning knob on its face, it began to pick up a weak signal. The Constable jerked his hand from the knob, leaned close to the big, single speaker, and listened. Although the signal was weak, it fluctuated to strong at times making it seem close. Virgil looked at the tuner. The red line was resting between police and the weather. Slowly moving it did little to improve the signal. Grabbing a pad and pen, he leaned close to the Motorola's speaker.

"Ites to recon. Ites to recon. Are you in place?" spoke a man.

"Never better," came back the second and much stronger signal of what sounded to be a young female.

"Damn," whispered Virgil as he settled back in his chair.

"Location. . ." said the weaker signal--an older man perhaps.

"Landing Road, just west of Cotton Plant and south of the farmhouse," answered the girl with the stronger signal.

"Damn it!" exclaimed Virgil.

Springing to his feet, he ran to the living room, and then looked out of the first window he came to. Peering past his car and on to the field across the road, he looked at the old, long-deserted shack Mrs. Gernell once used as a storage barn. There was not a light to be seen.

"Gotta be there," said the Constable. He ran to Jack's bedroom door and quickly opened the door.

The sudden of light, coupled with a dark silhouette at the open doorway brought Banjo up like a shot and Jack with him.

"In here, Jack, and make it quick," said Virgil. "We got company and if I'm right, they're too close for comfort."

Hearing the excitement, Marty stepped from her bedroom and paused in the hallway, looking at the two. Seeing they weren't stopping for her, she followed them into the living room and on to the dining room table where the radio was located.

Now quite close to the radio, Virgil placed his right, index finger across his lips. "Shhh," he hissed. "Be quiet and listen."

But now there was nothing but static.

"Did you pick up something?" whispered Jack as he reached for the dial.

"No-no," objected Virgil. "If we lose that position, we might not find it again. "The person with the strongest signal sounded like a young girl. She said she was west of Cotton Plant and just south of the old farmhouse." He slowly looked at Jack and whispered. "I think that's here. There's an old shack about fifty yards across the road from here."

"What about the other signal?" asked Jack.

"Hard to tell," answered Virgil. "Weak at best. Sounded far away-either miles from us as we travel, or very high in the air above us somehow." He looked up at Jack. "The weaker caller identified himself as <u>Ites</u>. But that's spelled E-I-T-S, meaning Eye in the Sky.

"Ohhh God," groaned Marty. "That's aliens isn't it?"

Jack grinned, looking at the young girl. "Marty, you've seen me in the 'Beast'. How alien is that?"

Looking sheepishly up at him, the young girl forced a half smile. "But you're an Angel. All of us very close to you know that."

Jack slowly shook his head. "It's getting harder and harder to live up to those expectations," he grumbled as he looked at the Constable. "Can you watch out for Marty right here for a little bit?"

Virgil slowly stood from his chair. Glancing at Marty, his gaze gradually made it to Jack. "You can't fight the government—Deep State, Black Ops, or whatever. I fear we're about to get between a rock and a hard place right here and right now. Will asked me to get you out of here if it got to this situation and we are close right now." He raised his eyebrows at Jack. "Will you let me decide that point?"

Jack took a long breath, as he looked at Marty.

"He makes sense, Jack," she agreed.

'I guess," agreed Jack with another, deep breath. "If that's what Will wants, but that will put Charlie in a queer spot."

"Well, let's just proceed with caution," suggested Virgil. "Do you have a plan?"

Jack nodded. "The only thing I know how to do is go look and see. I'm not much on waiting, Virgil. Every bone in my body is screaming to run the woods. Black Bottoms is as good as Insley Bottoms--woods are woods. If your radio girl is out there, I'll find her and whoever she is with." He looked to Marty. "Make Banjo a big bowl of Gravy Train and serve it to him in the kitchen. He can't come with me right now."

Virgil watched Jack toss his black toboggan to the couch and smooth his black hair down close to his head, pushing it down from his brownish-orange horns.

248

"Time to let the Beast out," said Jack, smiling back at the Constable.

"Jack. . ." Virgil placed a hand on the young detective's right forearm. "If you step into it out there, old Puff-n-Stuff will never trust me again."

Smiling, Jack pulled on his faded, denim jacket and headed toward the front door as Marth coaxed Banjo toward the kitchen with a big, Gravy Train bag. Pausing at the opened door, he looked back at Virgil. "There's a double barrel shotgun next to my bed if you feel the need. I'm gonna check with Charlie before I go looking. . .and I mean just looking. Stay off the radio. If we heard them, they might just hear us as well."

With that, Jack left through the back door and disappeared into the darkness. Calling the 'Beast' seemed now easy for him and with his eyes glowing, he could now see well in the darkness. It looked more like dusk to him as he circled around behind the old barn. The aroma of fresh beef and cornmeal fry bread greeted him as he neared the doors behind the old building. Choosing the smaller door, he gently pushed it and peeped through the opening he was making. Charlie was lying in a lawn chair on the far side of a grill now busily tended by Chee. Thomas was past him, looking toward the farmhouse through the partially open double doors. The one rattling pots and pans in Charlie's camper to the left was Jason Iron Eyes he figured. One truck was behind the open barn and the other inside the open area with them. Jack eased the door open a little wider and stepped inside, behind the Ford truck. Chee was still busy at the grill as was Thomas watching the house. Looking in the back of the truck, Jack noticed something covered in a green tarp. Slowly lifting its edge, he got a hint at what the old Apache had in store for the 'visitors'. On the side of three, wooden crates, bold, black letters spelled out U. S. Army-RPG-quantity 6. Taking a long sigh, he slowly lowered the tarp and then eased up behind Chee at the grill.

"Hurry with those plates," said Chee, glancing toward the Air Stream.

"Got 'em," replied Iron Eyes as he pushed open the camper's door and stepped out.

But as he did, and even before his foot found the first of the three, small steps, he looked straight into the Nephilim's green eyes. Now, clearly missing the first step, plates, cups, napkins, and utensils filled the air between him and the grill as Iron Eyes came tumbling to the hay-covered barn floor.

"What the Hell!" exclaimed Charlie. Struggling to free himself of his blanket and escape the folding chair.

Horned Jack quickly checked Thomas. The young Indian, apparently seeing the Nephilim, quickly left the scene through the still open front doors. Only when Chee noticed that Iron Eyes were locked on something behind him, did he figure out they were no longer alone.

"Jesus!" Chee spun around. Holding his spatula like a Bowie knife, he froze--mouth open and eyes wide. "Charlie?" he managed weakly as he gazed at the seven-foot apparition in the dimly lit barn.

"Chee, it's Jack I think," laughed Charlie as he dropped his blanket to the lawn chair. "Put down your weapon."

Visibly shaken, Chee looked from Horned Jack, to his shaking spatula, and then back to the Nephilim again. "Don't you knock?" he finally got out.

"Young Jack," started Charlie, trying to compose himself. "Why are you in the Beast?"

"We have company, old friend," answered the Nephilim with a tone much lower and guttural that what the man Jack would use.

"We do," agreed Thomas as he eased back into the barn and closed the front doors. "They're in the old shack near the woods on the far side of the road." He smiled sheepishly at Charlie. "I don't think they saw me. They don't have these far-away glasses." He held up his binoculars.

"Why did you go outside?" asked the old Apache, still smiling at him.

Thomas slowly shook his head as his gaze moved to the Nephilim. "Sometimes, one has to go where his feet takes him."

"Stay here with your Wolves, Charlie," instructed the Nephilim. "I will check out our visitors."

"There are three," warned Thomas. "All are in the old shack. But I don't see their vehicle anywhere."

The Nephilim nodded, looking at Charlie. "Are you good with this?"

Without a word, the old Apache eased closer to the Nephilim. "They are the deliverers of pain, Jack--they are the other Greys, the Clones I think. Look into their eyes. You'll see the color of ice. Do not trust them."

Jack nodded with a bit of a smile. "I'm not planning to talk to them at all."

"Good," grumbled Charlie. "If you have ta kill one, kill 'em all.

"Kill?" The Nephilim glanced at the others and then looked back at Charlie. "Is that what the RPG's in the back of the truck are for?"

Charlie stared back at the Nephilim. For the first time, the man, Jack, could see a side of the old Apache he had never seen.

"We have sent that same message to them back in the Nations, young Jack. We hope to send them one tonight-- the Shadow Wolves have teeth. They are here and watching. Perhaps the dark side of your government will get the same message. When this happens, you must leave, I think. They will be quick to come for us, but we will not be here." He motioned quickly with his right hand toward the back door. "Now go and let the Beast see this evil."

Jack backed slowly from Chee and quickly left by the same way he came. In just minutes, he was crossing the road about one hundred yards north of the old shack. As he ran for the cover of the woods, almost that distance away, Will's instructions rang in his ears--"You'll be workin' under Two Bears. The Shadow Wolves will run this show." *But does the Will know Charlie's intentions or how far he would go?* thought Jack as he entered the woods.

*   *   *

The night was crisp, clear, and not a breeze blowing at all. The Witch's moon lessened the light, but the countless stars seemed to make up for it, at least in the 'Beast's eyes it did. Jack could actually see his shadow at times as he ran and that didn't please the Nephilim at all. Night was his solace--his security blanket so to speak. Now, only the deep shadows of the woods could soothe the 'Beast'. Jack slowed dramatically. Shaking the blood from his fingers, he looked through the trees, searching for the old shack. Then, there it was, all but glowing in the light of the stars. The aroma of corned beef told on the strangers hiding in the old place.

Now what to do? thought the Nephilim as he crept up to the back of the building.

True to what Thomas said, there was no vehicle in sight. What few windows he could see looked so dirty, one could hardly see through them in daylight, let alone at night through a human's eyes. He remained still, listening to a metal utensil scrape the bottom of a tin can. Suddenly, the voice of a young man broke the silence.

"When do we move?"

The Nephilim's ears strained for the one who would answer.

"In a hurry?" asked what sounded like a young woman. "If this must be done, be sure not to harm anyone while doing it."

Laughter from a third person, an older male perhaps, proved that Thomas was correct again. Jack slowly looked about the place, but could see little from where he was crouching.

"Lights are still on," said the woman. "It's half past eleven. We should not rush this. We'll place the knock-out canister at 1:00AM."

"What about the dog?" asked the older man. "It's a bulldog and a big one."

"If the canister doesn't work on it, you can't kill it," said the woman. "Use the pulse gun on stun. It's soundless and doesn't leave a mark."

Now they had the 'Beast's undivided attention. Until the present, it had not become personal, but he was now fuming as he listened.

"After the canister works its magic, find the girl first, check the implant and then place the seed." instructed the woman.

"What of the two men? What should we do with them?" The younger man's tone seemed nervous.

"Leave them be," ordered the woman. "They will be sedated already. The less we do to draw attention to the impregnation the better it will be."

Now, Jack knew they had come with deadly force and failure on his part was not an option. Charlie's words 'kill them all' were now struggling to guide the Beast. If he failed, he might lose Banjo and Marty would end up yet another victim along with some of the Shadow Wolves as well. With his fingertips aching, the man, Jack, knew it was time to decide. Now, plainly in the 'Beast' he leaned forward but was stopped by someone moving about in the shack.

"I've had enough of this soda pop and corned beef," complained the older man. "We should have brought down better provisions. I don't think this canned stuff and sugary pop is healthy. I'm going outside to the nearest tree. This Mountain Dew stuff has just ran right through me."

The Nephilim froze, listening to the man hitting heavily on his heels as he made his way toward the back of the shack. The Nephilim wondered if Simjaza was watching. If so, would he step in if things turned deadly? Realizing he had waited too long and the woods were much too far to make a dash, he backed into the high weeds in the dark corner of the old shack. Now, squatting in five feet of Johnson grass, he watched what looked to be a middle-aged man step from the back door and onto the old, wooden, back porch. What light the stars provided through an eerie, yellow haze on the back porch and the

253

half-dead Johnson grass standing motionless before the stranger. Jack quickly pulled his attention back to the man still standing on the porch--blue, woolen jacket, brown pants, sandy-colored hair reaching to his shoulders, and facial features befitting an Englishman perhaps. Old Charlie's words 'clone and other Grey' immediately came to mind. But the Nephilim remained still, watching the one who was hesitant to move from the porch. He seemed to be staring at something up in the sky a bit south-west of them. Doing the same thing, the Nephilim spotted something Thomas had missed--a single set of bright lights forming a perfect triangle in the slightly dimmer stars.

Following the stranger to the nearest tree was no problem. He seemed to be talking to someone on a hand-held, chrome colored device and paying attention to little else. Choosing not to strike him in the head, the Nephilim quickly slipped his left arm down over the alien's left shoulder and under his chin. Now, with his feet off the ground, and his airway blocked, he was held there until he stopped struggling. Gently lowering him to the grass, the Nephilim took his device and what identification he had on him and then leaned close to his head. He was still breathing.

Now, the clock was really ticking. Jack had ten minutes or so before the man woke up. In a dead run, he headed for the back door, but when he burst through it, he found Iron Eyes and Thomas standing in the middle of the room. Thomas was looking down at the younger clone who had a strange resemblance to the man he had just choked out. But he was in much worse shape than the clone he had left under the tree. Now looking at Jack, Thomas held up the alien's weapon--a three-foot chrome rifle of a thing with a glass pipe for a barrel.

"What should we do with her?" asked Iron Eyes as he trained his Army .45 automatic on her. "She had no weapon," he added.

Lying almost flat on the floor, the young girl held a blank stare at the 'Beast'. "Who are you?" she asked angrily. "Solarians are forbidden here."

"He's not a Solarian," grumbled the male alien at Thomas' feet. "His skin is too dark."

"Who are you?" asked the 'Beast', causing the girl to flinch at his deep voice.

"Where are you from?" she asked, ignoring his question.

"Everywhere," replied the Nephilim. "I am a Watcher, and we are many. We watch everything. Your craft cannot hide in the air above this building and your ways with these people have become troublesome to us."

The smile upon Iron Eyes' face slowly widened, hearing the 'Beast's' reply.

The Nephilim leaned closer to her. Letting the talons of his right hand rest lightly upon her chest he looked into her hazel eyes. "You are not a clone. Who are you?"

"Captain Brook Williams, USAF Space Force with NASA," she answered as she glanced at Iron Eyes and Thomas. "Are you with those of the Nations?"

Jack slowly stood, looking down at her. "I am with anyone who defends their own people against those who would abuse them," he answered.

Captain Williams pushed herself from under the Nephilim and up against the wall. "What did you do to the other man?"

Jack turned to Iron Eyes. "He's in the back, passed out. Go and bring him, but do not harm him." He looked back at the Captain. "Where are these people from?"

Noting that the woman remained strangely quiet, Thomas slowly shook his head. "Not from here," he finally said. "Apsenthion. They call the planet Apsenthion. We know it as Wormwood."

"Say nothing!" shouted the older alien as Iron Eyes quickly pushed him through the back door. Stumbling at the Apache's shove, the alien landed beside the younger one. "What have you done?" he asked, looking at Jack.

But the older alien froze at the sight of the Nephilim's eyes and taloned hands. With his chin slowly dropping, he looked back at his friend.

"He's fine," said Thomas and then nodded toward the Nephilim. "This one just saved your lives."

255

In that instant, the younger clone quickly pulled another, silver device from his pocket and pressed its button.

"Damn it! He's called 'em!" exclaimed Iron Eyes as he kicked the device from the clone's hand." He then spun around to face the Nephilim. "You mentioned the ship. Did you see it?"

The Nephilim nodded. "It's very high and a bit to the southwest.

"How wide--a football field, and shaped like a triangle?" asked Iron Eyes.

Jack shrugged. "It was high. I couldn't tell, but the shape was right."

Suddenly, and before anyone else could say a word, the old shack began to shake so badly, it loosened the dust from the ceiling. A low-pitched hum began to resonate in the Nephilim's chest as the windows began to crack and break. But before anyone could figure out just what to do, bright lights flashed through the windows.

Iron Eyes ran to the still open front door. "It's the red Olds!" he shouted. "The Constable's here."

"Get out o' there!" shouted Virgil as he jumped from the car. "All Hell's fixin' ta break loose out here."

Now realizing that there were two Apaches missing, Jack turned toward the door to see Virgil rush in.

That old Indian's gonna--"

But it was too little and too late to do anything. The Constable's warning fell short by two, loud, hissing sounds followed by two, tremendous explosions, seemingly high above the old shack.

"Get out right now!" ordered Virgil. "Marty's in the car! Charlie won't come! And there's something about five hundred feet right above this place that defies description!"

Taking the cue, the now human Jack ran from the house, cleared the porch, and then headed for the Oldsmobile. Pausing at the open, front door, he looked up at the strange craft. Although burning in two places on the front edge, the vibrating hum was still there and didn't seem to weaken.

"Go!" shouted Iron Eyes as he pushed the young detective into the passenger side front seat. "We will be gone shortly, but not before we leave our mark."

"No killing!" shouted Jack, looking at Charlie.

The old Apache slowly shook his head.

"Get in!" shouted Virgil, now in the driver's seat.

Taking that cue, Jack dove into the Olds and shut the door. He could feel the big V8's dual exhausts roar as he scrambled for his seat belt. Secured, he turned and looked through the back window. Although the dust was considerable as Virgil headed for the pavement, he was able to spot two more, orange streaks streaming up and toward the strange craft.

"Damn it!" shouted Virgil. "Charlie's done hit 'em again"

"Don't look! Just go!" shouted Marty from the back seat.

As the exploding RPG's lit up the ground before them, Virgil slid the Rocket 88 out onto the paved road and hit the passing gear. All Jack could do was watch and pray the aliens would not shoot back.

"Are you all right?" asked Marty, staring back at Jack.

Only then, did the young detective spot Banjo. The loud explosions had sent him between the seats, looking glued to the floor.

"Thanks for taking care of my friend, Marty," he said, looking at the young girl. "I kind of had my hands full."

"That's OK," she replied without pulling her gaze from the happening. "But are you all right?" she repeated.

Jack nodded, placing a hand upon the Pitt's head. "I'll be fine just as soon as I learn that Charlie and his Wolves are out of danger."

"Out of danger?" exclaimed Virgil. He glanced at Jack with a look of disbelief. "Charlie just slapped an alien ship the size of the White House and probably, somehow, connected to it as well."

Marty giggled, watching Virgil's troubled expression. "Yep," she added, "and we all had ring-side seats."

Virgil held the Olds to a steady seventh-five as they headed back towards Drummonds on Highway 59.